KEEPER

OF MY DESIRE

BOOK THREE
THE IMMORTAL KEEPERS

HM HODGSON

First edition 2022.

Ebook ISBN: 978-0-6451286-8-0

Print ISBN: 978-0-6451286-9-7

Edited by Sarah Proulx Calfee, Three Little Words Editing https://threelittlewordsediting.com

Proofread by Jo Speirs, Nurturing Words

https://www.nurturingwords.com.au

Front cover design by Amanda Pillar from Smoking Hot Covers

https://www.smokinghotcovers.com

Inside cover design by Jacqueline Hayley with Marina Farcic

https://jacquelinehayley.com

❀ Created with Vellum

For my mum.
The woman who never let anyone
tell her 'you can't do that'.

PROLOGUE

The Higherworld
Four Decades Ago

In the Great Library, surrounded by bookshelves soaring up to its domed ceiling, the child's eyes widened. She couldn't help but reach out and trace the rainbow of colors that made up the old woman's mass of curly hair who sat beside her.

"Nay, child," her father scolded, shooing her hand away. "Do not touch Fate."

The old woman laughed—a twinkling sound too young for her wizened face as she opened the carved lid of the heavy box on the table. "Let the child have her wonder, Theron. She will face enough bitterness and battles in her life."

"Nay, surely not." Her father tightened the child into his side.

The girl squirmed, eager to see the contents of the box.

"Yes, Theron. But now, let us see what the Book foretells." The old woman reached into the box, lifted the Book, then placed it gently before the child.

The Book opened. But there were no words, no pictures, nothing but a blank page.

Suddenly the filaments of parchment shifted, darkened, grew into the shape of a sword rising tip first from the page.

"Reach out, little one," the old woman whispered.

"She is so young, Fate." Her father said, tightening his arm around his daughter again.

"All will be as it should, Theron. Worry not."

Drawn to the sword, the child reached out to touch it, and one filament of parchment pricked her fingertip. It was a minor sting, not enough to take her gaze from the sword in the paper, even as a bead of blood welled and stained the tip of the sword red.

Her father gasped.

1

THE HIGHERWORLD

In the quiet moments before night relinquished her grip on the dark, and the sun extended his arms over the day, Amadis donned a linen tunic for her training session and wrapped the straps of her sandals up her calves. She shrugged into her scabbard harness, swords already in place, and wound the leather straps beneath her breasts, around her torso and back up under her wings.

Her first sparring partner was scheduled for sunrise, so she would be there beforehand, limbered up and ready to hone her skill against whoever had lucked out for the early sparring session.

The ever-temperate air of the Kin's central lands greeted her with blissful silence and solitude, and in the dark she made her way between the longhouses to the farthest, oldest training ring.

She began by stretching and then moved through a combination of sword stances. But before she could begin her practice strikes, footsteps echoed in the dark from the direction of the longhouses.

She frowned at the still-dark sky. Her sparring partners were never early.

Finally, two figures emerged from the dark. She was only meant to be training with one today.

And then they stepped closer. It was her sire, Theron, followed by an unfamiliar woman, richly garbed in a fur-lined thick green cape, with golden hair framing a perfect face.

Amadis's gut tightened. Why was he here? And who was the stranger? But she kept her expression calm as she sheathed her swords and joined them at the edge of the training ring.

"Daughter, good tidings," Theron called.

"Good tidings." She nodded at her sire and then the stranger. "Is there a change in the practice schedule?"

"Training has been canceled. You have a Task."

"Me? But I have never—"

"Amadis. Angels do not speak when being assigned Tasks."

She shut her mouth and dipped her head.

"Now, your Task is in two parts and involves traveling to the Mortalworld."

What? She darted a look at her sire.

"Normally, the Council does not condone weapons to be taken on a Task; however ..." Theron glanced over at the woman, his expression tightening. "However, you have been requested for this Task specifically due to your warrior designation. Therefore, we have agreed that you will take your swords."

Her stomach dropped. *Belar's breath,* was he serious? Her first ever Task required her to be armed?

"Warden," the golden-haired woman called out. "May I speak to your child?"

"Of course, Freya." Theron dipped his head.

Freya? The Goddess of love, sex and war was here? Talking to Amadis? Why? How? Was this really happening, or was she still asleep and this was all a dream?

"Daughter," Theron said, his jaw tightening. "You may approach."

"Yes, Father." Amadis swallowed the lump that had lodged in her throat. "Hail, Freya." Amadis dropped to one knee and bent her head. Tried to keep the awe out of her expression.

"Hail, Amadis. And please stand, child. The second part of your Task involves the World Tree. What do you know of it?"

Now she *had* to be dreaming.

"The Tree is the connection between the three realms," Amadis whispered. "It is the most important being in all our worlds."

"And the Keepers?"

"They are the immortal warriors who guard the Tree. They stand in the way of those who would destroy the Tree, like the Order, to steal its power and take over the Mortalworld."

"Excellent." Freya nodded, approval lighting her eyes. "You will understand then why this Task is so important. You are to locate the next Keeper and see them called into service to the Tree. All we know is that this person is a child of Willow Grove, a village in the Mortalworld. India, a Keeper from my family, will be your contact in the region."

"Thank you, Freya. I will do everything in my power to achieve the Task."

"I wish you a safe journey, child. And for the sake of all our worlds, success." Freya dipped her head and then disappeared.

Amadis stared at the grass where the goddess had been. Had that really just happened?

"Daughter. Daughter?"

"Yes?" She spun back around.

"This is your first time in the Mortalworld. While your wings will be invisible to mortals, unless you choose to reveal them, your swords and scabbard are not afforded such stealth. Therefore, I have something to give you."

Theron held out his hand. A black metal ring lay in the center of his palm.

A lump lodged in her throat. "That was my mother's."

"Yes." Theron's jaw tightened. "Your mother's people spelled the metal so that when you wear the ring, it will glamour your scabbard, and none will see it. When your swords are sheathed, they too will be hidden from sight. Now, remember, you cannot reveal your Task purpose. And you are never, ever to reveal your true self to a mortal. You will need to find a location to base your search from—I recommend you find a remote place where you have less chance of having your identity revealed."

Gods, this *was* happening. Finally, she was undertaking a Task. She could prove herself a capable member of the Kin. And with a purpose more vital than anything she could have imagined being responsible for achieving. And she had something of her mother to take with her. *Belar's breath*, she had to prepare—

"Amadis," Theron called out. "There is one more thing. As a half Angel and the challenges you have with small spaces ... you have not always found acknowledgment among the Kin."

Challenge? Acknowledgment? Amadis snorted. Those were understatements.

"Daughter." Theron's eyes flashed.

"Apologies." She dipped her head.

"You need to know. Should you fail in your first Task, I cannot say that the Council will ever grant you another Task. Nor that you will find ..."

"Do not try to find the right word, Father. I know it already." Amadis couldn't contain a grimace and lifted her chin, staring back at the Warden of the Angels. *Acceptance.*

Less than one full day after receiving her Task, Amadis strode out of the Mortalworld forest toward her accommodation, carrying three pieces of luggage filled with clothes India Jones, her contact in the Mortalworld, had provided.

Belar's breath, this place—Australia, was it?—was so much more beautiful than she could have imagined. Silver-edged clouds floated in a stunning midday sky and reflected in the blue lake below. Two small dwellings nestled by the trees, and she walked past them to a tall building made of timber and glass.

Her lodging until the Task was complete.

Regripping her hold on the bags, she cast a quick glance up and down the porch. A driveway led from the lodge toward a road in the distance, but otherwise, it was just the buildings, the lake and the forest. Not another being in sight. Well, she had done as bid—found the most remote lodging possible.

An ornately carved sign hung on the front door "Welcome to Angel's Lakeside Lodge."

The hairs on the back of Amadis's neck prickled.

Blowing out a steady breath, she eyed the sign once more before pushing the thick wooden door open. A fresh, tangy pine scent drifted toward her. It tangled in her nose, and a sneeze worked its way up and out.

"Hello?" Amadis called out.

The door opened wide, revealing a room with soaring ceilings and exposed timber beams. Great expanses of windows overlooked the lake beyond, and a polished timber handrail high above drew her eyes up to a second-story internal balcony. Several couches and chairs sat around a huge stone hearth, the chimney climbing up to the ceiling.

What a breathtaking space.

But she froze on the doorstep.

Come on, Amadis. The room was incredible. Exposed, raw, rough and yet somehow inviting. Who would have thought the Mortalworld would have such welcoming spaces? And surely, with all this openness, she could do this. Uh-uh, there was no question. She *could* do this. Amadis took a deep breath and moved one leg, then the other, into the room.

She'd done it! She'd taken the step inside. But as the door swooshed shut behind her, she tensed, ready to fight the urge to race outside. Except ... nothing happened.

A sigh of relief escaped her. Thank *Belar.* Then she gave herself a mental kick. She was not weak. And being uncomfortable—some might even say scared—of small places was without question a weakness.

"Who are you?" A rough voice called from a darkened space beyond the remarkable room.

Amadis looked around. She was the only person there, so the comment had to be for her. "A guest?"

"You don't have a booking."

"Well, I think I do." A spark of awareness sang through her. She stood a little straighter. "They made it—*I*—made it for A. Jones."

A figure moved to follow the voice. Tall enough to fill the doorway, wide enough that at first glance, it appeared as if it was two beings, then it took a step into the light. Right then, the clouds shifted, and the sun shone through the highest window, casting a glow around the person—man.

Amadis jolted. It was the purest halo she'd ever seen.

"A. Jones?"

Amadis nodded, unable to make any other sound.

The man took another step, and the halo faded, deepened into a shadow as the clouds moved back over the sun. Instead, a very tall, intense man with a cap of short black hair stood before her. He wore denim leggings—jeans, India had called them—with a thick long-sleeved top. His deeply tanned face was hawkish with dark slashes of brows and carved granite cheeks. The only thing that tempered the fierce look was his generous mouth, set in a neutral curve.

Deadly. Dangerous. The words came to her in succession. Their absolute clarity had her instinctively reach back with her free hand to grasp one sword. But she caught herself just in time. This was a human—a mortal—what harm could he possibly pose to her?

She extended her arm in an awkward stretch in case the man queried her movement. But she needn't have worried.

The man walked—more like stalked—to a desk near the door where she stood. He jerked the lid of a rectangular black case open, revealing a surface filled with buttons—it was a laptop she recalled, and he tapped away hard at them. A moment later, he looked up, straight into her eyes.

An ocean of inky blue bore into her, and Amadis had to hold in a gasp at their glittering depths. Desire. This time the word came through slowly, languidly, rolling on a current of pulsing heat. She almost dropped the bags, had to shift one to her other hand to keep a hold.

"You put Mr. down as your title," the hawkish man said and swiveled the laptop toward her.

His gaze dipped to her bags, and Amadis wet her lips, forced her attention to the screen. Text filled the screen. Sure enough, the letters "Mr." preceded her name.

"See?" Hawkish continued.

"Yes, I can see that." Amadis shot him a look. Why was he regarding her so intently? She surreptitiously checked out his eyes. No aura shone around his irises. At all. Nothing for truth and nothing for deceit. How odd. She could always see if someone was telling the truth or not.

"Right," Hawkish said as he picked up a board with papers clipped onto it. He looked back at her for a moment and paused, then handed the papers to her. "Well, if you'd just sign against your name, and since you paid for the room up-front when you booked, you're good to go."

"Go where?"

The man stilled. With his massive height, he easily towered over her. However, given her father and most of her paternal Kin were of similar stature, his size did not faze her. But that current of warmth he'd sent through her set off an inner caution, like a warning beacon.

Though she didn't move back. She was here on a mission. This was her chance to finally prove herself. She couldn't afford to show any weakness, so she ignored the heat that poured off the man and looked at him, waiting for his response.

He looked directly back.

Amadis still couldn't see his aura to know his truth, but she didn't need any help to identify the look on his face. He was analyzing her. *Belar's breath*, had she given herself away already?

Maybe she could change his direction of thought. "You have a beautiful place here, Mr. ..."

"O'Connor." The man took a step back, and his face relaxed. His voice was mild, inconsequential even, but she had the sense he was still looking, still considering her. "But call me Daniel. I'm the manager and owner here. And you're my first official guest. So, what does the A stand for?"

Amadis considered his words. Combined with the normal tone he'd used, they seemed fine. But he still watched her. Were they meant to distract her, just as hers had been to him?

"My name is Amadis."

"Amadis. Don't think I've heard that before."

"Oh." Drat. Was her name really that uncommon? Amadis broke away from that perceptive gaze and looked around the room. Time for another conversation change. "When I first walked in, all this space, especially the beautiful timberwork, took my breath away."

"Thanks." Once again, Daniel just looked at her, but he turned away abruptly and looked around the space, too. Subtle pride crept over his expression before he glanced back at her. He nodded at the clipboard. "Once you've signed the form, would you like a tour, or I can just show you to your room?"

"My *room*?" Her heart jumped a beat. Did he mean this open, welcoming space wasn't where she was staying?

"Yeah." Daniel rubbed his jaw. "Where you're sleeping. This is a bed-and-breakfast, not a hostel or anything like that."

Amadis stared at the form he'd passed to her without seeing a thing. A prickling sensation crawled up her neck. Her shoulders stiffened. Oh no. No, no, no, no, no. This was *not* happening. She gripped the pen hard and forced herself to read the form. *Paperwork, Ammy. Focus on the paperwork.* Finally, the prickles receded, and her name—A. Jones— stood out enough for her to recognize it. A box with the word "signature" beside her name. Easy enough.

Amadis signed her name, another first, and passed the form back. Holding her breath, she observed the man's face for any sign of error on her part, but he just took the paper- work and tucked it away.

So she must have got that right. She bit back her sigh of relief. Now all she had to do was see where she was sleeping and not give herself away any further.

"Right, well, let me give you a hand with these." As Daniel reached for the bags, his fingers brushed the back of hers, and an electrical current sizzled all the way through her.

"Fu—hell." He jumped back.

Amadis dropped the luggage. What in all the worlds was that? Her pulse hammered, and she had to force herself to breathe evenly until it settled—a physiological reaction she'd not had since her early days of training.

"Whoa. Sorry about that. That's some serious static electricity." Daniel shook his fingers lightly.

Amadis blinked to dispel the moment of haze that his touch had caused and made herself nod.

"Let's try that again." Daniel turned away, picked up her bags with ease, and walked toward the stairs at the far end of the room. "Right, well, if you'd like to come with me."

Amadis briefly closed her eyes. Thank you, *Belar*. She'd passed the first step.

WELL, his first guest was pretty fucking unexpected, not that he'd had any set expectations of his first customer. But if he had ... it wouldn't have been Amadis Jones. The most unexpected person he'd ever met. She had, hell—what was the term she'd used? That was it. She'd taken his breath away.

He'd sensed her first. Those little hairs on the back of his neck, the same ones that had gone silent since he'd landed in Willow Grove, had pricked to attention. Moments later, her voice—husky, low, melodic—had echoed through the lodge. Icy prickles had swept over his body.

And then he'd walked into the lounge. Fucking hell, she was out of this world. Only small—hardly over five feet. But absolutely fucking perfect. Silvery hair chopped into a funky length around her eyes, and her eyes ... Hell, they were the clearest, most crystal blue, just like the snowmelt waters that rushed off the mountain.

Daniel's chest had seized like he was having a goddamn heart attack. His words had stopped. He'd lost his train of thought and had to start over what he'd been saying.

And even now, as she trailed him to her room, he could sense the way she looked around the place.

What the fuck was going on? Whatever it was, he wasn't in the mood for it. Hell, he wasn't in the mood for anything other than focusing on his business and making a living in a way that didn't include fighting other people's battles.

Forcing the crazy-ass reaction to a woman—his *guest*—out of his mind, he hefted her bags, one strapped over his shoulder and the other two in both hands, and nodded toward the next room and tried to be a good tour guide.

"Through there is the library," he said, voice rougher than he intended. "Use it as you like. And this is the guest dining room." He freed one hand to turn on the light switch. "Breakfast will be served in here, and we can do lunch and dinner, but you have to let me know. Plus, there are a few places in the town you might like to try out too." The locals had been great to him since he'd come, much to his surprise, and he planned on being just as helpful back.

"Do I let you know now?" she asked.

Daniel restrained a shiver at the husky words, purposefully avoiding looking into those too-perfect eyes. "If you like. You're the only guest tonight, actually, for the next couple of days, so it won't be any trouble. And dinner tonight's a beef"—he quickly recalled what Shannon had said before she'd left—"ah, a beef stew. With mash."

"In that case, yes please, to dinner tonight. Who's we?"

"We?" This time he had to pause as she had stopped too.

"You said 'we can do lunch and dinner.'"

"Oh. The 'we' are Shannon and I. Shannon's an old family friend. She's going to help me out with a few things, like cooking and cleaning. I'm only new to town, but Shannon's been here her whole life and can answer pretty much any question you have about the local area. She's not here at the moment, but you'll meet her this afternoon if you're around or at dinner if you head down."

Daniel took another step, kept going this time. He was going to get A. Jones into her room and then get some space if it killed him.

Thank Christ; she started walking again. "Right, so as I was saying, that's the dining room. The next door leads to the kitchen, and off that are my rooms—they're not for the guests, though. And then, if you come up these steps, we'll head up to the accommodation level."

As always, the urge to smooth one hand over the balustrade hit him, though since he was holding three suitcases, he gave it a miss. But that gleaming timber was a result of hours of his effort—hours of shaping and sanding and polishing. And he was goddamn proud of it. Plus, he just loved the feel of it. He'd always been drawn to wooden objects. And the opportunity to sink into something that he was in charge of and that let him work with his hands had been irresistible.

Daniel and Amadis reached the top of the stairs, and he took a second to stop. The view over the balcony into the great room below was the best right here.

He surreptitiously checked out Amadis's face. The awe in her expression sent a beam of pride straight through him.

Enough of that. He shoved the soft sensation aside and kept going to the very end of the landing and the last of four doors and awkwardly turned the handle.

He dropped—placed—the bags just inside the room and once again turned on a light switch, unnecessary given how much natural light streamed in through the windows.

"This is your room. You're on the end, so have a nice double aspect." He nodded to the views of the woods that surrounded the lodge. "Trees on that side. Lake through that one. And your ensuite is through there. It's only small but has all the necessities."

He stepped into the small bathroom and turned on the light. Not that there was a rule book on how to show your guest through their room, but what the hell, it seemed like a nice thing to do.

He turned back. Amadis stood in the doorway. Her face was gray, and a fine sheen—surely not sweat—covered her brow.

2

Deep in the belly of her god's Underworld home, Ri'Anit drew in a full breath. The first time she had done so without pain tearing through her. So, her internal wounds had healed.

Judging by the revelry that had taken place before her eyes, not yet twenty-four hours had passed since they had returned her broken body to the Underworld.

She attempted to move her head, and this time, the tendons and muscles that connected her skull to her body responded.

Not fully, but she turned enough to meet her god's eyes.

Irrika lay on her side, naked but for the platinum razor body-wire caught at her nipples and groin, shimmering beneath the glow of a thousand candles suspended above the altar of bones that held the perfection of her figure.

Black eyes, fathomless, drew Ri'Anit, and she tried to respond. Tried to move, to crawl, drag herself to Irrika's side. To pay homage to Irrika was Ri'Anit's right, not these other pathetic creatures who thought they could usurp her place.

Fire ripped across every single nerve as her attempt to move undid the mending already begun by her immortality.

But she did not give in.

Ri'Anit pushed again, heaved and retched as darkness hovered at the edge of her vision.

But she did not give in.

She would do this. She would be Irrika's First Follower again.

Leaking blood from wounds wrought by Irrika's own personal demon guard, Ri'Anit made one arm move, just one. But that was all she needed.

Amusement shone from Irrika's eyes, but Ri'Anit didn't stop.

Panting, fire screaming through every fiber of her being, Ri'Anit dragged herself over the other Followers, unheeding of their taunts and sneers, of their kicks and blows and knives that dug into her still useless limbs.

But she did not give in.

Hatred-led purpose swept through her. Harder, stronger than ever before. She turned her neck. One more inch gained.

"My god." She dipped her head. Waited.

"Yes?"

The languid tone did not fool Ri'Anit, and she kept her gaze locked on the ground. "I know I do not deserve it." She paused, had to retch as more blood welled from her reopened internal wounds. "But I will have revenge." She growled, the sound coming from the deepest part of her. The part now missing—that could not regrow—her magic. "I know the Keepers who guard the Tree. I know their town. And they think me gone. I am the perfect one to continue your quest, my god. And I *will* claim the mortal realm. For you."

A thousand tiny cuts flayed Ri'Anit's skin, pain flowing afresh with each slice, as Irrika used her power to punish her.

But it could have been worse. Hope sent her heart to glide.

"Rise, if you can," Irrika said.

Ri'Anit inhaled, ignored the returned pain. She would do this. Could do this. And, spurred by a quest for vengeance, she forced her wrecked body to rise.

The hoard at her back went silent.

"I know I am no longer your first. But all I need is one more chance to achieve your vision. I am your most devoted follower. And I will stop at nothing to do this for you." Fire raced along Ri'Anit's nerves as flesh and tissue reconnected. But she refused to groan, refused to spill a single tear. She let the fire blaze through her blood-filled eyes instead. "I. Will. Do. It."

Irrika flicked her tongue once; the forked length ran over her bright red lips as she surveyed the carnage, the result of Ri'Anit's last attempt to destroy the World Tree. Her gaze cut to the throng surrounding her dais, clearly weighing their merit. She flexed her long fingers, traced the gleaming clawed nails one by one.

"And how shall you, a powerless witch, achieve this feat?"

"Through my will to see you succeed. And my rage at those who dare resist you. I will strip every living witch of their magic if needs be and hurl their power upon the Tree until it is no more."

"Then you shall have your one more chance. And should you manage to steal a Mortalworld witch's magic, I will see your witch-fire returned." Then Irrika pierced Ri'Anit with her ice gaze. "But. If you fail, you had best hope the Keepers end your life, lest it return to me. For your death shall make these halls shriek for an eternity."

What blood remained in Ri'Anit's body rushed through her ears, sent her head to spin, but she kept her chin high, let her eyes burn. With hatred, and with the renewed need to kill, nay, to destroy the Keepers. Once and for all.

Daniel bit back a curse. What was wrong with his guest? She'd sneezed when she'd first arrived. Maybe she was sick. He moved to stand as close to the wall as possible and still allow her space to enter. Given his size and the fact the room wasn't huge, it was a squeeze.

"There's a pharmacy in the village. If you're unwell, you can head over. I can even drive you." Christ, no, he didn't want to do that. But it was too late. The words had already come out.

"No, no. Thank you." The woman set her lips—now colorless—into a straight line, and he swore she even stiffened her back before she left the doorway. She visibly took a deep breath and then turned around in a circle.

Daniel would have taken a step closer to the wall, but he was already up against it. He stared down at her cap of silver hair. What the fuck was she doing?

Whatever it was, she suddenly stopped and looked at him. Those eyes sucker punched him again.

"Apologies for that." She bit her lip, and color flowed back into the plump curves.

Daniel held back a groan. Those icy prickles raced back through him, only this time with an undercurrent of heat.

"This is embarrassing to say," Amadis continued.

Daniel looked from those now red lips to the curve of her shoulder, where her plain white long-sleeved shirt revealed surprisingly firm curves of muscle, then down to the feminine sweep of her chest. She was packaged just perfectly.

Christ, he was looking at her chest. He wrenched his eyes up. Had he been busted? But she was staring out the window and only then glanced back at him. Thank fuck.

"You see," she said. "I have a small fear—no, not fear—a small level of discomfort, with closed spaces. But this room is fine. It will be absolutely fine."

Focus on her words, focus on her words. Daniel forced himself to keep his eyes on her forehead and finally processed what she'd said. Was she trying to convince herself or him? Whatever, he had to get out of there.

"Well, thanks for filling me in." Pushing off the wall, he risked another look at her eyes. Bad move. Pain, deeply banked, lurked within them. It spoke to him on a level he knew all too well. Hell, he should get out of there. But ... he held in a sigh, raised a hand. "If it's an issue, your phobia, that is, you can—"

"Nay—I mean no. No, thank you, Mr. O'Connor." Her slim hand popped up, palm out. "I am absolutely fine and will stay right here in this room."

AMADIS BARELY HELD IN A CURSE. She was going to get it together. Going. To. Get. It. Together. She took another breath, forced herself to look out the windows—the room wasn't so small after all. Resolutely, she ignored the walls and ceiling closing in on her.

But she needed to be alone. Needed to unfurl her wings and be herself, just for one moment. That's all.

She turned to her host and worked hard to keep her voice low and even. The threads that she pulled on to maintain her facade of calm frayed further and further. No way in all the worlds was she going to unravel in front of this man.

"Thank you again, Mr. O'Connor. I am fine, though. I'll be leaving shortly to go for a walk, so might not see you until dinner."

Amadis held her host's gaze and waited. It took a moment, but Daniel nodded and left the room, saying nothing further.

She swung the door closed.

A ball of lead weighed her gut down; her heart thudded faster, faster through her. *Belar's breath.* She had to focus on something else—a movement outside the window caught her attention. Branches of a tree swaying softly, calmly, in the breeze that rolled through the forest.

Perfect.

She took a deep breath, swayed from side to side in cadence with the leaves and branches.

And slowly, her heart reduced pace. The walls stopped bulging. The urge to get out into the open receded.

Amadis sighed, relieved she'd made it through the panic attack. Closing her eyes, she backed up to the same wall

Daniel had leaned against. But the moment she made contact, a tingle worked up her spine.

Oh gods, she wriggled out of her sleeveless jacket and bounded into the center of the room. Got there just in time for her wings to unfurl in a cracking snap. Pain sliced from her shoulder to the medial joint, then radiated to the tips.

Biting back a cry, all she could do was roll and stretch her joints until finally, the burn receded, and a shimmy worked its way down her body. At least that wiggle meant her wings were okay.

So much for gently easing her wings from their cramped position. Ha. If her host hadn't left when he had—well, that would have been one way to break cover.

But she still took the time to inspect the black expanses. They were her greatest defense and, considering how tightly they'd been furled for such a long time, they'd fared well. But then, she'd worked hard to be ready for whatever Task the Kin ordered. Hours, days, years of training with *Daudhi* and *Dagr* for offense and her wings for defense.

And look at what she'd done! Her eyes widened, and she spun around. She'd entered a room barely large enough to hold her wingspan and hadn't vomited or run outside. And in doing so, had taken another step toward fulfilling her first Angelic Task: ensuring the ongoing protection of the World Tree.

Belar's breath. She'd been so absorbed with her trial she'd lost focus on the Task. Well, no more. Adrenaline surged through her. She was going to prove herself a capable member of the Angelkin. Finally.

But she had one more thing to do before she furled her wings. Reaching back with both hands, she grasped the hilts of her swords and withdrew *Daudhi* and *Dagr* in one smooth motion from their scabbard. The balanced blades, made from a rare Underworld ore, crossed above her head, metal ringing as she lowered them for inspection.

Thin silver gleamed under the bright light. Not one imperfection marred their surface.

She swiftly sheathed the weapons and then furled her wings and checked her reflection in the bathroom mirror. One pirouette confirmed the spell that hid the scabbard was intact—not a single sign of her swords was visible. She was ready to go. Providing no one touched her back, she'd easily pass as a mortal.

Time to get to work.

HIS FIRST EVER GUEST WAS LIKE some goddamn otherworldly being. And what the hell kind of thought was that? Daniel shook his head forcefully, pushed away the crazy notion and focused instead on reality.

His instincts had led him true for eighteen years as a soldier, and while they'd been dormant since he'd moved here, they'd fired up the moment he'd seen ... no, that wasn't right either. The moment he'd *sensed* Amadis at his door.

And they rode him hard now, saying something was not right—not true—about A. Jones. Both the booking and the person. Daniel's website had been live for all of an hour when his first booking had come through.

Even though his lodge was in the foothills of Mount Baw Baw, the locals had cautioned not to expect too much in the way of business given he was opening well into winter and most visitors planned their trips to the mountain in advance. Plus, he was new, so he couldn't exactly rely on return business.

But he'd worked for months to get this old place turned around, and long after he'd technically been ready, he'd finally hit the button and made the website live.

Though frankly, a slow start was for the best, given his desire for contact with people was still goddamn low. But he'd done it, and when the site had opened up, it was like bam—here's your first booking.

His guest just happened to be ... suspicious.

Was she lying about her identity? Was there some underlying reason for her stay? Sure, she'd looked the right image in the long-sleeved T-shirt, the sleeveless puffer vest and walking pants. Even the sneakers had been right. But they'd all been new, with no wear marks on the shoes, even the creases in the pants looked like they were off the shelf. Again, not such a big issue—lots of people purchased brand-new stuff before they went away.

And then there was the reservation form. Who got their title wrong? Although maybe they wrote it differently where she was from. She was a British resident according to the address she'd used for the booking. Her accent kind of fit, although even that wasn't quite right. And he'd met a fair few Brits over the years in the armed forces, though they had a variety of accents just like Aussies did.

But still. There was something about her ...

Daniel shook his head. Maybe she was just trying to hide, period. Hell, hadn't that been as much of his own reason for coming here? And it really didn't matter. She was a guest. A paying guest. As long as she kept to herself, she shouldn't cause any problems.

And he still had work to do. His guest had arrived right as he'd been about to put out coffee and tea. He might only have the one guest today, but his website stated he offered refreshments, so that's what he was going to offer. Although Ben—hell, all his old army mates—would laugh if they saw Daniel pushing a tea trolley.

Heading back into the kitchen, Daniel grabbed a cloth and wiped the trolley down, its two large, spindly wheels on one end, flat feet for stands on the other, the brass legs and trays. It was too fine for his taste, and he might even make one for himself one day from a nice timber. But this one had been practically free at an estate sale, and since it was in good condition, it seemed a shame to waste it.

What about people who didn't drink coffee or tea? That idea was completely alien to Daniel, but apparently, some people were anti-coffee. Should he be branching out into hot chocolate? That sounded like a more difficult prospect. Although maybe they did hot chocolate in sachets like instant coffee? He'd have to check it out because he wanted something warm for any future guest when they came in after a long forest walk.

He picked up the kettle to fill it with water. *Walk*. That's what Amadis had said—she was going for a walk.

Hell. He'd been so focused on getting out of her room, getting away from the pull of her eyes and her body, that he'd completely missed her comment. Did she even know where she was going?

Daniel stopped what he was doing and went still. The lodge was an old building—the original had been built on this site over a hundred years earlier—but even with several modernizations and then his own intensive overhaul, the place creaked and groaned with the best of them.

No sound came from above.

He sighed, ran a hand over the short hair on his head. Should he check on her? She could basically head in three directions—the trail to the north would take her around the lake, sure, but the lake was bloody big, and it was a good twelve-hour hike before the path emerged out of the forest, crossed the gorge higher up, which alone was enough of a barrier, and then wound back on the other side of the lake into the village.

If she walked the trail to the south, the trek into town was only an hour.

But if she headed east, into the state forest, well, she could go in that direction for days before she'd find anything other than snakes and spiders and ticks.

And it was fucking winter. She'd need more than that sleeveless jacket if she was going to head out for any stretch of time. Plus, this was Victoria. The weather was as unpredictable as you could get.

Hell. Looked like Daniel was going to get some fresh air after all.

His first guest was already putting him out of his way. They bloody well better not all be like this.

4

The lakeside trail that led from the lodge into the village of Willow Grove eventually opened into a sweeping expanse of grass, with play equipment in the distance and several small buildings visible after that.

Amadis had walked past beautiful trees spearing into the sky and smaller ones covered in tiny, round yellow blossoms with the sweetest tang. Everywhere she looked, the flora was hardy, rugged, in a mix of dusky greens and browns and golds. She'd had to force herself to stay on the trail and not get distracted by the forest.

A signpost stood at the front of the grassy area. "Willow Grove, population 569". So, she had just under six hundred people to work through to identify the next Keeper.

Her heart picked up pace.

And while she had to start her reconnaissance, the lake, shining an inky blue beneath the late afternoon sun, called to her. That blue was the same stormy hue as her host's eyes.

Amadis blinked. *Her host's eyes?* She pursed her lips. Thoughts of her host should be the farthest thing from her mind, except to ensure she didn't trip herself up, given she'd have to spend some time around him.

At least she'd crossed him off her list. He'd described himself as new to the area, so he couldn't be the "child of the village" that had been the description to aid in the search for her target. But the woman he'd mentioned, Shannon, might be a great resource if not the actual target of her Task.

But regardless, as the sign said, she had some 560 others to review.

And review them, she would. As soon as she'd been to the lake. The lovely, non-reminding-her-of-her-host's-eyes, indigo-blue lake that lured her off the trail.

Grass, springy beneath her feet, buoyed her steps all the way to the water's edge. Gentle ripples crossed the lake, pushed by the breaths of wind that swirled down off the mountain.

It was stunning. It was life. It was perfect.

The clear icy air, sweetened by the fresh water and the forest beyond, filled her lungs, and she lifted her chin to the sun, lips curving. What a wonderful, natural, simple yet amazing world.

What she would have given to let her wings stretch and take flight right there, to lift, slip through the air and rise with the current. To join the wind as it swirled over the lake.

"It's a bit cold for a swim," a masculine voice called out from behind her.

Amadis yelped, and the spongy ground beneath her feet gave way, and gravity pulled her toward the water.

Then someone grabbed her arm, pulled her back from the lake's edge. The scent of pine and tang tingled at her nose.

"Whoa, I got you," a man's voice said. "You're not going to fall in."

Daniel. She was close, right up close, to her host. Amadis leaned forward, automatically protecting her wings from being crushed against his chest.

"What are you doing?" She hissed over her shoulder. "Let me go."

"Doing? I was stopping you from falling ass-up into the lake." But he shifted back and dropped her arm.

"I wasn't falling anywhere." She spun around—he couldn't be near her back again.

"I didn't mean to scare you," Daniel muttered. "You were about to topple into the water. Are you steady now?"

Deep indigo eyes surveyed hers. Her heart skipped, started again. Faster. Harder.

Had she been a mortal, perhaps the aid would have been required to avoid falling into the lake.

"Thank you, but your help is not nee—" Oh dear. She had to pretend it was. "I mean, yes, I am okay now. Thank you. For ..." Daniel's face was close—too close.

"For ...?"

Amadis moistened her lips. As she did, Daniel's eyes tightened, his jaw clenched. A tinge of color hit high on his carved cheeks. He was fascinating. And he was waiting.

"Thank you for pulling me back from the edge. I was close to, um, falling into the beautiful water." She shut her mouth. She'd never been close to falling in the water, and having to fake it made the lie sticky on her lips.

His mesmerizing gaze trapped her. Had he caught her lie?

But even that thought evaporated, as the tang of pine, a

surge of heat, wrapped around her.

With the afternoon sun shining down, coating them in gilded, warm rays, Amadis moved without thinking and reached up, sliding one hand over his jaw.

She had to touch him. Hot skin, rough with stubble.

A growl rumbled from deep within him.

The sound broke through her distraction. What if mortals weren't as open to touch as Angels? She jerked her hand back.

"Sorry, I shouldn't have done that." Heat flooded her cheeks, and she shoved away from him. Space. She needed to get some space from this male.

"Hey, careful—" he called out.

But it was too late. Amadis stepped on the soggy edge where the grass gave way to the water.

Daniel reached out again and grabbed her arm, but she was already tipping back.

She could've flipped onto the shore, but instead of giving herself away, Amadis fell into the lake, icy water rushing to meet her feet and her legs.

She gasped. But the bitterly cold lake didn't go above her calves. A little water wouldn't hurt her.

Except, the lakebed kept giving way. What in the worlds? She wobbled back as the ground sucked her feet down.

"Daniel—" She grabbed his arm.

"Shit, Ms. Jones—Amadis—don't pull so hard."

"What? I can't stand!"

"The lakebed here's mud, and it's deep. Just stop struggling."

"Mud? My feet are being sucked into the bowels of your world by mud?"

"Bowels? What the hell? No. Just a foot or so. Here, take my other arm, too. I'll pull you out." A smile hit his mouth. "From the bowels."

"Are you laughing at me?" Amadis glared at her host. It wasn't her fault it had seemed like the lake was trying to drown her.

"Of course I'm not laughing at you. With you, yes."

"Oh?" She eyed him, standing dry and smug—and chuckling—on the bank. "Then why am I not smiling?"

Still grinning, Daniel leaned out further, offering both his hands to her, feet squelching in the grass, right where hers had been. He opened his mouth to say something, but before he could speak, Amadis pulled hard, toppling him into the water flat on his face, stomach, thighs.

He came up with a roar, water sluicing off his body. "Fucking hell."

Amadis blinked. That was a curse she hadn't heard before. But oh, revenge was sweet. Daniel's face said it all.

"Did you—how did—?" He rolled to his knees, his thick-fleece zippered jacket ballooning with water, clearly making it hard for him to get his balance. He shook his head, and icy droplets sprayed everywhere.

"No! Don't get me wet," Amadis said.

Daniel's eyes narrowed, fierce, assessing hers.

"What?" She lifted her hands. "I'm just trying to get out of the water. But yes, I am laughing now, too."

"Yeah, sure." His body gave a mighty shiver.

She eyed his broad chest as he found his purchase in the mud, like her. He was massive. And that was saying something, considering the immortals she'd trained with for decades.

Oh no. She cut her gaze away from his form and propelled her mind away from the thought. She was not here to get caught up by an impressive mortal.

Although perhaps making him fall into the water hadn't been the wisest option.

She bit back a sigh. Her rotten temper. But he'd spiked it with his comment, and when he'd laughed at her, the urge to get him wet had surged. And now, here they were. She should have been better than that, though. She was an Angel. Or meant to be. Maybe this was why they hadn't given her a Task until now. She was too impulsive. Too prone to emotion.

Maybe what she needed was some space from him. She couldn't afford to get distracted, not when her mission was so important.

Then Daniel unzipped his sodden jacket and tossed it on the bank.

Another shiver shook through him, and once more, his chest drew her eyes. He wore a thin black long-sleeved shirt, some kind of innerwear that molded to every hard, delineated curve of muscle. Ridges lined his stomach, his nipples were tightly peaked, and his arms curved in giant sinuous ropes.

Amadis bit her lip to stop it from making an inappropriate sound. But wow. Simply wow. If she wasn't here for her Task, she would be more than happy to spend more time in the water with her host.

"Hell, this water's freezing," Daniel said. "Come on, let's get out. Want to give me a hand up?"

Cold? She was on fire.

But then another shiver shook him. *Belar's breath.* He

really was freezing. That wasn't good. A mortal could die from such low temperatures.

"Here, let me help," she ordered.

They grasped each other's arms, and Amadis sucked in a breath, because with the touch, another surge of heat blew through her.

Her eyes flew to Daniel's. He met hers, too. Dead on.

Did he feel this heat as well?

A cloud shifted above them, and the sun once more broke through. A ray of light, golden, warm, hit them both.

Wrapped them in the moment.

"Hey, you guys need help?" a feminine voice, laced with amusement, came at them from the bank.

Amadis blinked, the spell broken. Daniel blinked too and shifted away from her.

"Here, you go first," he said, and pushed her up onto the shore, then he dragged himself up beside her.

Loss—the moment, his touch—echoed inside her. But she ignored the disappointment. The interruption was just as well. Once more, her host was distracting her.

She turned with purpose to the person on the bank.

"India. Hello, again." Amadis smiled up at the striking dark-haired witch-Keeper standing on the bank. India had arranged the accommodation at the lodge and lent Amadis her surname for the booking.

"Ah, hi," India replied. "I was going to pop by to see how you were doing, but luckily saw you here as I was driving past."

"Thank you, that is very kind. I am afraid my host lost his feet and landed in the lake. And I too."

5

Burning pain could be a disadvantage, but Ri'Anit refused to let the fire arcing through her body get in the way. She'd killed hundreds of beings in her quest to become First Follower—she'd lost her magic and had almost lost her life force.

Almost. But she was back.

As the portal ejected her into a darkened alley in the Mortalworld city of Melbourne, her feet connected with pavement, and the pain slammed through her again.

She bit back a cry, even though only the grimy walls would've heard her. There could be no weakness. No distractions.

She was there to kill the Keepers who guarded it and steal their magic. And then destroy the World Tree. From here on, everything she did would be in that endeavor. Which meant she needed two things: an army and magic.

And this grubby building where her predecessor had marshaled his soldiers would be her starting place.

She pivoted, the ends of her heavy coat swirling around

her black high-heeled boots, and slammed the door open to the warehouse.

Three immortals, all buoyed with stolen death magic, swiftly looked up—and all recoiled. She didn't care. These beings were once again hers to command.

Ri'Anit let the door grind shut. The squealing of heavy metal a balm for the cacophony of pain and hate and vengeance raging inside her.

She jerked her chin at the three Followers. "The portal needs closing. You are now my seconds. Close it. Then you will bring all our Chapters to me. We have found the region where the Keepers live, therefore we have found the Tree as well. Our soldiers are useless in any other location. One of you will then take your Chapter and scout the exact location of all Keepers. The other two will send your Chapters to bring me magic. I'll kill every single witch in this world if needs be to get the magic I—Irrika—needs."

6

An hour after falling into the lake, Amadis sat on the couch beside India as Daniel stoked the fire in the great-room hearth, his shoulders hunched over his task. Either side of him, soaring expanses of window rose from the built-in seats to the ceiling, affording a perfect view of the lake beyond, but her gaze was caught by the wide expanse of his back.

"So, what did you say brings you to Willow Grove?" Daniel asked, his attention still on the fire.

Amadis cut India a quick glance. India traded the look, as cautious as Amadis. The answer was something Amadis couldn't share. Nor could India.

"Oh, I don't think I mentioned that." Amadis blinked. Coming up with a reason for her trip hadn't been covered in her preparations. "Well, you see, India is a—"

"Friend," India said.

"—cousin."

"Well, we were so close as friends that we feel more like cousins." India frowned at Amadis. Amadis shrugged at

India. She had no experience in making up this kind of story.

"Close cousins?" Daniel paused, expression impassive as he eyed them both.

"You have it perfectly." Amadis nodded.

India groaned.

Daniel's brows rose, but without a word brushed his hands on his clean jeans and stood.

She followed his movement as he straightened to his full height.

A jab to her ribs had her frown at India. Oh. She'd been staring. She cleared her throat and tried to find something else to talk about. "So, the fire's nice." She turned to India. "Are you able to stay for some time this evening?"

"Not tonight, I have to work."

"Where do you work?" Daniel tilted his head.

Amadis stilled. How would the Keeper answer this question?

"I'm a freelance copy editor," India said with an easy smile. "And I have a piece due, so need to get back to it."

Wow, India was telling the truth—a halo of gold ringed the witch-Keeper's eyes. This woman was a Keeper *and* had a job? As in a job that had a purpose other than keeping the World Tree safe?

Amadis had been looking forward to talking to India purely in her role as guardian to the Tree. After all, India had received the call from the World Tree—something Amadis had only ever dreamed of in her wildest imaginings. But the woman was clearly more than only a Keeper.

～

DANIEL HAD to work hard to keep in a sigh after Amadis's cousin—friend—whatever she was, left. The two women had been about as subtle as an ax to the head. But what was behind their kookiness?

They were opposites. One tall, dark, with some serious cat eyes going on. The other was tiny, delicate, silver-gilded, and so fucking attractive he wanted to get skin on skin with her every bloody time he looked at her.

Hell, maybe he was the loopy one.

Daniel scowled. Getting hard over his first official guest was not the way to start a business. He bit back an oath and somehow forced his gaze away from the couch. Looked at his watch instead.

Bloody hell, it was almost 6:00 p.m., which meant he should be offering his first guest dinner. But after today, he needed a drink more than anything. A strong, rich brew. His mouth almost watered in anticipation.

"Ms. Jones, it's almost dinnertime. While I get that underway, can I get you a coffee or tea? Wine?"

"Yes, please."

He blinked. "Any preference?"

Amadis looked at him sideways, like she was measuring him. What the fuck for, he had no idea.

"Whatever you are having will be lovely," she said.

"I'm having coffee. The brew of the gods. How do you take yours?"

Amadis chewed on her lip—fuck, why did she have to do that all the time?—before finally nodding. "However you do."

"Really, no preference?"

"Well, I haven't had this godly brew you talk of before, so no. No preference."

"Ah ..." Daniel tried to find the right words but had a serious moment of brain failure. Never had coffee? Who was this woman? "Okay, let's focus on the most important thing here. You haven't had coffee before."

"No."

"Never?"

"Yes. Never." Amadis shrugged. "Why is this important?"

"Important?" Daniel almost spluttered. "Lady, you are about to have an introduction to the world's finest beverage." He didn't even stop when Amadis rolled her eyes. "I'm serious—and believe me, I've had a lot of beverages in my life. But there is one single drink I guaran-goddamn-tee you I'm drinking every day. And this is it."

"You are very insistent about this beverage. Thank you; I would be delighted to try it."

Daniel glanced sideways at his guest. Once again, her words juxtaposed her image. The funky haircut, the casual clothes. But who spoke like she did?

"Right, and then I'll get on to your dinner." If the fine hairs on the back of Daniel's neck rose any higher, they'd be longer than the ones on his head. But he didn't say anything. Yet. "Now, you didn't mark down any dietary requirements on your booking, and tonight's meal is going to be a beef stew. Does that suit?"

"Beef stew? I will try that as well. But I am more interested in the godly beverage you drink every day."

"Right, well, in that case, I'm going to make the finest batch of coffee I've ever made." And induct this ... this heathen into the world of coffee worship. Then spend some serious time figuring her out.

While he was in the kitchen making the perfect brew, the back door opened. Shannon bustled in, arms full of grocery bags, the winter breeze rolling behind her before she slammed the door shut with a thwack from her hips.

"These are the times a wide backside is useful." She laughed and waggled her eyebrows.

"You should've called me. I would've grabbed these from the car." He stepped over and took the shopping from her hands.

"Sweetheart, I've been carrying more bags than these for longer than you've been alive. Now, sorry I'm late with dinner. Julie Simmons went into labor, and the baby didn't want to wait. No surprise with it being Julie's fourth and all. Luckily, I was in town when I got the call, so I was there in time to catch her." Shannon laughed.

"Fourth? At home?" Daniel couldn't keep the smile from his face. "Man, they breed country girls strong out here. And I'm just making coffee for our first official guest. She doesn't seem too hungry just yet. How about you join us?"

"Well, I'll take a tea. That would be lovely. And given it's bloody cold out here, very welcome."

"Head into the lounge, warm up by the fire, and I'll be in soon. By the way, our first guest isn't a Mr. Jones; it's a Ms. Jones. Goes by the name of Amadis."

"Amadis Jones." Shannon rested back against the bench, all casual. But her gaze sharpened.

"Mm, is the name familiar?"

"Oh, not the Amadis, and that's unusual enough that I'd recall it, this being such a small community and all. But the

Jones name, well, that's very familiar. We have a long history with the Joneses around here. Wonder if she's one of them."

"Why does that sound ominous?"

"Oh no, nothing like that. More of a friendly family rivalry." Shannon pushed the hair back from her face. "Even so, the Joneses are a well-known part of the local community. I'll go talk to your guest."

Daniel snorted. Country people were a breed apart.

Once the hot drinks were ready, he piled them onto a tray and backed through the door into the great room.

"Coffee and tea are ready," he said as he turned around.

A frisson of something raced through the air—a current of unseen electricity—that fired up along his skin, and as quickly as it was there, it disappeared. Fuck. What was that? He glanced around the room. But there was nothing that could give off a shock like that.

In front of the fire, Amadis and Shannon stood face to face, staring at each other.

Shannon wasn't tall, but what she lacked in height, she made up comfortably in her sturdy frame. And yet, with the two of them standing, facing each other, it was tiny Amadis who held the balance of power. Her chin was lowered, and her body tensed as if she was going to leap into action.

It was like they were squaring off. What the fuck was going on?

Right, enough was enough.

He set the coffee tray—made of local mountain ash that he'd turned and polished to bring out the hue of the grain— down with a rap on the side table. Both women turned to him.

"Okay, it's time." He crossed his arms. "What's going on here?"

Amadis cut him a look but returned her attention to Shannon.

Shannon folded her arms over her chest too.

"Uh-uh. Don't ignore me." He blew out a breath. "And don't give me some BS answer. I've dealt with enough of that over my life not to need it right now. So, come on, 'fess up."

Suddenly, both women relaxed. At the same time.

"Nothing's going on here, Dan." Shannon smiled and took a seat on the couch closest to the fire. "We're just getting to know each other, and I'm over here warming up. These old bones feel the cold more and more every day."

"Ha, old? You just helped deliver a baby. That's not old."

Amadis gasped.

"I am old." Shannon gave him a look. "Old enough to be semi-retired, anyway."

Amadis turned fully to Shannon. And not in the same I'm-about-to-fight-to-the-death stare they'd been trading only moments before. In a way that suddenly, he wanted to have her look at him.

Uh-uh. He scowled at himself. This was his first guest. Probably wasn't the most professional thing to get down and dirty with your customers. Plus, something wasn't on the up-and-up with A. Jones.

First her, then her cousin-friend, and now Shannon was acting all weird.

But then Amadis darted to Shannon.

He had the loco urge to grab the smaller woman, stop her from doing harm—like that was even a possibility—when she dropped to the couch beside Shannon.

"You delivered a baby?" Amadis said. "Are you a midwife? That is one of the most important tasks a being can have. And you did that today? That must have been incredible."

Shannon smiled, a genuine curve to her lips and appreciation lighting her eyes. "It was incredible. And on this occasion, it was more like catching the baby." Shannon's smile widened. "I like you. You've got an appreciation for the important things in life."

Daniel laughed; it turned it into a cough when two sets of eyes swiveled to him. "Good to see you two getting along now. And don't think I missed how you changed the conversation. But fine, coffee and tea's ready, and I'm not wasting good brew." He nodded down at the tray. "Now, Shannon, you might be a certified tea drinker"—he ignored the roll of Shannon's eyes—"but Ms. Jones, *you* are in for a treat."

Shannon looked at him like he was the one who'd gone mad.

"I'm ignoring you on purpose, Shannon. You don't realize—this is our guest's very first coffee."

Shannon pursed her lips and cut Amadis another look.

Daniel approved of her suspicion, but right now, they had more important things to do. "Okay, Ms. Jones." He waited until Amadis looked at him. Ignored the spark of energy, the way his heart picked up pace when she set her gaze on him. "I drink my coffee straight—how do you want to try yours?"

"Ah—"

"Now, now, if this really is your first try, ease into it," Shannon said. "I'm a milk and sugar woman myself." She picked up her mug of tea and took a sip. "You don't want to scare your taste buds off first sip."

"Well ..." Amadis turned to Shannon.

"Uh-uh, don't listen to Shannon; she's a watery-sweet-tea drinker. Trust me, you go into coffee drinking with the purest flavor first. Get your taste buds accustomed to the best from the start."

Shannon snorted.

He laughed.

"Wait." Amadis held up both hands. "You two are making it impossible." A smile crept over her face, and her eyes lit from within with a pure richness of laughter that outdid the strongest coffee taste he could ever recall.

That light called to him, made him want to smile right back, bask in the warmth of her.

Daniel's pulse, already beating hard, picked up pace.

Harder. Faster.

And then Amadis took the cup from the tray. "I'm going to try it both ways. But that means without your sugar and milk first."

Still smiling, she glanced at Shannon before raising the cup to her mouth—that lush, perfect mouth—then looked at Daniel over the rim of the cup. As she blew softly across the brew, steam lifted, shrouded her eyes for one second.

But then she sipped, and her gaze met his.

Surprise, delight, satisfaction filled her gaze in succession—a look he'd given her with a simple taste of coffee.

A shaft of desire hit him hard in the gut, heated him, spread to his groin in a rush. Fucking hell, he wanted to see that look on her face beneath him, above him, *because* of him. Not some goddamn coffee.

A surge of ice doused the heat. What the hell was going on? He was thirty-six. Not a teenager with a crush.

Focus, Daniel. Willow Grove was about the simple life. The quiet life. And no fighting. These women with their secrets and weird behavior bloody well better not be bringing anything like that to his door. Hell, he'd rather Amadis pack up her bags and find another hotel than anything like that.

Peace. Quiet.

He repeated the mantra in his head as he turned away. Blew out a surreptitious breath. "Right, I'll get onto dinner. You, ah, enjoy your coffee—however you want."

And he squashed the satisfaction that blazed from giving her that look.

fter dinner, Amadis closed the door to her bedroom, the handle locking with a quiet snick, and waited for the telltale bunch of her muscles, the pace of her heartbeat to pick up. The dread to leaden her belly.

Sure enough, they all arrived, but nowhere near as strong as earlier.

She took another steadying breath and worked through the moment. Focused on the window ahead, on the solid ground beneath her feet.

Irrational. Irrational. She repeated the word, over and over, with each deep, slow breath she forced into her lungs as she waited for the fight-or-flight instinct to surge.

Except instead, the lead weight eased, her muscles relaxed.

That was an improvement. Cheering inside, Amadis grinned. Had she conquered that reaction? She sat down on the edge of the bed, suddenly more at ease than she'd been in the Mortalworld yet.

And what an evening. The food had been an unfamiliar

experience. Chunks of meat cooked to be so tender it had fallen away as she chewed it, drenched in a thick, rich sauce. She had used a bread roll slathered in butter to scrape every drop from her plate.

Mortals ate well. Very well. Everything the Angelkin consumed—bread and proteins—was designed for energy production only. Nothing ever made her tongue dance or her mouth water.

Her host hadn't joined her, muttering something about having to work and that he would grab a bowl later. But Amadis hadn't minded. Getting space away from him had given her room to breathe. Daniel was ... he was ... Intense. Massive. Perceptive.

And that perception could be a problem. She sensed his unease, or perhaps disbelief, when some of her comments must not have made sense. She was working hard to blend in, but everything was so new—exciting— unusual, and she wanted to see it all and experience it all while she could.

Except she was here on a mission. And that led her to possibly the worst problem with her host. He was fascinating. The urge to touch him, to get close to him, skin to skin, overwhelmed her every time they were near.

What was it about Daniel that was so captivating?

One thing was certain, though. He was a distraction. One far more interesting than the cars and the house and the food.

And she couldn't afford to be distracted.

She needed to focus on her Task and find the next Keeper so they could be called into service to the Tree. Someone who was *a child of the village*. Not that she was looking for an actual child. The World Tree would never call a child into service.

No, she was looking for an adult who had grown up here. Gods, please let the person still live in the village; otherwise, her Task was going to be even harder. But she had a starting point, the 569 permanent residents.

At least Shannon had shared information on some of the locals before she'd left for the night. Amadis had filed away every comment as the other woman had chatted about their little community.

And Shannon had been lovely. She'd recognized Amadis as a witch even with Amadis's low-level powers, but also as someone not from the Mortalworld. And once she'd determined Amadis wasn't a threat—although that had taken Amadis answering quite a lot of Shannon's questions as honestly as she was allowed—the older woman had opened up about Willow Grove and the surrounding areas.

So tonight, it was time to use that information and set out to find the next Keeper. To finally let her wings free, complete a full reconnaissance of the region, and put her decades of training to use.

Once again, Amadis eased the constrained muscles of her wings out one by one. The powerful muscles and tendons that grew from scapula to wing were the tightest, and she stretched them over and over until all the kinks were free.

Finally, that involuntary shimmy trembled through her.

Amadis changed into a black shirt perfect for night flying, secured her swords in their scabbard, and fastened the sheath on her back.

As she eased up to the windowsill, the total dark of the

forest beyond called her name, beckoned her into the veil of shadows and night.

With a leap, Amadis took off.

Her wings caught the air, and the updraft against them had her soaring high into the trees within moments.

A car engine rumbled somewhere off in the distance, and the rustle and snap of animals moving through the forest echoed around her. But otherwise, she was alone.

She turned, hovering to look at the lodge.

Dim light spilled from the windows on the main level, but the rest of the building was dark. Had her host gone to bed already? He'd disappeared after serving dinner, so she had no idea where he was. Just in case he was still awake and looking out into the forest, she dropped further into the trees, her wings blending into the shadows, the leaves her curtain.

She stayed still for a moment ... no movement or change in the lights. Perfect—she was free to move.

Across the moonlit lake, the lights of the village of Willow Grove shone.

Her powerful warrior wings, strong and built for the night, propelled her into the sky. Another time she would have enjoyed the crisp, clear air, the way the stars called out with their joy and light, but all her attention was on the lights of the village across the water.

She landed silently near the one building in town that housed a drinking establishment—Shannon had called it a pub.

Ahead, twin beams of light bloomed in the distance, synchronized, traveling toward her, followed by the rumble of a motorized engine. A vehicle.

Amadis tucked her wings in tight. These mortals certainly were surprising with their grasp of technology to make living easier.

The car must have stopped close to the pub because suddenly the motorized rumble ceased.

Well, this was it. She'd made it. She was in the village where she would find her quarry. Where she would finally complete her first Task and prove to the Kin she was fit to be part of their community.

With a deep breath, Amadis walked around the two-story building until she was at the front door. Light shone from two large windows, and inside, villagers were gathered in small groups, talking and drinking and eating.

Following the muted chatter and music that echoed from within, Amadis entered the building.

The curious gazes of half a dozen mortals—men and women—including her very own host, met her.

Daniel sat alone at a high table, drinking an amber beverage. He slowly withdrew the glass from his mouth and placed it squarely in front of him.

What was he doing here?

His fierce eyes traveled over her. And everywhere his gaze touched, heat tingled.

Amadis had never had a reaction like it. Hadn't known it was even possible.

When his eyes drew back to hers, the pull of the indigo depths almost had her step to him. And then he frowned.

Uh-oh. Had her glamour dropped? She twisted the metal ring around her forefinger. No ... the subtle tingle still vibrated over her skin, so the magic was still present.

So, what else had caused the scowl? Well, she didn't have

time to worry. She nodded at Daniel and then surveyed everyone else present.

A young man, barely on the cusp of adulthood, served drinks behind the bar. Two white-haired elderly gentlemen sat at the bar; they were holding hands and were deep in conversation about something nice, judging by their smiles.

Two stocky men sat side by side at another high table, and a man and woman sat facing each other at a low table.

Where to start first? And was it the polite thing to acknowledge her host before she began interviewing everyone else?

And if she did, would that be productive or a hindrance to her Task?

The two stocky males, wearing jeans and thickly woven checked shirts, stood up from their high table, picked up glasses and came toward her. They moved fast, given how unsteady they both were on their feet.

The taller of the two attempted to smooth down a tuft of reddish-brown hair, then jostled with the shorter man.

She had to crane her neck to look them in the eye, and they each had the brawn of a fighter. Could one of them be her quarry?

Their gazes were bright and, going by their gait and odor, influenced by whatever they were drinking. She balanced her weight evenly across both feet in case she had to make a swift move but did nothing else.

"Hey," Red Hair said to her. "You're new to town, ain'tcha?"

Amadis tilted her head, replayed the words over in her mind until she understood what they meant. "Yes."

Red Hair smiled, a cute grin showing off two dimples

that most local females no doubt found attractive. "I knew it." He struck his friend in the side with his thick elbow. "Didn't I tell you?"

"Yep. You said." The friend grinned, too. Apparently not minding the strike.

"Hey, maybe this will be my lucky day twice."

"And why is that?" Amadis didn't hold back a smile. These two were amusing in their earnestness.

"I'm an uncle. Again. My baby sis had her baby." A tear worked out of Red Hair's eye.

"Okay, boys. Why don't you let Ms. Jones sit down and get comfortable, given she must have walked a damned fast three miles to get here, and I'll get you another drink. To celebrate your newest family member."

Amadis barely contained a jump as Daniel's gravelly voice echoed from right behind her. Heat crackled where he stood behind her. It tempted her to lean back into him. Wrap that heat around her.

She stepped forward. Refused the temptation. "Mr. O'Connor. Lovely to see you again."

"Hmm." Daniel eyed her for a long moment. Too long.

Heat worked through her cheeks, but she didn't look away—couldn't have, even if she'd wanted.

Suddenly he blinked and ducked his head. "So, can I get you that drink?"

"Oh, well, that's unnecessary."

"Hey, I insist. You being my first customer and all. What would you like?"

"To drink?"

"Let me guess. Whatever I'm having?"

"Yes, please. And while you do that, I'm going to offer my

congratulations once more to your friend. I'll meet you back at your table."

A frown touched Daniel's face before he pivoted and stalked to the bar.

The tension and the heat in the air cleared.

Wow, that had been him? His physical presence, not just his physique, was truly unlike any other she'd known. But none of that mattered.

Focus, Amadis.

She turned back to Red Hair and his friend. They both appeared to be in their late third decade, surely a time of physical prime. Now, what clues could rule them in or out?

Not that she had a specific guide on what to look for.

The conversation with the chatty pair was easy enough and revealed they were born and bred in the community and worked in the local mechanic shop.

But nothing gave her any sign that they may be the one. She held in a sigh. This Task might be harder than she'd thought.

And then Red Hair stood up. "Now, you being a foreigner an' all, I'm going to be the … the …" He turned to his friend. "Whaddya call it? Yeah, that's it. I'm gonna be your officially welcome committee." A beaming smile lit up his broad face.

"That is very kind of you, but I don't need any, um, committee."

"Uh-uh, you can't say no. It's the only right thing to do."

"Oi, I'm the one who should be the officially committed." The friend also stood up.

A loud sigh echoed over Amadis's shoulder. "Chris and Jake," Daniel said, "here are those drinks I promised. And since Ms. Jones is staying in my lodge, I guess that makes me her *official* welcoming committee. But that's mighty good of you both to offer. I'll be sure to let you know if we need any help." Daniel held a tray of three drinks, and he deposited two of them on the table and lifted one toward Amadis. "I got you a lager since you wanted the same as me and all."

Right, well, at least she'd spent a little time with the two men. She could experience this lager and then move on to the others in the room. Amadis mentally added Chris and Jake to her list with a question mark. She couldn't cross them out entirely, but her instinct was to say no.

And right now, her instinct was all she had to go on.

The obvious sign of a Keeper was a person who could offer some type of service to the World Tree. Either in defense or offense.

Daniel gestured ahead of him, apparently asking her to precede him to the high table.

Holding in a sigh, she took a seat on the stool nearest the wall so no one could come up in stealth behind her.

Once he'd sat down too, Daniel took a slow sip of his drink and eyed her.

Oh, she was to drink now, too. She inwardly smiled. Time for another new experience.

The glass was icy to the touch, and the condensation not quite comfortable beneath her grip. The malty smell got her nose twitching even as she drew the glass to her mouth, then a metallic taste hit her lips.

It was a type of beer. She had tasted a version several times over the years in the Kin lands, but that Higherworld beverage had been too bitter to enjoy. This lager was crisp and light, yet with a burst of malty flavor. Wow. All that taste in one mouthful?

"I'm guessing by the scrunch of your nose you don't like it?" Daniel said.

"Um, this isn't dislike—not exactly. It's unusual but interesting. And it packs a lot of flavors into one tiny sip. But then all of your tastes have done so today." The crisp malty flavor was more enjoyable with the second taste. "It's amazing; the more you drink, the less unusual, and the more interesting this gets."

"Slow down, bevy-bess; you're only a lightweight. Wouldn't want you to get drunk and have to find your way home in the dark."

"Lightweight? I'll have you know I am as strong as—"

"As?" Daniel cocked his head, raising his glass again.

Amadis snapped her mouth shut. She'd almost let slip something right there, and that was bad. She considered Daniel for a moment. He appeared casual, the comfortable position of his body side-on to hers. But his eyes ... those indigo portals told her something else.

He was gauging her. Her radar went on high alert.

"As strong as the next female." She left the glass on the table. "But you're right; I don't want to become drunk and ... walk back to the lodge."

"How *did* you get here so fast?" Daniel's brows lifted almost off his face. "And where's your jacket? You must be bloody freezing."

Belar's breath. This male was being difficult. She looked around, tried to find a truthful answer that would satisfy him. Amadis bit her lip. She'd already had to lie numerous times, and she'd been in this realm for a little over twenty-four hours. What kind of Angel was she?

"Did you hitch a ride?" Menace suddenly oozed from Daniel.

What did hitch a ride mean? Hitch was to move or jerk something into a different place. That was a word she knew. But the context threw her. She moistened her lips as viable options flew through her mind.

"Listen," Daniel said, "I know you hear tales of how hitchhiking's a cool thing to do and all, but it's not. It's absolutely not okay to hitch a lift with a stranger, okay? You never know who's in the car, what their intent is. There's been ... let's just say some pretty awful things have happened to hitchhikers over the years. And you're so tiny; you'd be an easy mark."

Tiny? Amadis's brows rose high. *Easy*?

She was more than capable of taking on any person who might wish to do to her something awful.

Right before she jumped off her seat and showed her host exactly how easy she wasn't, she stopped. *Hitchhiked*, ah ... now she understood. He thought she had picked up a ride from his lodge to the hotel with a stranger, and apparently, this was a dangerous exercise.

Now his comments made sense. Amadis clenched her hands in her lap to keep from springing up and proving herself and her strength.

Let him think that's what she'd done; that would be much more helpful than having to create some other plausible explanation for how she'd come into town so quickly. But then his comments triggered another thought.

"Are you saying there are people here who are dangerous?" Her heart picked up pace. A dangerous person might have the kind of fighting skills the World Tree would see as a benefit.

"Locals?" Daniel recoiled. "Well, no. I mean, I don't know everyone, obviously. But I haven't met anyone dangerous. But the thing is, you still get people traveling through. And you wouldn't know. That's why you just shouldn't do it."

"Right. Well, it's good to know the dangers of hitchhiking. Thank you." Subject-change time ... again. And time to escape the beam of that unwavering indigo regard. "So, this is your town's standard place to gather?"

"Gather is one way you could describe it. As you'd have noticed, Willow Grove is pretty small, so there's only the one pub here. Jenny-Lee Ellis runs the place, and that's her son Alex behind the bar."

Perfect, she could learn more about the town and its people from Daniel and make use of these few minutes. Amadis let her host talk, all the while resisting the heat that poured off him—swept invisible fingers across her skin, urged her to move closer.

More gravelly words flowed, and all her focus shifted to him. Desire coiled low in her belly. His firm lips shaped the words; the line of his throat was defined when he sipped his drink. That carved jaw flexing with each movement. His powerful hand wrapped around the glass. What else could those fingers wrap around?

Her pulse jumped. Gods, how would all that heat and muscle feel to touch—

"So, that's the town. Listen, I'm beat, gonna head back. Do you want a lift? Now that you've sworn off hitchhiking and all. It's too cold to walk back, and even if you had the right gear—which you don't—it's not the best idea this time of a night, even if we are a small town."

The spell broke. Amadis blinked.

Gods, how had she lost time again? She hadn't even taken in the words he said.

She blew out a short breath. The couple who had been at the bar had left, and even Chris and Jake appeared to be leaving.

No, no, no, *no*. She'd missed her chance. She pushed aside the beer.

"So you didn't like it?" Daniel asked.

"I'll pass on any more of this beverage." Amadis couldn't contain her grimace. "It distorts perspective."

And please let it be the lager playing with her focus. Because there was another explanation—her host. What if he was hampering her on purpose? He could be an agent for the Order. India had explained a little about the Order's recent efforts to destroy the World Tree. Although the Keeper had been certain she and her fellow guardians of the Tree had ousted the Order from this region.

But no, Amadis had sensed no death magic, in fact, no magic of any kind in Daniel. The only oddity was that she could not read his truth.

She gave her host one more glance as he shrugged those mighty shoulders into a sturdy leather jacket. Her mouth went dry. Hah, there was no need for him to purposefully hamper her—he drew her attention like a night breeze would tempt her to lift aloft and dart along the currents.

And then he turned back to her.

Fast.

Too fast for her to avert her eyes—and once more, his

indigo gaze captured hers. She automatically sought his truth and once more failed. Instead of his truth, a sea of beckoning heat met her.

But this time, she steeled herself. Concentrated on an image of the World Tree as it had been when she'd come to the Mortalworld. *The towering trunk, large enough to hide a dozen fighters, holding aloft arm after arm of limbs that pushed long bright leaves into the soft morning sky.*

That was why she was here. To find the next Keeper— the next warrior who would guard the Tree and ensure its existence into the future.

She was here for a purpose. Not a male. And with that, she extricated herself from the moment. Finally, she summoned an impersonal smile.

"Thank you for the offer; however, I'm going to stay here a little longer."

"Here?" Daniel's eyebrows rose.

"Yes, I would like to talk with ..." She turned to the bartender. What was his name? "Alex."

Daniel's gaze cut to the bar. "Right. Well, see you around, Ms. Jones."

DANIEL SCOWLED and jammed his hands in his pockets as he strode out of the pub. He ignored the way the stars sparkled down at him, kind of like the way his guest's eyes sparkled, ignored the blast of icy air, ignored the fact that Amadis would fucking freeze if she tried to walk back. Not his problem.

And it wasn't like they had easy access to taxis or a car

service all the way out here. Her options were to walk back or hitch another ride.

Still, not his problem.

But he couldn't ignore the shiver that shook through him at that thought.

Damn it. She'd said she wouldn't hitch again—but Ms. Jones was young, and he could recall plenty of times he and Ben had gotten into trouble, and they'd been older than she had to be. She was what, maybe early twenties? No way was she more than that, going by her clear, smooth skin. Even if her eyes, those lakes of meltwater, sometimes held a depth of experience that he only ever saw in the mirror.

Fuck. Even as Daniel unlocked his SUV, he rocked back on his heels, looked around.

A noise at the pub door caught his ear, and he turned as Chris and Jake staggered out. So it was just Ms. Jones and the bartender left.

He could at least make sure the locals didn't cause her any grief. Chris had looked very interested. But soon enough they staggered off into the night, disappearing down the dark road heading out of town.

Maybe Ms. Jones would stay the night here with the kid —Alex was certainly more her age than Daniel. His gut seesawed.

Oh hell, he was jealous. Of a kid. Daniel shook his head at himself.

No way he was going there. Ms. Jones was a customer, and that was it. So what if she was sexy as all hell and made his heart pump just looking at her? He had a lifetime of experiences that made him the absolute worst guy to even think about having a relationship with—not that anything like that was even on the cards for him.

He was after a simple life. Quiet. No more bullets and carnage and death.

Images whirred past his eyes—the black of the night dissolving into an endless bone marrow of desert, the icy air heating beneath an unrelenting sun; his best friend shoving him aside, taking several rounds heading straight for him. Daniel's heart and stomach and fucking world dropping alongside Ben to the ground.

Daniel froze. The familiar arrow of stress ricocheted through him.

Flashback. Just a flashback.

He took a deep breath, pushed it down through his core, through his thighs, through his calves, to his feet. Pressed them hard against the ground.

Took another breath, deeply in. Out.

And the tension receded.

Fuck, it had been ages since his last episode. He needed to get back to the woodshed. To get his hands moving and his mind calm. His palms itched to feel the grain of timber beneath them.

He cast one last glance at the pub. The front door was closed; he cursed and got into his SUV. But even as he turned his key, the hairs on the back of his neck prickled, one by one. He ran a hand over his neck, looked around again.

He knew that feeling—or had when he was in the army.

Nothing stood out. No overt sign of danger, or even covert. Hell, they were in the safest, sleepiest town he'd ever known. It must be a holdover from his anxiety attack and the flashbacks.

He checked the pub again. Nope, no movement.

Fuck it. He pulled out of the car park and headed home.

Fifteen minutes later, Daniel pulled his SUV into the detached garage and strode into the lodge through the back entrance.

The smell of dinner still lingered in the air, rich with beef and herbs. His stomach grumbled.

Of course. He hadn't eaten any dinner. He quickly reheated a large bowl of the chunky aromatic mix and set about eating it at the kitchen table. After he'd cleaned up, he went into the great room and turned on a lamp, left enough light that his guest could make out the way to her room if she was back before morning.

He was walking back out to the workshop when a crunch in the leaf litter nearer the lodge caught his attention.

He tensed, swiveled.

A shadowy blur of movement darted back into the woods. Disappeared.

"Hey!" Daniel yelled, racing to the edge of the forest. The dark canopy of the trees loomed high; solid trunks blended into the night, a deep, unending void.

He stilled, let his eyes adjust, but no motion came. No sounds other than the result of small creatures on the forest floor, the swoosh and crack of limbs and branches.

What had that been?

He turned away, doubting his own eyes. Then another crack, loud, sharp, came right at his back. He pivoted again.

A soft swoosh, almost a sigh, breathed into the night, and a flurry of winged things took flight in the canopy.

Birds, bats, their screeches and calls a cacophony that overshadowed everything else.

Fuck. That was not right. He took a step past the demarcation of tended lawn to brush and forest scrub, but the stuff was too thick for him to pass through silently.

And the trail into the forest was on the other side of the lodge.

The hairs at the base of Daniel's neck rose once more—the prickly buggers. Something had been right here. Right at his back.

8

S tanding over the remains of the fallen Order soldier, Amadis lowered *Daudhi* and *Dagr*. Moonlight, where it broke through the canopy, glinted off what silver shone beneath the dark wet stain of blood covering the swords.

Her arms shook even as she watched the body and head for signs of regeneration. None came.

Her breath whooshed out, and Amadis staggered for a step, caught herself before she tripped into the scrub. She didn't want to make any more noise. Daniel was close—so close that had she reached the lodge minutes later, the soldier would have skewered him.

She carefully looked around. The scrub and night and her midnight wings hid the scene from Daniel's view from where he stood at the edge of the woods. But she needed to attend to the remains before her host came back with a light, or morn lit up the forest.

Amadis grimaced. Her first kill hadn't been part of the plan.

But she'd done it—would do it again to protect the innocent and to protect the World Tree. That was the end goal of her Task, after all.

Although *Belar's breath*, why were the Order here? And was this why Freya had called on Amadis for this Task?

Amadis held herself still until Daniel turned, his face cast in a million mysterious shadows, and walked back into the lodge.

Only after light shone inside his rooms did she kneel and carefully wipe clean her swords using the foliage about her. And then she shot into the air toward the residence of the Keeper Thrane.

He and the other Keepers needed to know about the Order's presence, and she needed insight into how to find the next guardian of the World Tree.

Even if the Keeper was not present, he had barrels of Higherworld salt that would consume the remains of the Order soldier.

Amadis had been to the residence when she had first arrived in the Mortalworld, and as she raced high above the terrain on a current of air, she easily identified markers of the land to guide her back.

A light rain began to fall around her, and she dove to the ground, moving as fast as her wings would take her, and landed close to the Keeper's cottage.

Light shone from within the home, and before she had even approached, the front door opened.

India stared out at her.

"Amadis?"

"Excellent, you are here. Is this where all Keepers live who guard the World Tree?"

India blinked. "Ah, no. Not all of us. Mind you, there are

only three of us—Thrane, Nate and me. But I've been …
spending a lot of time lately here. Nate—he's also my cousin
—and I live at the farm over the hill. So we're all close by."

An enormous figure—even larger than Daniel—moved
into the doorway behind India. Thrane. The Keeper who
had been in this realm for hundreds of years. He wore
denim jeans and a sweater that hugged what was a very
impressive physique. He placed a hand low on India's hip.
India didn't appear to mind.

"Oh, I understand," Amadis said as she put the Keepers'
body language and actions into context. "My apologies for
the lateness of my visit; however, I need your help. And
something has happened that you need to know about."

"No worries. And please, come in. We can talk inside. It's
freezing, and the rain is starting to pour." The witch-keeper
held out a hand, and the rain stopped above Amadis's head.

"You have so much power," Amadis blurted. "Sorry, I
know it's not good form to discuss a witch's strength. I just so
rarely get to talk to other witches—let alone someone who
can control the elements."

"No worries. And I know you're a witch, too, but yeah—I
never know how much other witches want to talk about
their magic either." India's green eyes sharpened.

"My craft is minor, from my mother's side. What is—"

"All right, ladies," Thrane said with exaggerated
patience. "As India said, it's effing freezing out here. Let's
take this conversation inside."

"I don't recall the cursing part." India turned around
with a sniff.

A rumble moved through Thrane's chest, and a lazy
smile curved his hard lips, softened the planes of his face.

Amadis looked between the two for one moment before she followed India.

The narrow corridor caused a shiver to trickle down her spine. *Please, please let her not lose control in front of the Keepers.* But thankfully, India led her into a book-filled room with a high ceiling and room enough Amadis could spread her wings if needed.

It appeared India and Thrane had been in this room as the lights were on, a fire was crackling in a large stone fireplace, similar to Daniel's, and two mugs of some liquid, perhaps even the coffee that Daniel loved, sat on a table.

"Wow, you have a personal library?" Amadis asked.

"Thrane's version anyway." India smiled and looked around. "Do you have anything like this where you're from?"

Amadis couldn't help but draw closer to the walls lined with shelves full of books. Had even reached out to touch one before she pulled her hand back.

"Yes and no. We have libraries, of course. There's the Great Library where Fate lives. But in my home, nay. Although most Angels have access to the Great Library at any time."

"You're not most?" India tilted her head.

Amadis drew in a short breath. Over the years, she'd pleaded with her father to let her go to the library—especially once she gained her immortality—but after the incident, he'd refused to let her leave the Angelkin lands. She pushed the memory away.

"Nay, I am not most," she said carefully. "But it is why I am here now. When I first arrived, I told you that part of my Task here in the Mortalworld was regarding the World Tree."

"Mm. And Thrane mentioned you might not be allowed to tell us your mission ... Task, or something like that." India moved farther into the room and sat on a large seat. She reached up and took Thrane's hand—he'd moved to stand at her side but didn't sit.

Amadis let her Angel sight hover between the two Keepers. The truth of them blasted out at her. Not just a couple but bonded in the way of supernatural beings. A connection that would last for eternity.

It made her heart skip for a moment. To witness such a bond was rare. And for the briefest second, the desire for such a connection for herself sung through her. But that was one feeling she couldn't force, and certainly none of the Kin would ever see her as such.

"Your Thrane has it right," she said with a smile. "We do not normally reveal our Tasks." She took a deep breath. "However, given tonight's events, I think you need to know. So ... my Task is to find the next Keeper and bring them into service to the World Tree."

Thrane stiffened, and India shot up from the couch.

"What do you mean—the *next* Keeper?" Thrane said.

Amadis shook her head. "My instructions didn't go into that detail. All I was told was that I had to come to a place called Willow Grove, find the child of the village who will be the next Keeper, and bring them to the Tree so they may find their fate."

"But the Tree always calls the Keepers. Why on earth would it need help now?" Thrane's brows tightened over his eyes.

"I don't know," Amadis said. "But I have pondered that same question, too. Though I have to tell you that tonight, an Order soldier was at the lodge where I am staying and attempted to kill a mortal—"

"What the fuck?" Thrane appeared to shimmer for a moment, and the next second, he had a giant sword in his hand.

"Where are they now?" India's eyes flew from her mate to Amadis.

"Worry not. They are dispatched." Amadis made a calming motion with her hands. "Their skill was low and nowhere near up to withstanding my swords. But I will need your assistance to dispose of the remains, and then we need to ensure no others are close by."

"Holy shit," India whispered. "Are you okay?"

Amadis couldn't help the frown that hit her face. "Of course. I mean, I have trained for this event for decades."

India's eyes locked on her for one moment and then they widened with comprehension. "It's a thing, isn't it? Your first kill. Even when you know it's the only way, it's still a thing to know you've taken a life."

"Yes, it is." Amadis forced herself to take an even breath. "But I believe the need is more urgent to deal with the remains, lest Daniel discover them. Are you able to help? If you can, I will stay with the remains until I see the soul depart this world."

"Yes," Thrane bit out. "Right this way."

"Thank you." Amadis breathed out a sigh of relief.

"You can see souls? Is that an Angel thing?" India asked as they left the cottage.

"Nay, it is from my mother's side of the family. She was a witch from the Underworld, not Angelkin. I have little inheritance from my father."

India's gaze flew to Amadis's wings.

"Well, yes, they are a definite genetic trait."

"After we deal with the body, you need to tell us more about your Task. And how we can help." India shared another look with Thrane.

"Right," Thrane said, nodding at whatever unspoken communication had passed between the two Keepers. "Let's get Nate, too. Once he's here, we'll work up a plan for the defense of the Tree. We need to know if this soldier was a straggler from Annalise's attack or something else."

Amadis's blood quickened. She was here now, part of planning with the Keepers. Except she wasn't one. And she had her Task. Her blood chilled. "I will assist in any way that might help the Tree. But my Task must take precedence. I need to know the qualities that make a Keeper so I can narrow my search."

"Well, Nate, India and I are all different," Thrane said. "But we're all fighters in our unique way. I'd start there."

"You know, finding us another Keeper will definitely help the World Tree." India glanced over to Thrane. "How long has it been since you had this many Keepers?"

"Well over a century. And for you all to be called now, I have a sense something is coming. Something big. The last time we had multiple Keepers, the Tree came very close to annihilation."

THE RAIN HAD PASSED by the time Amadis returned alone to the body in the woods. India had offered to come with her, but Amadis had declined. She'd been the one to take this life. She would be the one to see the soul into the next world.

In the last hours of the night, she scattered the salt over the remains, then stepped back as the mineral dissolved into skin and hair and fabric, consuming everything it touched.

Around her, the forest stilled. No leaves rustled. No animal whispered through the brush and scrub. And in the silence, as the last grain disappeared, a sibilant whisper grew. The murmur turned to mist, and then the soul lifted into the air.

It hesitated, seemed to hover over the ground where its former body had fallen. And then it rose sharply into the air. Disappeared.

Amadis exhaled, only then aware she'd been holding her breath, and clenched her fists to stop her hands from trembling. It was done. One less Order soldier searching for the World Tree.

A spark of awareness rushed over her arms and neck. The World Tree. The entire reason she was here. Perhaps that was where she needed to go to find some ... clarity.

With a swoosh of her wings, she flew into the air, then banked sharply to skim the treetops of the evergreen forest, icy air streaming over her feathers.

She flew unerringly toward the Tree, her knowledge of its location as much a part of her as breathing, and when she reached it, she dropped through a gap in the canopy, into the clearing at the base of the Tree.

When she'd arrived in the Mortalworld through the Tree days earlier, she hadn't taken the time to acknowledge —to meet—this ancient.

Using her meager magic to see in the pitch black, Amadis walked between the giant roots that grew in and out of the earth until she was at the massive trunk. In the dark, the bark was indiscernible, but she didn't need magic to see it. The Tree hummed with a life force so strong it carried to her through the air like waves of electricity.

Warmth bloomed in her chest, and an image of tree branches dipping in welcome flew through her mind.

"And hello to you, too, Tree," Amadis murmured as she wrapped her arms around the Tree and hugged it back.

That warmth eased through her, and everything inside her relaxed. And suddenly, a new vision played in her mind.

An Angel child with midnight wings, hair messy, skin streaked with mud and scratches, walked hand in hand with an unknown dark-haired woman toward the Tree. Around them, the clearing was brightly lit with sunlight streaming through gaps in the forest canopy.

The youth reached out a hand and touched the Tree, and a smile broke out on her serious face. And then another being appeared—Amadis's father. He dropped to his knees, wrapped the child in his arms and looked at the dark-haired woman and said something.

His words were obscured, but the woman nodded and held out her hand. Amadis's father placed a small jar filled with something into the woman's palm and then covered her hand with his, bent his head. A wind blew through the clearing, sent leaves spiraling into the air, branches crashing into each other, whipping the ends of everyone's hair. When the leaves subsided, only the woman remained in the clearing.

The woman stared at the Tree for a long moment before

she turned and walked back into the forest, disappearing into the trees.

"*Belar's breath*," Amadis whispered. "That was my father —that child was me. But who was that woman? And why is she ... familiar?"

Warmth gathered again in her chest, along with an image of the Tree's branches dipping.

"So you can show me images and feelings, is that right?" As soon as the Tree sent another confirmation, she nodded. "Then I *have* been here before. Before this week, I mean. I knew you were familiar. And I need to ask you a question—I was sent here to find the next Keeper."

An icy wave washed through Amadis, and then a new image entered her mind. In a dimly lit clearing, a group of people stood at the World Tree; they were the Keepers and Amadis, and then through the forest from all directions, soldiers raced in, cutting down the guardians where they stood.

Next, a volley of magic launched over the soldiers' shoulders into the limbs and branches. At first, the Tree remained steady, but suddenly the mighty trunk bulged outward, then inward. A crack of energy split the air, and the World Tree shattered into a million pieces.

And then the vision disappeared.

Amadis jumped back from the Tree. "What by the gods was that?"

AMADIS STARED out over Willow Grove Lake. The grassy bank was crystalline with icy dew. Glints of gold cast by the first rays of the rising sun shimmered over the serene waters. Towering trees surrounded the lake, dark sentinels motionless in the still air.

Motionless like the last whisper of death before the body and soul part. Like it had hours earlier, courtesy of her swords.

Serenity wasn't a notion she thought of often. Although Angels aspired to the state, the closest Amadis could get was during her practice sessions.

Absently, she played with the midnight ring on her finger. The warm metal was from her mother's world—a tie to a land Amadis hadn't been to since the incident and to her mother's family, who she'd not seen since either.

A breeze rolled across the lake to dance about her legs. It raced up her back, lifted the ends of her choppy hair before darting off back across the lake toward the forest. Toward the World Tree, the entire reason she was in the Mortalworld.

A scent carried gently on unseen wings; fresh, tangy. Alluring.

She turned around as Daniel walked toward her, holding a mug, steam rising to blend in with the misty dawn.

"Morning," he said, his voice gravelly and low. "I, uh, normally come out at sunrise with a coffee, right here. To take in the start of the day, you know?"

"It's beautiful," she murmured. Speaking loudly seemed ... wrong somehow. Like it would break the beauty of the moment. "Sunrise is my favorite time of the day. And you have the perfect place to watch it."

"I'll bring two coffees tomorrow since you're an early riser."

She just smiled and nodded; she didn't correct his notion she had just awoken, when in truth, she had been awake all night.

He stepped closer, nowhere near touching her, yet somehow his presence was tangible. For long minutes, they stood there, silent, until the sun had risen above the trees and the dawn sky had lightened to a pale blue.

"So, what are you doing for the day?" Daniel finally asked, breaking the silence.

"I'm going to see more of the town, perhaps visit with India."

"Hey, don't move," Daniel whispered. "Look into the trees now." He slowly raised his hand and pointed at the brush. "Those are wallabies. They love to eat the new grass first thing in the morning."

"Oh wow," she whispered back. "They're amazing. You get to see them all the time?"

"Most days, yeah."

"You are so fortunate to have them right here with you. Part of your world."

"Yeah, I guess so. Anyway, I have to head in and get breakfast ready. But hey, tomorrow morning, then? For coffee? Sunrise?"

"I'd like that."

9

____

The following morning, Amadis finished her night patrol once again on the lakeshore. She smiled when Daniel joined her in the near-dark, carrying two steaming mugs.

"Hell, it's freezing. Here, take this, it'll warm your hands. And where the hell are your gloves?"

"Thank you for the coffee." Amadis accepted the mug Daniel handed her. "And good morning to you too."

"Sorry. Morning," Daniel muttered. His cheeks reddened. He opened his mouth as if to say more, but then he shook his head and faced the lake, his bicep brushing her shoulder.

A slow, low-burning heat gathered in her belly. She should move, should get away from his delicious, tempting heat.

But she didn't.

In the silence, warmed by the coffee and the giant, serious man at her side, she took in the daily birth of the sun. They both took a sip from their mugs. Could there be a more perfect way to start the day?

Her shoulders slowly dropped as the tension she'd carried since the Order attack dissipated. Over the past twenty-four hours, looking around the village, talking to locals, and patrolling the grounds of the lodge, Amadis had reached a final conclusion. The Kin had sent *her*, a warrior Angel, to this realm. So, she was going to help this world, the Keepers, and the World Tree—no matter that she wasn't a Keeper—for as long as she was here on this Task. And if that meant taking more lives, then that was what she'd do.

That, and make the most of every moment with this mortal. He was bewitching. It might've been a while since she'd last been skin on skin with another person, but his interest in her was still clear. And *Belar* knew Daniel drew her like a lodestone every time she was near him. Surely, she could manage to enjoy his presence and not let it get in the way of her Task?

She eyed him over the rim of her coffee mug. "You live in such a beautiful place. I had no idea it would be so peaceful here." A smile curved Amadis's mouth, and she cradled the mug against her chest.

"I think that's what drew me here." Daniel brought his mug closer to his chest, too. "That and Shannon. She was a good friend of my mum's, before my mum passed away. When I told Shannon that I was looking for something ... different to do, she suggested this place. But don't get the wrong idea about the quiet. Wait until you hear a male koala calling for a female. The sound they make is as chilling as any tale about demons and hell."

"Koalas? Those cuddly animals with tufts of hair in their ears?"

"Yep. Those little guys that look like a kid's teddy bear. They're on the move this time of the year, so you should spot a few while you're here. All part of the magic of this place, I guess." He turned back to the lake.

"The other day, you said you were new to town?" Amadis couldn't contain a frown as she considered Daniel.

He slowly nodded, though his gaze stayed locked on the water.

"Yeah. Kind of. I came here for the summer holidays a few times as a teenager and loved it. So when I was looking for somewhere to run a business, this place made sense."

"May I ask about the name?"

"Angel's Lakeside Lodge, you mean?"

"Yes." The choice of the lodge's name had been making the back of her neck itch from the moment she'd arrived. Amadis eyed him over the rim of her mug as she took a sip of the hot brew. Daniel's lips twisted and then his cheeks reddened again.

"Angel is—well, *was*—my nickname. A mate in the army gave it to me. As kind of a tribute to him, I kept the name for the lodge."

Belar's breath. He'd fought in an army?

"You were a soldier?" she asked as casually as she could manage.

"Yeah. And I guess that's why I came here. The peace of this place compared to where I'd been."

Sensing Daniel wouldn't open up if she probed too sharply, Amadis mirrored his stance. But she wanted— needed—to know more about this mysterious mortal.

"Well, you certainly found the place for peace," she softly replied.

A tiny internal ripple shook her; the events two nights earlier had not been peaceful.

She cleared her throat, dislodged the lump that had knotted there. "May I ask what you did in the army?"

Daniel stilled. Clearly not comfortable with her question.

"Sorry if that was too personal," she said. "You don't have to answer."

"Nah, it's okay." He sighed, still staring out over the lake. "It's a normal question people ask. I was just a combat engineer."

"Why did you leave?"

This time Daniel turned to look at her. Pain radiated in his eyes. She wanted to ask more. Wanted to find out all about him. But that was only for her—to ease *her* curiosity. And right now, that was not what Daniel wanted.

"You don't have to answer that," Amadis said. "I am just ... curious, I suppose. About you. But that was too personal."

Daniel's eyes flared.

Gods, was blurting that out too much? Her cheeks warmed. But she *was* curious about Daniel. Nay, more than curious. He was a flame—the opposite of the icy perfection of the Angelkin world. And she wanted to get close enough to be scorched by his fire.

She blew out a low breath, forced herself back to the view. Let the warmth of the wonderful sun fill her from the inside out.

But her gaze was pulled to something even more

wonderful. Daniel's legs were braced apart, his broad shoulders turned like hers, his granite jaw gilded.

Irises, the deep slate blue of a stormy ocean, crashed into hers.

The gentle heat grew richer, deeper. Simmered, then boiled within her veins. It pooled in the pit of her stomach and deep between her legs.

Her heart began to hammer.

Daniel's lips tightened, and his eyes dropped to her mouth. Her skin tingled as if stroked by that look alone.

And suddenly, more than anything she'd ever wanted, she wanted to kiss him. Wanted to know his taste. His feel.

He lowered his mug.

She shouldn't. The first tenet of an Angel's Task was to stay focused on the goal. But that warning drowned beneath the heat pooling low in her belly, the coffee, him ... the chance to experience this Mortalworld on a level far deeper than any other.

She lifted on her toes. Flicked a glance at his sculptured lips, then back to his eyes.

But he didn't move. Did he want to kiss her? Then his gaze deepened, the pulse at the base of his neck began to visibly beat. But still, he didn't move.

His body heat; it coiled around her, worked its way under her skin. Until there was no choice.

Amadis rose as high as she could, eyes locked on his until they were a breath apart. But he was too tall for her to make that last distance.

She grasped his forearm, pulled him down. His eyes flew wide. His mouth curved and then met hers.

Coffee, heat, desire crowded her senses.

And then his tongue stroked her lower lip.

Her heart thudded painfully in her chest before it beat double-time to the sound of the blood roaring through her veins.

He did it again, and with a moan, she met his tongue with hers.

His arms tensed hard beneath her hands, and a growl worked up and out of him, reverberating through his chest.

Her body reacted. Suddenly, everything in her wanted to be closer. Touching him. Surrounding him. Surrounded *by* him.

Amadis's mug fell from her hand, hitting the ground with a thud.

She rocked back.

Heart still pounding, she hauled in a shuddering breath. She'd wanted a Mortalworld experience, but this ... this wasn't an experience. This was soul changing. From a kiss.

Was a mortal kiss meant to do that? Was this why Angels were warned away from mortal entanglements?

Something that enticing, overwhelming, was dangerous.

A chill prickled over her skin with icy fingers, no less cold than the waters of the lake they stood beside.

Right as the rumble of a car engine echoed through the morning air, followed by the crunch of tires over gravel at the front of the lodge.

Amadis blinked.

Daniel frowned.

"Hi, anyone here?" India's voice rang out.

Gods, India was here? Amadis threw a quick look at Daniel. His face was impassive once more, but the fire wasn't entirely banked in his gaze. She cursed under her breath and turned around. This man was too hot, too tempting.

Task first. Always the Task first.

"What did you say?" Daniel asked.

"Me? Nothing." Amadis picked up the dropped mug and hurried ahead of him toward the lodge right as India walked around the side of the building. The witch-Keeper's pretty green eyes widened as she looked at the lake.

"Morning," India said. "What a beautiful place to watch the sunrise. Even if it's freezing cold."

"Good morning," Amadis muttered. Cold? She was on fire.

"I know it's early, but I had a guest arrive unexpectedly, and they ... that is, he ... needs somewhere to stay, and I thought about this place. Daniel, do you have a room for another guest?"

"Yeah, I mean yes. Of course. I'll head inside if you want to meet me in the great room?" Daniel cut Amadis a glance, his gaze still full of that delicious heat, before he disappeared inside the lodge.

And then a new voice echoed from the front of the building. It held a warm, soothing timbre, yet with a lilting formality that was oddly familiar. And then a man emerged from around the building.

"Hello, there. Lovely to meet you," said the second-most stunning male Amadis had ever seen. Long straight black hair swept over his broad shoulders.

She gasped. Enormous white wings gleamed like starlight at his back.

"You're an"—she lowered her voice—"Angel. But I know every member of the Kin. Who ... how—"

"I am an Ex. And I am—"

"Moyarn." Amadis's breath whooshed out. Holy gods. Moyarn, *the* Moyarn, was here.

"And India is correct when she says I need accommodation." Moyarn stepped nearer, and while he wore dark jeans and a dark knee-length coat, it was immediately clear he was not of the mortal world. *Belar's breath,* his eyes were silver. Pure liquid silver. And they took her in from her head to her toes. "And you are?"

What was the protocol for dealing with an ex-Angel? This wasn't something that had been covered in Amadis's training. The Fallen had departed the Higherworld millennia ago—at least that was the story told to young Angels.

Amadis opened her mouth to introduce herself when India came back outside, followed closely by Daniel.

"Hi. I'm Daniel," he said. Judging by Daniel's casual acceptance of Moyarn, he was unable to see the ex-Angel's wings. "I'm the owner here. And you're who India wants the room for? I just need some information to complete your booking."

"Hello, Daniel. I'm Moyarn." The Angel held out one perfect hand in the traditional grip of these mortals.

"Moyarn?" Daniel said. Although he was smiling, his gaze cut to Amadis. "Another name I haven't heard of before."

"I know, it's an unusual name." The ex-Angel chuckled.

"Huh. I'm getting used to those."

But there was a tone in his voice, like how it had been outside when he'd spoken about the army, that didn't ring true. Amadis's stomach twisted.

What were the risks if Daniel suspected they were not who they said they were? Possibly very little—Daniel could ask them to leave, but that would only be a hindrance, not the end of her mission as she would stay until her Task was done.

But the fact that she'd come across an Order soldier right here? What if more came? They would care naught for these mortals. And the idea of Daniel, or Shannon, or any of the locals she'd met so far being in danger made her stomach twist farther.

No, she needed to stay right here. So they needed to keep Daniel's suspicion allayed.

"Right, well, how about we head inside, and I'll get your room sorted?"

They followed Daniel into the lodge, and he walked over to the desk where he'd checked Amadis in and opened his laptop.

"So, Moyarn, welcome to Angel's Lakeside Lodge."

Don't look at Moyarn. Don't look at Moyarn. But even though she could sense the ex-Angels' regard, she managed a calm expression and kept her focus on Daniel.

"If I can just grab your details," Daniel continued, "I'll get you sorted. What's your last name?"

Moyarn stiffened. Amadis had to turn this time—right as his gaze cut to India.

No, no, no, *no*. She could practically see the Fallen Angel's thoughts. *Belar's breath*, he couldn't use the same name. That would absolutely scream something was not right. She raised a hand, tried to catch Moyarn's eye—

"Jones," Moyarn said.

Amadis caught India's gaze. The other woman mouthed, "Oh, shit."

"Jones." Daniel stopped, hands hovering over the keyboard. His eyes narrowed at Moyarn. "Let me guess, cousin?"

Amadis rushed forward. "Yes, you see, we're all related ... distantly."

Daniel's eyebrow rose as he surveyed them all. But as his eyes landed on her, their blue was tainted with something accusatory that made her stomach twist harder. Like he expected more from her.

"Right."

The warmth from their kiss had completely dropped away.

Suddenly a door slammed in the kitchen, and a breeze rushed in, swirled around the lounge, carrying the tang of blood on icy fingers.

Goosebumps prickled over Amadis's arms.

Shannon appeared in the doorway a moment later, clothes askew and torn, scratches marring her forehead.

10

———

Adrenaline slammed through Daniel, and his fight-or-flight instinct engaged. Distrust and hurt—goddamn fucking *hurt* of all things—whipped away, along with the memory of Amadis's smooth, silky skin, her lush, intoxicating scent, as he took in Shannon's state.

He raced across the room and grabbed Shannon right as her knees wobbled, and the creases around her soft brown eyes tightened.

"Here, Shannon. I've got you. Let's get you to the couch."

Shannon nodded and leaned all her weight into him as he steered her across the room and eased her onto the cushions. Daniel knelt on the floor, held her chilled hand while she caught her breath. He eyed the deep scratches, more like gouges, dug into her skin.

At his back, the scent he associated with Amadis grew stronger, so he knew she'd approached. Sure enough, she sat beside Shannon.

"Here, let me look at you." He kept his gaze on Shannon and thoroughly inspected the wounds. "Right, I've got a medical kit here and can clean you up, but a couple of those scratches look deep, like you might need a bit more than just a plaster. Are you injured anywhere else? And what in the fu—hell happened?"

Shannon's eyes darted to Amadis and India, then stopped on Moyarn. Her already pale cheeks lost every ounce of color.

"Hey, don't go fainting on us," Daniel said. "Lie your head back."

Shannon resisted a little, her gaze still glued to Moyarn.

"It's okay, he's one of us." Amadis leaned forward and began to stroke Shannon's other hand.

"One of who?" Daniel frowned at his guest.

But Amadis ignored him and kept her gaze on Shannon. "You're safe now. And Daniel is right—please tell us if you're hurt anywhere else? And then, what happened?"

"Something chased me as I was walking here, and I ... I fell over." Shannon's hand shook as she gingerly felt the skin around her forehead.

"What the fuck?" Daniel surged to his feet. "Where? Who was it?"

"I don't ... I don't know." Shannon started to tremble, and she looked at Amadis as if the smaller woman was her lifeline. "I—I got away, just in time, and ran here."

"Let me look." Amadis leaned over Shannon's forehead. "India, you need to see this."

"Why?" Daniel stayed close to Shannon. "What are you looking for?"

"Ah, animal scratches," India said. "We've had some trouble with ... dogs around here. Just recently."

"Dogs? Shannon, you were attacked by dogs? Was it a pack or just one? I need to see where it—"

"Daniel, don't go out there." Amadis's glacial gaze flashed at him.

Whoa. He'd never seen eyes turn so iridescent before. Then her words struck him.

"I can take care of myself," he growled. "And we can't just let wild dogs roam around. I'll call the police."

"Please," Shannon said, "listen to the wit—to Amadis. She's right. You can't go out there. Not until we make sure it's gone."

"I should go," India said. "I have a connection with the local police, so I'll go let them know about the *dog* attack now. Moyarn, come with me."

"No, India. Not yet." Amadis stood up and planted her fists on her hips. She stared hard at him, that glacial tinge still present in her eyes, causing the hairs to rise along Daniel's neck. It held him in thrall as she searched his face —looked for something, though *what*, he had fuck all of a clue. Finally, she pursed her lips and nodded.

"Daniel, we may be able to convince you that this was a dog attack, but *Belar's breath*, we *shouldn't*. Though first, we need to see to Shannon—erase any trace of what they tried to do." Amadis's jaw clenched, then she sighed and turned to India. "He needs to know."

Shannon gasped, and at his back, India swore. But Amadis shot them both a hard, commanding glare. The kind of glare his old CO would give the unit when they knew they were heading into shit but didn't have a choice. One that didn't seem possible from such a ... a feminine little thing like her.

"Ladies," Amadis said, "Daniel needs to know, and he's going to guess once we cast a spell to help Shannon heal. And if he knows, then he can be on guard. And clearly, that is necessary. We can't let him go out there thinking he's looking for a mere dog."

Daniel recoiled. "Did you just say 'cast a spell?'" He shoved his hands on his hips and stared at them all.

India muttered an oath. Shannon emitted a squeak. Both turned to look at him.

"Yes." Amadis glared up at him from beneath her brows, a feisty kitten. The memory of their kiss snuck back to him, the silken lush curve of her lips, her honey taste. His fists clenched at his hips. Not the fucking time for that. He shoved the thought away.

"C'mon. Get the fuck—" He cut Shannon a look, then lowered his voice. "Amadis, get serious. What's going on?"

Amadis's gaze lowered to his lips once—as if she'd had the same thought as him—then snapped back to his eyes. Steely determination blazed from her eyes. Her chin set.

"Right. I can understand this is hard," she said. "But you have to trust me. Us. It will be easier to show you the first time." She turned back to Shannon. "Now, I'm not a ... a ... very good witch. That is, not a ... a *real* witch. But India is very strong. Would you let her perform a healing spell to help your wounds mend?"

Daniel cursed. What did Amadis mean, not a real witch? And what the hell was with all this witchcraft BS all of a sudden?

"Thank you." Shannon slowly nodded, lips still pursed. "But you stay here with me, Amadis."

Daniel couldn't stop his eyebrows from rising. Shannon

hadn't exactly been trusting of Amadis when they'd first met.

"Of course, Shannon." Amadis moved aside and gestured India closer.

The tall, dark-haired woman gave him a quick appraising look but then sat at Shannon's side.

"All right, I'll do it." She picked up Shannon's free hand. "But my magic isn't like anyone else's either."

Moyarn snorted, and Daniel eyed him carefully. Mild curiosity showed in the man's expression, but nothing more. Were they all in this together?

But then an odd buzzing crackled through the air like static. The fucking hairs on the back of Daniel's neck pricked up again.

Shit. He stood aside to make sure he could see Shannon and keep ahead of whatever kookiness was going on here—

Shannon looked straight at him. Her soft brown eyes widened, and the torn skin on her forehead evened out; the angry tinge faded. While the blood remained, the skin cleared.

"What the hell?" Daniel jerked back, stared at Shannon's face. "Where did—what did—"

"Oh, Daniel, this wasn't the way ..." Shannon whispered.

"Wasn't the way what?" Daniel clenched his fists at his sides, restrained himself from leaping over the couch and scrutinizing her forehead. How in the fuck had that just happened?

His jaw ached; he was holding it so tight, and he looked at each of the people present; everyone stared back at him. Shannon was ashen, scared. India was frowning, maybe angry. Moyarn was still fucking curious. Did the bugger's face never change? And then Amadis, his first official house-guest. Her full lips were set, and her lake-blue eyes flashed at him. Pure, clear determination.

But why? He blew out a hard breath.

"Right," Daniel said. "It's time to cut the bullshit, people. This is my place. My business. And I don't know what kind of ... of"—he tried to manage his language, failed—"*shit* is going on here. But I have just opened this place up, and I don't need anything threatening that right now." He glanced at Shannon and winced when her lips trembled. But then his eyes were drawn back to Amadis's. They stayed on her. "You need to tell me," Daniel said, "right now, what the fuck is going on."

"Yes, I—we—do. But first, India, thank you for your magic."

"No worries," India replied. "And for what it's worth, I support you on telling the truth given the situation."

He turned back to Amadis, but she had her back to him, leaning over Shannon.

"You should rest while the spell completes within you," Amadis said. "May I bring you something to refresh you while you rest? One of those teas you like?"

"Thank you, that would be nice. But I agree that Dan needs to know. Everything. And I have things to share as well." Shannon tried to smile, but her lips wobbled, and her eyes didn't leave Daniel.

"Shannon, what are you talking about?" Daniel ignored the queasiness in his gut. Tried not to stare at the skin still smoothing out on Shannon's forehead.

India coughed lightly. "Ah, I need to check the perimeter. Now. Moyarn, you should come with me."

Daniel noted through his peripheral vision India dragging Moyarn out of the room. But his eyes still didn't leave Shannon. Her face had turned a kind of puke green.

The roiling in his stomach turned to lead.

Something told Daniel he should be running in the opposite direction, but he steeled himself against the urge and instead brushed past Amadis—somehow ignoring the surge of heat that flowed with that simple contact—and sat on the other side of the couch from Shannon.

He tried to look elsewhere, but the healed skin on her forehead caught his attention. He forced his attention back to Amadis. "All right. Let me have it."

"Have what?" Amadis frowned.

Daniel barely held in a growl. Why did she take everything so literally?

"He means to tell him what you want to say." Shannon sighed. "But I think I should go first. Amadis, why don't you have a seat over there? Stay close in case this doesn't go right."

Amadis eyed him as she took a seat on the couch, perched right on the edge.

"Okay, whatever," he muttered. "What is it?"

"Well, you know your mother and I grew up here. Heck, I've known you since you were a child." Shannon moistened her lips.

"Yeah, so what does my mother have to do with anything?"

"That's what I need to tell you." Shannon started to wring her hands. "It's such a small town, no wonder we were so close. But we had something else in common. We were both witches."

He stared at Shannon. "Witches?" Had she hit her head when she'd fallen?

"Yes." She stared back at him. Face pale. Lips trembling. The skin on her forehead still fucking clearing.

"Wait. Just wait a goddamn minute. Mum—*my* mum— was a witch? And you, too?"

Shannon nodded, gaze still on him.

"Like, what does that even mean—witches? You do spells and shit? You think you've got special powers to make stuff happen?"

"Well, yes to the spells. And yes, we can influence events, and some of us have extra-special abilities. But we are all different."

"You actually believe what you're saying. I can see it in your eyes. And this is something you decided to tell me, *now*?"

"You see—" Shannon's forehead—her *healing* forehead —creased as if she was going to cry. Something oily slicked through his gut. Was this real?

"No." He jumped up as if he could run away from what had been said. Stalked to the window. "No more fricking woo-woo explanations. I can't deal with this right now."

11

As Daniel stared out toward the lake, his back stiff, hands clenched at his sides, every muscle in Amadis's body tensed, and she barely managed to stay seated.

Belar's breath. Daniel's mother—a witch—was born in Willow Grove. Would that generational link make him also a child of the village? Was *he* her target?

The pieces fit. He was a soldier, experienced in fighting.

Although if his mother was a witch, why didn't Amadis sense any magic about him? Was it linked to why her Angel sight couldn't see his truth? What else might he be impervious to?

"Daniel, please, I have to tell you this," Shannon said with a shaking voice. "Your mother left here when you were just a baby. She told me then that if something happened to her, she'd arrange for you to come back here. And then you did, twelve years later when you joined me for the summer holidays. At first, I didn't know how to explain your mother's gift. You were so lost without her. So I thought to wait until you finished high school. But then you up and joined the army and haven't been back … till now."

Amadis held in a sigh. She had to prove if Daniel was the next Keeper, but the tension between Daniel and Shannon was too much for her to let go unchecked.

"Shannon, be at ease," she said. "You have been hurt and need to rest. This distress is not good for you."

Daniel whirled around. Remorse tightened his features, and Amadis silently cheered. Of course he wouldn't want to cause the older woman harm intentionally.

Outwardly, she kept her face calm as she spoke to him. "This news about your mother is a surprise."

"That's one word for it." He scrubbed a hand over his hair and cut a glance at Shannon. "But it's done now. No need to go and get upset. It was just … I wasn't expecting to hear someone say Mum was a … a …. Christ, I can't even say it. Can't even say I believe it." But his gaze darted to Shannon's forehead.

"Daniel, you should make Shannon a tea. I will help you." Amadis nodded toward the kitchen.

"Man, you have balls. You're ordering me about, in my place?"

"I haven't heard that term before, so I don't know what balls you refer to. But yes, I am ordering you to make your very dear friend who, from the sound of it, has looked out for you since you were a child, a cup of tea to make her feel better." She set her chin and glared at him.

"Okay, okay. Of course I'll make her a goddamn tea."

Amadis sent Shannon a tight smile before following Daniel into the kitchen, although as she reached the door, it closed in her face.

Hmm, this might be a little harder than she'd thought. But she'd dealt with hard-headed males all her life. Look at her father. One mortal wasn't going to get in her way.

She squared her shoulders and pushed open the door.

"So, you got me in here," Daniel demanded from where he leaned against the timber dining table, his arms crossed, biceps bulging. "Why?"

"Well, tea to start with." Amadis forced her gaze back to his face. "And I will have a coffee if you can make that, too."

"Fine!" Daniel threw his hands in the air. He grabbed a small steel-colored urn and took it over to a faucet and sink in front of the window. With jerky movements, he turned a handle, and water poured into the urn.

Amadis couldn't help herself; she had to peer around him to see how Daniel made the hot beverages these mortals loved so much.

Daniel stopped the faucet and whirled around. He rammed the urn straight into her stomach.

"Oomph."

"Fuck. Sorry."

"I am fine." Amadis waved his concern away. "I have had much worse in training." She rubbed her stomach and looked up.

Mistake.

Blue eyes crashed into her again, their intensity like riding the turbulent waters of storm-driven waves, of giant peaks and impossible troughs.

Amadis's heart began to pound. Who was this mortal male?

Her eyes dropped to his lips. Memories of their kiss

raced through her. They drew her in, and instinctively, she rose high on tiptoes and—

Oh no. She dropped back down to the soles of her feet. Daniel's lips were pulled tight, and that glittering gaze was hot, feral almost, on her. For her.

He wanted her kiss too. A feminine thrill rushed through her. Had their kiss wrought the same reaction in him? It was impossible to know definitively, but something in that heated gaze whispered yes. And that he wanted more.

Her blood warmed, and in her core, an ache grew.

But this was not the time. Maybe there never would be. Disappointment flared in his eyes when she moved away.

Focus, Amadis. The Task, always the Task. Her father's words replayed over and over in her mind.

As soon as she had soothed out the tension between Daniel and Shannon, she was going to identify if Daniel was her target. The news that his mother was a witch, even if he had no discernible power, only made her more certain. So it was time to get to work.

"I can see you are hurt by Shannon's words," she softly said. "And I am assuming this is to do with your mother. However, Shannon is an elder and injured. Please let her explain her motives to you further after she has rested and is fit to talk to you again."

Daniel set the urn down on the counter and flicked a switch at its base. Then he leaned back on the counter, crossed his arms again. Her gaze drifted back to his biceps.

Focus. The Task. She wrenched her gaze back to his face. *Again.*

"Listen, there's a ton of crap going on right now. But

believe me, I don't give a fuck about the details. I just want to live my life in peace. Finding out that my mother called herself a witch is ... is ... it's insane." He tightened his arms and looked away. "But it also doesn't matter at all. I'm not some little kid who needs to hold his mummy's hand."

Amadis held in a sigh. No sight was required to see Daniel was lying.

But why?

A bigger sigh escaped her as the true reason for his comment hit her. And her heart cracked a tiny fracture for him. For the pain he was in. But how to address the topic? And if she did, would it even help? She moistened her lips.

"Daniel, the loss of a parent—any parent—is a terrible thing. And you do not need to hide that."

"I'm not hiding anything." Daniel's head shot up. "And this isn't about my mother."

Amadis kept her gaze level on Daniel's. She didn't let her disbelief show. But she wasn't dropping this either. "When did she leave this world?"

"Stop. Stop making this about my mother. This is about Shannon dumping this witch shit when I'm just starting my business. It's about what the fuck you're all doing here. And about who the fuck you are." He scrubbed a hand over his short hair before he blew out a hard breath. "Never mind. Listen, I think you and your crew should head out. There are rooms over in Willow Grove at the hotel. I meant what I said earlier. This place, my business, is just getting started. I don't need any weird shit going on to jeopardize that."

The boiling water in the urn rose in volume, and Daniel turned to it, his back an implacable wall.

Amadis stiffened. There was no way she could leave yet

—she couldn't fail this Task. The near attack on Daniel. The foiled attack on Shannon. The fact that Daniel was more and more looking like her target. Their kiss. For all those reasons, she couldn't just walk away.

"Daniel, my apologies for disagreeing with you; however, I don't think it's possible for us to leave yet."

Daniel slammed his hands on the counter and pivoted. His blue eyes turned hot, lit with a dangerous edge. The air grew heavy. Her eyes dipped to his lips. And *Belar's breath*, his eyes followed to hers. He stepped closer.

"I want you so fucking much," he whispered. "But fucking hell, I want you to go."

The blood in her veins grew thick, pulsing in rhythm to her heart as he moved closer still. The large kitchen evaporated, and it was just Daniel and Amadis.

His spicy scent curled around her, stroked her with heated fingers. A shiver thrilled through her, and she lifted her chin, kept her eyes on his.

He reached out with both hands and gripped the table's edge behind her. Caged her. His jaw clenched.

She swallowed, tried to meet his gaze, but got caught on his lips. Their curve tightened, and she couldn't stop herself —didn't even try—but reached up and stroked them.

Daniel inhaled sharply and then shifted his jaw, nipping the pad of her thumb.

Fire bloomed in her core. Her nipples pebbled. *Belar's breath*, she wanted more.

And then his firm lips met hers. No hesitation. No tentative rub. His tongue parted her lips, plunged inside.

A wave of heat poured over her, obliterating everything else.

A growl rumbled through Daniel's body, and Amadis answered it, moaning into his mouth. She met his tongue, tasted him back. Heat, glorious intoxicating heat and spice funneled through her, just as it had with their first kiss. She slanted her mouth under his, burrowed into him.

She had to get her hands onto his skin. She searched for his shirt, lifted the hem, and then, finally, hot skin was beneath her palms.

An arc of fire shot through Amadis where they connected, and Daniel hauled in a sharp breath. In a flash of movement, he crowded her hard against the table, the timber edge jamming into her back, and finally, his body pressed into hers.

All of him.

Gods, he was heavy and hard against her, and she was about to combust if she didn't get closer. Thank the gods he picked her up and sat her on the table, pushing between her thighs.

A sharp crash and smash of something echoed on the floor behind them.

Amadis tore her lips away from Daniel's. "What was that?"

Daniel flicked a gaze to the floor. "Some cups. Saucers. Nothing that matters." He leaned back down.

Belar's breath. Once again—the lure of this male had overwhelmed everything else.

She shakily inhaled, somehow managed to withdraw her hands from all that delicious, heated skin—and laid her palms instead against him. Pushed.

A moment later, his eyes opened, his head lifted. His

parted lips still held the same intent as hers had, and turbulent seas shone from his gaze.

"Daniel, this—us kissing—it distracts me. I came here, as in right now, to help you and Shannon make peace. Because I need your concentration for something else. This ..." This crazy, burning, clawing need to touch him. She cleared her throat, waving between them. "This—if we do this, it can't get in the way. I will not let it get in the way."

"This"—Daniel's brows drew tight as he mimicked her hand motion—"is perfect. But I meant what I said—you all need to leave."

Amadis drew in a tight breath. "You don't understand; I can't leave."

"Yeah, you can. It's pretty simple. The door's right there."

"No, I can't. This is about more than just you and me. This is about the World Tree."

"Huh?" Daniel stilled.

Amadis went to smooth a hand over his arm but came up short. She couldn't risk touching him, not if it would lead to more of those drugging kisses.

"Daniel, the World Tree is the most important being in all of the worlds. Without it, there would be no connection between our worlds, but more, there would be no protection for those in the Mortalworld." She looked at him in earnest. "There are immortal guardians called Keepers who protect the Tree—and there is no finer duty than that of keeping the World Tree safe."

"Stop. Just stop with all the loopy shit. I mean it." Daniel spat out a laugh. "This, the hots between us—fine, it's real. But that other shit—the lying. That has to stop."

"I am not lying."

"Bullshit."

"Daniel, I'm not. That is the truth. You saw the magic for yourself."

"Who ... what ... are you then?" He folded his arms.

The moment of truth. Did she—should she—tell him? What if revealing her identity was the only way to achieve her Task? Going by the distrust on his face, there was no other option.

"I am ..." She took a deep breath. Gods, let this be the right thing to do. "I am an Angel. And I have been sent here to Willow Grove on a Task—technically as part of my first— to find the next Keeper who will join the war to protect the World Tree. I believe now you are that being. To prove if you are indeed the next Keeper, you need to come with me to the World Tree."

"Right." The scowl on his face deepened. "Clearly, you didn't hear me the first time. I said cut the BS and tell me what the fuck is going on here."

"I have no idea what BS is, and therefore, how to cut it; however, I have told you what is going on here. But there is more. And I understand this is a challenging concept given your previous lack of insight into non-mortal world matters, however—"

"That—that there is the BS." Daniel waved a hand. "Bull. Shit. As in a lie. There aren't Angels, or demons, or witches, or some bad bogey man running out of the bushes."

"But, Daniel, you saw it. You saw Shannon's wounds mend. What else would it take to convince you we are real?"

～

DANIEL SCOWLED and ran a hand over his hair. Of course, she couldn't prove it. Except, Shannon's wounds *had* mended. Before his eyes. His mouth dried up. His heart raced.

A chill flew across him, goosebumps following in its wake.

For years in the army, he'd been at the forefront of battles and incursions and attacks, and never once had he been injured. Nothing.

That was why Ben had branded Daniel with that god-awful nickname.

Angel. A fucking joke.

Monster is more like it. Because Daniel should've been hurt—hell, he should've been seriously injured multiple times over, but nada. Unlike everyone around him in his unit.

The pain of that alone had worn at his conscience for years.

But what if?

He shook his head. His mother had died years ago, but he remembered her—she'd been loving and fun and normal. No witchy shit. Sure, she'd liked crystals and rocks and he could recall her playing with a deck of cards all the time. But that didn't make her a witch.

And he'd know, right?

He snorted. Fuck this; no way was magic real. This was total crapola. He set his jaw.

"Listen, Ama—" He bit back a growl. He needed to get purely on a business footing here. "Listen up, A. Jones, or whatever you call yourself. There is nothing you can say to convince me that magic exists. That my mother was a witch, and that I am some goddamn special person who has to join an imaginary war. Because even if you were for real, even if what I saw out there with Shannon was right, and I'm not living some existential fucking nightmare right now, there is no way in hell I will ever join a war again. I am done with fighting other goddamn people's battles and wars. I came here for peace. For the quiet of a small, simple town and to live that life forever. Hear me?"

Amadis's face paled. And he almost reached out a hand to somehow soften his message and appear less monster-ish. But hell, he was what he was. And these people needed to get the fuck out of his world. Now. "So, I'd appreciate it if you could just pack up whatever you've got going on. And leave."

Amadis narrowed her eyes. Not intimidated at all. Which he grudgingly respected.

"What if I can show you?" She lifted her chin. "You say there is nothing I can say to convince you, but what if I can? What if you can see with your own eyes and feel with your hands that what I say is true?"

"Whatever." He snorted.

"I'm serious." Amadis jammed her fists on her waist. "If I can convince you that something exists that you didn't know previously, will you listen to what I have to say about the World Tree? And let us stay? I have a terrible fear that if we leave, you and Shannon—anyone who comes to this place —will be at great risk. And I know you would not want that. We—Moyarn, India and I—are the best protection you can have."

Damn, but she was a tough little thing. He bit back an oath.

"Fine. Go ahead. Prove what you're saying is the truth—and that there's some *terrible* danger only you can handle. Then you can stay." He crossed his arms. "I'm waiting." He inwardly rolled his eyes. This World Tree BS was a whole new level, but maybe this was the fastest way to get her and the others out of his hair.

An image of Shannon's skin mending flashed through his mind. Uh-uh, this was all batshit. And the only thing he wanted right now was to find out the truth about his mother and then get rid of these kooks and get back to the whole reason he was here. Peace. Quiet. A normal fucking life running a normal fucking business.

Amadis fiddled with a ring on her hand, then she took a deep breath and took it off. Placed it carefully on the table.

Out of nowhere, twin strips of dark leather straps studded with beaten brass appeared, wrapping around her breasts and rib cage, rising high to her shoulders.

Holy fuck. He staggered back into the bench.

Then she slowly raised both arms above her head.

Okay, the move was straight-up sexy. But he'd had a hard-on for her since she'd walked into his place, so that was nothing new.

And then, in a graceful arc, maybe the most graceful movement he'd ever seen, Amadis crossed her arms and pulled out two fine-tipped swords from behind her.

She swiveled the swords, metal singing as the blades kissed in midair, and brought them down to her sides.

"Ah ..." He tried to blink but couldn't tear his gaze from the swords, the leather. Things that had not been there only moments ago. Was he going mad?

"Nay, Daniel. You are not seeing imaginary things."

"So what—you can read minds, too?" He scowled.

Amadis looked directly at him. "Nay, 'tis only that your expression made it clear you do not believe your eyes."

"You think?" A short laugh escaped him. "This is batshit, Amadis ... Ms. Jones ... whatever your name is. Seriously batshit. Or I am. Hell, maybe I really have finally lost it, like Ben did." Poor bloody Ben. Had this been what it was like for him?

Amadis frowned, and her eyes shone with something— maybe sympathy. Fuck that; he wasn't after anyone's pity. He straightened up.

"Okay, so maybe I'm not losing my marbles. But this is —this is—"

Amadis chewed her lip for one moment, then sighed. Her eyes appeared troubled, but then she lifted her chin.

"Daniel, there's one more thing I can show you, but—" She swallowed like she had a lump in her throat. "But this is one rule every trainee is taught never to break when we come to the Mortalworld."

"There's more? Amadis, I don't think—"

But she didn't listen to him; instead, she stepped over to the kitchen table. She ran a hand over the worn timber top, then turned, squared her shoulders. A steely look grew in her eyes again. And then two dark shapes formed high on her back.

They extended on both sides of Amadis, arcing out in great midnight sweeps. Their top curve was smooth and even, while the underneath was scalloped ... like ... Holy shit.

Feathers.

His stomach dropped. And every single fucking thing

inside him stopped. Like the whole effing universe was holding its breath.

Wings. They were wings. And they were beautiful. Stunning. But they were wings.

"I'M NOT LOOPY, AM I?" Daniel said through pale lips, rocking back against the counter.

Amadis's heart wanted to soften, but she had to hold firm; she needed Daniel to recognize the truth.

"No, Daniel. You have not lost your mind. You are finally seeing me."

"And Shannon? Your friend India?" Daniel nodded his chin toward the lounge.

"They are witches. Technically, we are all witches."

"Technically?" Daniel scowled.

"I am also a witch, though my craft is negligible. That is why technically." Her shoulders wanted to deflate, but instead, she forced a shrug.

"So if you're all witches, why did Shannon get all tetchy when you first met?"

"Shannon is wary of outsiders—and she had no idea if I meant her, or you, harm."

Daniel eyed her swords. "Do you mean with those? They look pretty damn sharp."

"This is *Daudhi*." Amadis slowly turned her swords, the light bouncing off the razor-sharp points. She swiveled her left hand and then her right. "And this is *Dagr*. They were gifts from my maternal grandmother. And no, Shannon was not fearful of these. She had not even seen them. She recognized I had some magic, that was all."

"Your swords have names? Doudi? And Daggar? Does that mean something?"

"Yes, to my mother's people, their names mean death and day."

"Death day. *Right*. Okay, so you have a freaky set of swords—and not just their names—but why be scared of magic if Shannon's also a ... whatever you call it?"

"Witch. And she was scared because some with magic use it to hurt, even kill, others. Which is what almost happened today."

"The attack on Shannon?"

"Yes. Somehow Shannon got away—she thinks the soldier who tried to take her was inexperienced, and she was able to use her power to get away before he could complete the spell to steal her magic."

"What the fuck? Steal it?"

"There are those—both witches and non-witches—who want power that is not theirs. But not all witches are like that."

"And my mother?" Daniel blanched. "She was a witch too?"

"I am sorry to say I do not know about your mother. I have never met her."

"No, I didn't mean that. My mother died a long time ago —you wouldn't have even been born."

Amadis opened her mouth and then closed it. Was now the time to tell him how old she was?

"Shit, I don't know," Daniel continued. "I thought maybe

you all have some kind of witch group or something. A coven, right? That's what you call it."

"Ah, I see what you mean. Well, you have some things right and some things wrong there, Daniel." She took a deep breath. "You see, I have been alive for over four decades, so technically, I have been alive at the same time as your mother."

"Hold on." Daniel's eyes widened, carefully looked her over. He held up a hand. "You're how old? How can you look like ... well, how you look?"

"Immortality."

"Shit." With unsteady hands, Daniel pulled out a seat and dropped into it.

"And yes, some witches in Mortalworld call their groups covens. Others, like practiced here, simply align themselves in familial or extended familial groups. I am just not one of them."

Amadis blew out a short breath. Daniel had such a lot to deal with. Did she tell him the rest? At least he showed no resistance to their world now.

"What else is there?" he asked.

"Why do you say that?"

"You're pretty easy to read, especially now I know what the hell is going on here. And clearly, you're mulling something else over. Come on, might as well lay it all out. It can't be worse than what else you've already told me."

"Read me?" Hold on, she was meant to be the one with the sight of truth, but for some reason, it seemed to be backward with this male. But maybe he was different for a reason. Because he was who she was here for.

She swiveled her swords once more, smoothly sliding

them into their sheath. Daniel's eyes tracked their movement, and heat rose to simmer in their indigo depths.

An answering heat began to boil deep within her, but she forced herself back to her Task.

"Daniel, there is something in you that is different from all others."

"Me? You're talking about me? Not you."

"Yes, you. You are immune to my sight of truth."

"Ah, what?"

"I can see a being's truth in the words they speak. And I can see everyone else's truth, except for yours."

Daniel's face darkened. But he didn't say anything.

Amadis took another fast breath. "And that is why I think you may be the reason I'm here. I meant what I said about the World Tree needing its Keepers. My Task is to find that being."

Her stomach dipped. Once she'd found the Keeper, she'd be called back to the Higherworld.

Suddenly the internal kitchen door opened, and Moyarn stepped into the room, his black jacket swirling around his knees. "Amadis. Daniel. We ... need you out here. Now."

"Moyarn, I am here on a Task." Amadis frowned. "You must still recall what that means. And I believe I have just found my target. Is your need more urgent than that?"

Moyarn's silver eyes cut to Daniel and understanding lit the carved planes of his face, but he still nodded.

"Yes. Yes, it is."

"Fine. But Daniel, you and I need to finish this discussion."

"That wasn't a discussion—that was a bomb full of you know what."

"Now, now. No fighting." Moyarn held the door and gestured for them to head through.

Amadis did so, caught a hint of something warm and spicy as she passed close by the Fallen Angel. He smiled down at her, silver eyes flashing, and she couldn't help but smile back.

Daniel muttered something under his breath and followed into the lounge.

12

"Where are my witches?" Ri'Anit demanded as she strode up the porch of the pitiful little farmhouse. The late-morning sun highlighted flaking green paint and damaged weatherboards. Her lip curled.

She deserved far better for a base of operations. But at least the pathetic building was tucked behind a high hedge and set well away from any road. And the old man who'd lived here had been easy enough to dispose of. Pity he hadn't any magic to take, too.

The soldier guarding the entry paled as he opened the door for her.

"Well?" She flicked the end of her coat and cut the guard a look.

"In—in the kitchen."

Anticipation zinged through her. Finally, magic would pulse through her veins again.

"My First," one of her second's called from the shabby lounge room. As he spoke, five other soldiers sitting with him rose to their feet. They dropped their gazes to the floor as they passed her and exited the building.

"Well, Second? Why do you stop me?"

He walked over, expression tight. "We have lost communication with another Second. He was scouting for another remote base of operations and never checked back in."

"What useless Seconds you have proven to be. And I understand you have only located two witches?"

"Ah—"

"What?"

"We lost one of the witches before we could bring her in." The soldier bowed low at the waist, although dared raise his eyes to her.

"You what? After making me wait days for two mere witches, you lose one? How?"

"I ... I needed more power. I tried to conduct the transfer as soon as the witch was down—"

"How dare you steal from me?" Ri'Anit whipped out her dagger and struck him hard, slicing the third through the side. He cried out and fell to the ground. She dropped to his side and plunged his knife into his heart. Twisted the blade. "Their magic is mine. *Mine.*" She stepped over him into the small kitchen.

Her only female Second stood in the middle of the kitchen. At the soldier's feet, a body lay crumpled in a puddle of blood.

"One witch?" Ri'Anit spat, cutting her second a look. "I need more. Get me more witches."

The Second backed away, bowed low as she did.

"I shall see it is done, First Follower," the female whispered, wisely keeping her eyes cast down.

"And get rid of the body in the lounge." Ri'Anit couldn't contain her snarl as she knelt in the blood, uncaring of how it would stain the black denim of her jeans. She jerked her chin toward the door. "Leave me now. This task is mine alone. And keep your men away, lest they join this one, until I call for you." And once she had the power, she would command her army properly. Although she would need to test the new magic. "Wait. Have just one of your men stay behind and stand guard at the door. But he is not to enter. I will call him in when I am ready."

"Which do you—"

"Any."

"Yes, First Follower."

As soon as the door closed, Ri'Anit grasped the witch by the hair, taking no notice of the face or form. Blood still leaked from the body, and that was all that mattered. If the heart had stopped, there would be no life force remaining to steal their magic.

"You shall be my rebirth, witch. My god thanks you."

She got to work carving Irrika's mark into the witch's forehead and quickly whispered the words of the rite. She touched her open palm to the sluggishly bleeding cuts, and as she whispered the last word, a surge of energy shot through her.

Power. Strength. She rested back on her haunches, tilted her chin up as pure energy poured through her at the transfer from the witch to her.

"Yes, yes!" she cried out as her witch-fire returned, coursing through her.

She dropped the witch and strode to the kitchen door, wrenching it open.

"My first." The soldier there dipped his head immediately.

She eyed him for a moment, then stepped closer. "Eyes on me," she ordered.

He lifted his gaze immediately.

Well, he was obedient. That was a good start. But for the spell to work, she needed his body. She tapped one blood-stained finger on her lips.

"I have need for your services as more than just a soldier." Ri'Anit held his gaze and licked her lips slowly. "If you say yes, I shall ensure your time here is more enjoyable than you could ever have imagined. And you may find your rank rising higher than ... fourth."

He inhaled sharply, and instantly the scent of his arousal bloomed in the air. Her lips slowly curled. He was already hers.

"But," she said, shrugging, putting on a show of being open to his dissent, "if you prefer me to go to another for this"—she ran a hand over her breasts, down to her groin, almost humming at the pressure of her hand—"task. Then, of course, so say." She didn't add that if he refused, she'd dispatch him immediately.

His chin dipped once, but his eyes stayed locked on hers. Good.

"I am fully at your disposal, my first."

Perfect. Now she had magic, she was going to see how far she could push it. And it was going to start with a sex spell to bind this one to her. All she needed was his orgasm to make it happen—and she deserved her own enjoyment after all she had been through.

"Yes, yes you are." She grabbed his cock through his pants and pulled him into the bedroom nearest them.

She pushed him back onto the bed and pulled his pants over his hips. An impressive cock sprung free and rose high into the air, glistening at the tip. Better and better.

She shoved her panties aside, and in one move, straddled his hips, slammed onto him, her body clamping over his cock.

"Press me here, hard." She grabbed his hand and placed his fingers on her clit.

Then she rode him fast, and her orgasm erupted, and she rushed through the binding spell.

With a deep breath, Ri'Anit inhaled the scent of her release—and his—and shivered as the residual tingle of the spell to bind him through orgasm echoed through her. Yes! She had the power to make this work.

She stood up. "Dispose of the remains in the kitchen and give word to my second to find more witches. Then return to me here. I have more need of you."

Because she did need more. More of the hum of power coursing through her veins, more power to bind her soldiers to her will. More death at her hand. All to get her closer to the destruction of every single Keeper and that cursed Tree.

13
___

Amadis walked into the lodge's lounge room, the door swooshing shut behind Daniel and Moyarn as they followed her out of the kitchen. India and Shannon stood beside the hearth, winter sunlight diffusing through the windows around them.

Although their eyes widened when they saw her, neither seemed injured. Moyarn had called her away for this? Then both of their gazes shot to the front door of the lodge.

Theron—her *father*—stood just inside the front door.

Amadis's stomach dropped, and she stumbled to a stop.

Daniel ran into her back. "What's going on? Hey, who are—"

"Not now," Moyarn hissed.

She ignored Daniel's questioning look as he stepped around her. Thankfully, Moyarn grabbed Daniel's arm and pulled him over to fire with India and Shannon.

They all stared at Theron. But although her father's jaw clenched, his gaze locked on Amadis and didn't shift.

A lump lodged in her throat, though she forced calm to

her countenance. Why had he come? Did he know she had revealed her wings? Had she transgressed in some other way?

"Father," she called out, somehow keeping her voice steady when her heart was pounding.

"Daughter." Theron spoke as calmly as she. But he flicked a look at the group by the fire, and all too familiar tightness pinched his features.

"What is your purpose here?" She squared her shoulders.

"I ... needed to see how you were progressing."

Amadis clenched her jaw. *Belar's breath,* he was assessing her?

She lowered her voice. "You've never checked on another Angel's progress. If you didn't think me capable, why did you give me this Task?"

"Nay, it is not that. I am not here in my capacity as Warden."

"Oh no? I know you have held me back from Tasks." Amadis couldn't stop her lip from curling. "No doubt afraid of my failure, that it would reflect poorly on you. That my ... fear made me unsuitable to take on the purpose of being an *Angel.*"

"*Amadis*, I did not hold you back from fear for myself or my reputation."

"Then why? I have been ready to take on Tasks for two decades, yet only now have you given me a purpose other than training. Why now?"

"You were not ready. You said yourself, your fear—"

"—has not held me back once?" The question she'd been asking herself a million times tumbled out, and she challenged her father—something she had never done. Ever. Amadis, the dutiful daughter of the Warden, never spoke out, never challenged authority, never provoked. Until now. "Why all of a sudden have I been given my first Task, treated as part of the Angelkin?"

"Daughter ..."

"*Father.* I need to know. And don't try to lie; my sight of truth will show me. Was it to do with Freya?"

"Yes." Theron's lips thinned. "She specifically called upon you. Her belief is that you alone can complete this Task."

"What? But you are the Warden—*you* assign the Tasks." She slowly shook her head as the guilt on Theron's face made sense. "But you'd never have sent me of your own accord, would you?"

"No. No, I would not have. Though let me repeat, that was not only for me. Use your sight to know this truth: I ... I almost lost you once. I did not want, *could not*, face that again. Could not ask *you* to encounter again what happened last time. When we lost your mother."

The blood left her head in a rush, and Amadis swayed for a moment.

Instantly, the walls closed in. But she forced herself to breathe long and low, repeating her mantra until her mind settled.

Finally, she looked back at Theron.

"So that explains why I finally received my first Task. It does not explain why you are here."

Theron's gaze broke away, and he looked around the room—eyes widening at something over Amadis's shoulder.

His jaw clenched again—this time so hard his cheek ticked. "Do you know who they are?" he whispered.

She glanced over her shoulder and followed Theron's gaze. "Daniel and Moyarn? Well, I believe one is the target of my Task. The other is an ex-Angel, and someone whose swordsmanship methods are taught in the training ring to this day. It has been an honor to meet him."

"An honor? Daughter, he Fell and left the Angelkin. He is not worthy of talking to you, let alone being in the same lodging. And the other ..."

"Daniel?" She cut a glance at her host. He was staring at Theron with outright suspicion, which just showed how smart Daniel was. "What about him?"

"He is the child of the one who saved you." Theron's eyes tightened, then his voice dropped. "When you were kidnapped, we went to his mother for help. After she located you here in the Mortalworld, she then went to the extra effort of returning you to us. But your kidnappers then pursued her in vengeance—and they eventually ended her life, just as they ended your mother's."

Amadis sharply inhaled, pivoted to Daniel.

"What now?" Daniel asked. "Amadis, why are you staring at me like that?"

"Oh, Daniel. I am so, so sorry."

"No. Uh-uh." His face clouded over, then he cut a hand through the air. "No more fucking life-changing revelations from you. In fact, you know what? I've had enough of all of this. And fine—you can stay. But I'm going to my shed. Don't disturb me. Especially you." He glared at Amadis.

Moyarn unfolded his arms from across his chest. "Why

don't I join you? I can help answer some of those questions you must have running around your head."

"You see, that's exactly what I *don't* want. So no, you *guests* can stay in here. I'll be outside. In *my* shed."

As Daniel stalked out through the front door, he cut Theron a hooded glance. Theron returned the look equally.

Amadis eyed Daniel's back as the door slammed behind him, then turned to face the room and planted her hands on her hips.

"Well, that did not go well. How long will you be staying?" she asked Theron.

"Long? I am not staying at all. My duty awaits me in the Kin lands now, lest Tasks go unassigned. And if you have indeed identified your target, then your Task is complete, and you will not be staying either."

Amadis held in a breath. No—she wasn't ready to go yet. But how to make this work? She stared at Theron for a long moment. There might be one way ...

"Well, the exact words of my Task were to see the next Keeper *called into being*. Yes, I think Daniel may be that person, but I will not know until the Tree confirms it. And then he must accept the call. *That* will be when my Task is complete. And while I am here, these people—this place— has needs of me. Us. You and Moyarn, too. The World Tree needs us."

Theron cast a fast look at the others before he leaned down. "Amadis, you are an *Angel*—"

"Half."

"An *Angel*, regardless of your mother's bloodline, and you know you cannot get caught up in the matters of mortals." His lips thinned.

"But these people—most of them—are not mere mortals. They know of the World Tree, of witches and magic. And this is not just a Mortalworld matter. The Order are here. And if they are present in this village, then they think there is a way to achieve their goal. Here."

"*Amadis.*"

"You know I am right, Father."

"What I know is that you have a Task to complete. Angels do not get involved in other matters while their Task is unresolved."

"I agree; the faster I bring the next Keeper to the Tree, the better. But I am a warrior. And I am here. I will help."

"Nay." He slashed a hand through the air. "This is not your fight."

"You always taught me that the World Tree comes above all. Without it, the mortals we are tasked to aid will have no hope. And we will never set foot in this world again." She risked a glance at the others, then bowed her head. "I have never disobeyed you, but I cannot in good conscience let these people go unprotected when I am here. When my swords have never been better placed to protect. And I cannot believe you would ask me to."

A low cough at her back had Amadis turn around.

Moyarn stepped over to them. "Forgive the intrusion; however, might I suggest this conversation pauses while we work out the best course of action to ensure the safety of these humans and the World Tree right now?"

"You would dare talk to my daughter?"

"Yes, I would," Moyarn said, crossing his arms to match Theron. "As much as I'm sure it pains you to be talking to an

Ex, I think we've got more important things to worry about than your Angelic scruples."

"Makes sense, hey?" India said as she joined them. "And ah, hello, I'm India."

Amadis slanted her father a look. His jaw was locked so hard she doubted he could have gotten a word out if he tried. But he did dip his head.

Amadis took pity on him and made the introduction to the witch-Keeper. Theron's innate curtsy would make him hate to be seen as anything other than the genteel Warden of the Angelkin, at all times polite, courteous, and never failing at social graces.

After the niceties had been observed, Theron grabbed Amadis's shoulder and whirled her around. "You must leave here now. You should not be around an ex—"

"Stop. I am here on a Task. One you have said came from Freya herself. So no, I cannot leave. And you know that."

"Not even one week, and look at what you are becoming." Theron's face paled. "I cannot tell you strongly enough, this is your first Mortalworld experience. Please, do not let this place taint you or your choices. You are an Angel."

"Half, remember? And hasn't that been the issue all along? That my mother's blood is so different from everything the Angelkin stands for?"

"You know not what you say."

"Ah, yes I do. I've lived it for four decades. But I thought we were past that when you gave me my first Task."

"This. *This* is why I came," Theron said through clenched teeth. "To make sure that you do naught to irrevocably damage your future as a member of the Angelkin. Amadis, please reconsider your actions. I will say it again—I do not want to lose you. Either from this life or from our world."

Theron sharply inhaled, then his icy gaze, so like hers, was hidden as he pivoted and strode out of the door.

Well, that conversation had not turned out as she had wanted. Two men had just stormed out of the property, and she found herself only wanting to go after one.

Belar's breath, this was not easy. A burning sensation in her throat had her stiffen. Oh no, she would not cry. Not in front of anyone. She was strong. She'd survived the terrors that had haunted her dreams for years. She would not cry.

She turned to India. "Given there's been two attacks in two days, we need to set up a perimeter and keep watch. But I have to ask—do you recognize any magic in Daniel?"

"No. Not at all. And it's the first time I've ever met a blood-child of a witch with zero magic."

"At least the Order won't be coming for him specifically then. But we still need to be careful."

"I'll head out now and do another sweep of the grounds," India said. "But I won't be able to stay for long. I need to be on watch back at the Tree, too."

"Why don't we divide it up? If you head out to the forest, I'll patrol the lakeside."

When she reached the water's edge, she blew out a long breath. Tried to find her balance. Why did males have to be so ... so ...? She wanted to stamp her foot.

But that would be a sign of lack of control—something an Angel never did. Well, not until now. She stomped her foot.

Energy shot through her. *Belar's breath,* but that felt good. She did it again.

No wonder Angels were considered so uptight. They never gave in to their emotions, never let themselves be free with their reactions. Or maybe they didn't feel? Hadn't she tried to make herself feel nothing for such a long time? Well, maybe it was time to stop trying to hold everything in. Time to let herself feel.

"May I join you?"

Amadis whirled around. "Moyarn. You move surprisingly quietly for one so big."

"And you are surprisingly emotional for an Angel of the Angelkin." The corners of his silver eyes scrunched.

"Half. And that's the problem."

"Ah." Moyarn nodded. She could tell he wanted to ask more but clearly read her lack of interest in discussing that further. Instead, he turned to the lake and placed his hands in the pockets of his long black coat.

"It is a special place, is it not?" he asked.

Amadis let the beauty of the waters, more turbulent than when she'd been out earlier, take her focus. "I didn't realize the Mortalworld could be so beautiful."

"It's a special place to undertake your first Task."

"Yes, it is. And yes, I am the oldest first-timer ever." Amadis tried not to let her muscles tighten. Failed.

"Well, if you have found your target in our host, then you are doing a good job so far." Moyarn tilted his head as he regarded her. "It was a long time ago, but I recall miscalculating my first Task up completely. But that was before your father's time."

"You?" Amadis couldn't keep the surprise from her face.

"Me. This was before the World Tree had been created, when there was only one plane of existence. But even then, our god believed in the mortals enough to send his agents to aid them when he felt needed. But I took the wrong action, and it cost my Task dearly. It took a lot of help before I could complete my Task. Sadly, with mortals, there are some damages you cannot undo."

He turned silver eyes to the lake.

Amadis let him have the silence but finally couldn't contain her interest. "May I ... Can I ... ask a question?"

"Let me guess. Why did I leave?" Moyarn grimaced.

Amadis nodded.

Moyarn's chest rose as he inhaled deeply. "After the World Tree was created, we—some of the older Angelkin and I—believed that the ability to do more good in the world of mortals, in all of our worlds, lay outside the lands and dominion of the Angelkin.

"Back then, the rules were ... strict. No tolerance for stepping outside of the edict of the Warden and the Kin Council was allowed. And we were meant to be perfect. The perfect instrument to guide mortals through their lives. But we were never perfect. We were created with foils and traits that even we could not stamp out completely, no matter how hard we tried."

Amadis's stomach twisted. Perfect was her least favorite concept. Since the incident, her fear of enclosed places had always placed her on the outer edges of the Angelkin society. And she'd heard the whispered words. *Imperfect. Not worthy. Not a real Angel.* And with her mother's genes, well, that had just given the Kin even more fodder. But Amadis had blocked them all—had ignored everything but her training to be the best sword fighter in the three worlds. And now she was here, ready for this.

But could she do more good if she wasn't Angelkin? If she were called to be a Keeper, her heart's most secret desire, then the Angelkin would have no say over her. But maybe there was another way—like Falling?

No, leaving the Kin was not the answer. Not for her. She had seen her sire's truth when he'd spoken of his fear of losing her. And she didn't want to leave him. For those who Fell, who chose to live a life outside of the Angelkin, they were never allowed entry again.

"Thank you for telling me. There is little shared with younger Kin about the ex-Angels. But when they—you—are spoken of, it's negatively. Your actions are ascribed to motives of selfishness rather than goodness. That you would rather be in this existence for your own benefit rather than others."

"Of course." Moyarn sighed. "Because the Kin don't want to lose their Angels. It doesn't have to be that way, although I know the old guard have held that thought for millennia."

"Angelic lore has it that you carried out thousands of Tasks?"

"I stopped counting. But I would say so." A grin flashed over Moyarn's face.

"You are still spoken of with regard in one area—your skill with the sword. They even teach your lessons in the training ring."

"Really? I thought they would have refused to teach my techniques after all this time."

"No, oh no. The opposite. I trained in your method for decades once I was able to wield the full sword."

"Well, that is ... pleasing. Oddly enough." His eyes narrowed. "You are a warrior Angel?"

"That was the designation that Fate wrote into the Codex. And the truth is, I don't have many Angelic skills. In fact, I only have one—the sight of truth. But I am one of their best warriors. That is a truth I also know."

"Wow, that's impressive."

"Sadly, I haven't had the opportunity to use my skills, until now."

Moyarn cut her a sideways glance. "You know, I came here for another purpose. But I can see that it would be beneficial for me to stay until the Keepers—and you—have the current situation under control. If I'm going to remain here and help, we need to be able to work together. Fight together. Which means I need to know your fighting style. We should practice, find a rhythm that works for us."

Her heart picked up. Train with Moyarn? The master swordsman whose methods had skilled Angels for thousands of years?

"*Belar's breath*, I would love that." Amadis blew out a slow breath. "We can train between the woodshed and the forest. That way, if someone approaches by water or road, we won't be seen."

14

These people were fucked-up. No other word for it. Alone in his woodshed, Daniel snorted as he grabbed the nearest chunk of raw timber, the scent of eucalyptus calming him even as he sat down at his saw.

He pulled on his protective eyewear and leather apron, switched on the machinery and got ready to take his mind off everything.

The wood was warm beneath his hands. His thumb ran over each knot on the uncut side, over every groove on the other. This was real. This here, this thing that was heavy in his hands.

This was what he believed.

Not the rambling fantasy of a hot woman, her crazy friends, or Shannon, the person he'd trusted more than anyone else in his life. Or had, anyway.

Daniel positioned himself in front of the machine. What to make?

He created functional things that had a purpose. His

finished pieces filled the cupboard in the corner—bowls and plates and chopping boards.

But right now, Daniel let the wood turn in his hands; let the saw guide him as it met variations in color, in texture.

And minutes later, he had a weirdly shaped, useless piece of art in his hands. Fuck. He shut the machine off in a hurry and slammed his goggles on the bench.

What the hell had made him make this? Had to be all the kookiness—and the kooky people—no other explanation for it. And look at what he'd done earlier—he'd let them stay for fuck's sake. He snorted. Looked like he was the kooky one now.

And then, with the buzz of the saw gone, a faint echo of ringing strikes echoed around the shed walls. What the fuck was that?

Daniel dropped the creation on the bench, refusing to even look at it, and headed back outside.

Amadis and Moyarn had their swords out and were trading blows. The scary fucker towered over her—close to double her size.

Daniel's gut tightened. How could anyone attack her? She was tiny.

But it was clear they were just sparring.

Amadis's wings were tucked tight at her back, and her swords, wicked tips glinting in the light, flickered through the air with each strike.

She'd dropped her jacket, and in her tight jeans and white shirt, she spun, thrust, withdrew, her body dancing in the winter sunlight, more beautiful than anything he had ever imagined.

But was this real? Had he fallen asleep, or worse, had an

accident and died, and this was some fucked-up afterlife? Except, it wasn't fucked-up. It ... she ... was beautiful. No, that wasn't even right. Stunning. Breathtaking.

A shiver ran up his spine. Amadis was ethereal.

Moyarn called out to her, what sounded like words of encouragement, and then paused; he held a sword high in a strike pose before stepping back and letting Amadis attack again.

"They're something else, aren't they?" India said softly behind him.

Daniel stiffened. He'd been so caught up in the beauty of Amadis's moves that he hadn't even registered India's approach.

He shifted so she wasn't at his back and cut her a glance, ran a hand over his neck. "Ah, yeah. You could say that."

"I just did a perimeter walk and didn't see anything dangerous," India went on as if talking about perimeters was everyday conversation. "We'll take it in turns to keep an eye out."

"What, no sword?" Daniel nodded at Amadis and Moyarn. "By the look of them, I thought you'd all have swords or something."

"Swords aren't my thing. But they are my partner's. I'm going to swap out with him and have him come here." Her green eyes seemed to glow for a moment. "He should meet you."

"Let me guess. He believes in all this woo-woo stuff, too?"

"I don't think you can keep your disbelief much longer." India softy laughed and nodded toward Amadis and Moyarn.

Daniel scowled. Maybe he could ignore some of what he'd seen and heard. His gaze drifted back to Amadis ... but those wings.

Then Moyarn stepped right into Amadis. Too close. Daniel almost jumped out of his skin, barely holding himself back from barging into their training session. He could practically see the masculine approval in Moyarn's eyes from all the way over here.

"He's not going to hurt her," India murmured.

"Yeah, guess not." Except he'd never thought Moyarn was going to hurt Amadis. Nah, the fucker had other things on his mind.

And everything in him screamed *mine*. But Amadis wasn't his anything. One or two kisses meant fuck all.

He angled his body so India wouldn't see his physical reaction and crossed his arms.

"Fine," he growled. "My disbelief is suspended. What next?"

India nodded again toward the sword fighters. "Let Amadis tell you more about the purpose she thinks you have. If she's right, it's a damned important one."

"Whatever." Daniel sighed. "I can't see that being the case in any way, shape, or form. But it's getting close to lunch, so once they're done ... with whatever they're doing ... I'll be back inside. Doing my job, since I can't get any peace out here either."

Normally woodworking was the one place he could center himself, get away from the thoughts and dreams that had followed him back from the war. But now, even that was gone. An image of the useless bit of nothing he'd created flashed in his mind. See? These fricking people and their woo-woo were following him everywhere.

He bit back the grunt he wanted to deliver and skirted around the two doing battle.

As he passed them, Moyarn gripped one of Amadis's arms, positioning her for what appeared to be a lesson.

Something dark sprouted in Daniel's chest, and a growl rumbled through him. He almost stepped off course right into the middle of a fucking sword fight to tell the newcomer to take his hands off Amadis. The only hands that should be there were Daniel's.

But he'd been a trained soldier for eighteen years, and he marshaled his body, forced his legs to walk the direction his brain—not his dick—said to go. He stomped into the lodge through the kitchen entry, letting the door slam behind him.

"Daniel?" Shannon called out from the lounge.

"Yeah, it's just me," he yelled back. "I'm getting started on lunch."

"Do you want a hand?"

Hell no. He couldn't face Shannon just yet. "No. Ah, you stay there and rest. I've got this."

He swallowed the lump that rose in his throat. Shannon injured. His mother a ... a ... witch. Amadis, with her silky lips and deadly swords, and her fricking wings.

His chest tightened, and he tried to inhale—struggled to breathe.

Daniel needed to work his way through all this shit before he looked at Shannon again. Because he didn't want to hurt her feelings, and right now, he was as raw as the chunks of timber in the shed. And he needed to find some ease.

Fucking hell, he needed to find his peace. He'd had it—up until all this crap had started.

He blew out a slow breath, planted his feet squarely on the ground and clenched and unclenched his fists for the space of four heartbeats, focused on counting in time with his breathing.

Finally, he shook out his hands.

Roughly an hour later, he piled a heap of rolls and sandwiches onto platters on the dining table and put out all of the cups and saucers and things needed for hot drinks. The urns on the tea trolley were filled, and he wheeled that over as well.

"Lunch is ready," he yelled outside through the kitchen door. Then, steeling himself, he ducked back into the lounge. "Shannon, can I get you a sandwich and a coffee?"

Shannon shifted on the couch where she sat with her leg still raised but didn't respond. He stepped closer.

Damn, she'd fallen asleep.

With a sigh, he eased her other leg onto the couch and gently turned her so she wouldn't wake up with a kink in her neck. But she would wake up cold, so he grabbed one of the throw blankets and dropped it over her lap, then took one of the sandwiches he knew she liked and put it on a plate, set it aside. She could eat later.

After the ... attack, rest was probably the best thing for her right now. She'd just had her seventy-fifth birthday, and while she looked like a strong, capable woman, you couldn't underestimate the effects of trauma. Even after the physical wounds had healed.

He eyed the now-healed scrapes on her forehead. The only physical reminders were the hints of blood he'd missed when he'd first tried to clean her wounds.

Daniel went completely still. His stomach dropped.

Fuck. This was real. The woo-woo stuff was real.

A ringing clanged in his ears, and he shook his head to clear it. So, what did that mean? What had it meant for his mother? Ice settled in his gut.

And what exactly had Amadis meant earlier about his mother? Her father—hell, the man didn't look old enough to be that—had said something to make Amadis concerned.

Well, he was going to fucking find out. He couldn't let this go until he knew what had happened to his mother.

But he wasn't getting involved in any fricking war. He'd been there, done that, and had promised himself he wasn't ever going back. And he had a purpose here—one he needed to get back to.

DANIEL HAD JUST CLEARED AWAY the lunch dishes when the murmur of voices—three he knew, two he didn't—echoed from the front of the lodge. He took a deep breath. What next?

Sure enough, Amadis pushed the kitchen door open. "Ah, would you be able to join us?" she asked. "Out here."

"That's the softest I've ever heard you speak," Daniel said.

Amadis eyed him, nibbling on her lip. He bit back a groan; those bloody silky, lush lips were going to be the death of him. "C'mon, out with it." His voice came out gruffer than he expected.

But Amadis stiffened, and fire lit her gaze. Huh, so the little thing didn't like being told what to do. He filed that away.

"Since you ask so nicely, I need to tell you that you have new visitors. India's partner, Thrane, and her cousin, Nate. Thrane is a Keeper. Nate is a … I think they called it a police officer. They call him a detective."

"And he's on the up with all of …?" Daniel couldn't stop his mouth from dropping open. He waved a hand around the air. "This stuff?"

"Oh yes, most certainly. He is also a Keeper."

"Fine, I'll finish up here and be out soon. Dinner is going to be a giant pot of spaghetti bolognese, given I wasn't expecting so many people here for dinner. And anyone who doesn't want it can get themselves something else, from somewhere else. In fact, they can feel free to head into town and have dinner at the pub."

"You are sounding very grumpy again, Mr. O'Connor." Amadis sighed. "But I understand why, and I shall pass your message on. Please join us when you are able."

"Bloody hell," Daniel muttered as Amadis left the kitchen. This day had gone from fucked to fucking worse.

Finishing up the sauce, Daniel turned the heat down low to let it simmer, then washed his hands and left the privacy—safety—of the kitchen.

His gut churned, but he kept his face impassive as he let the door shut with a loud snick behind him.

Amadis, Shannon and Moyarn were on a couch near the

fire talking to two strange men who sat opposite them. All five turned to face Daniel.

One of the men was tall and lean with blond hair and an easy smile. He was vaguely familiar ... Daniel mentally clicked his fingers. He'd seen the man at the local Warragul pub on one of his rare trips into the bigger town for supplies. But something in the way the blond-haired man held himself spoke of a readiness to strike, the opposite of the easy-going smile. Daniel put him in the category of "do not be lulled into a false sense of security."

The other man was a giant scary-ass motherfucker—no other word for it—with a hard face and dark hair and eyes. Hell, there was something about him ... But Daniel racked his memory ... couldn't pin down where he'd seen him before. Except, he had. Somewhere. Sometime. And every-thing about him shouted, do not mess with me.

Daniel slowly nodded. That was a vibe he could get with.

"Okay," Daniel said, "so apparently, you are all for real, and this whole other world exists out there. Who's gonna fill me in?"

"Yes, I knew you'd come around." Amadis jumped up. "You couldn't be that thickheaded to ignore what your eyes were telling you."

"Ah, thanks. I think."

"That might not be the best way to get Daniel to *come around*," Shannon muttered.

"Don't worry." Daniel shook his head. "I'm not so *thick-headed* as to mistake what our guest here said as an insult."

"Perfect," Amadis said.

Daniel traded a look with Shannon.

"So," Amadis continued and waved him closer, "let me introduce you. Daniel, this is Nathaniel Jones."

Another Jones. But Daniel just held out his hand. "Hi."

"Hi, call me Nate. I've seen you in Warragul a couple of times, right? At the Warragul Grand Hotel."

"Yeah, I've grabbed dinner there a couple of times. So, Amadis tells me you're a cop?"

"Yep, I am. The Grand is a regular meeting place for most of the cops in town. My girlfriend, Sim Morris, runs it. Although it's shut down for a few days." Nate gave the last man a whack on the back. "And this is Thrane."

"Not another Jones?" Daniel asked.

"Me?" the big man said. "No. Just Thrane."

"Right, well, good to meet you and all that. So?" Daniel crossed his arms and held Thrane's gaze. "Let's talk."

Thrane rubbed his jaw but didn't say anything.

Then Amadis stepped over and placed a hand on Thrane's arm. "Keeper," she said softly, "you know my Task, why I am here. And I am telling you, now is the time."

But Thrane just stared at Daniel, dark eyes assessing.

"Listen here," Daniel ground out. "I've agreed to hear you all out. And yeah, given the shit that's gone down, Amadis and crew can stay here. But I want to know what this danger is so I can keep an eye out too. And I don't want any secrecy. You—as in all of you—came here, to my place. My home and business. Shannon was hurt here, on the way to my house. So, if you've got something to say, say it."

Amadis dug her hands into her hips and stuck her chin out. Glared at them all—but mostly at Thrane.

"Keeper," she all but growled at Thrane. "Daniel is right. Tell him."

"Fine, Angel. You can stand down."

Amadis nodded and sat back down beside Shannon.

Daniel took a seat in one of the armchairs and placed his feet squarely on the ground.

"Okay. I'm ready. Hit me," Daniel ordered.

"I am a Keeper, as is Nate," Thrane said. "We guard the World Tree."

Daniel cut a look around the room. Everyone looked back at him, almost expectantly.

"Right. You guard a tree. Amadis said that earlier. What else?"

"Not just any tree. The World Tree. It is the lone connection—and protection—between the realms. It was created millennia ago by the old gods to define each world. It secures the Underworld through its roots, the Mortalworld through its trunk, and the Higherworld through its branches."

"Let me guess—they're like heaven and hell?" Daniel asked.

"That's how they've come to be portrayed by mortals after thousands of years apart from them. But they are so much more than that. They are continents and oceans and mountains and deserts like here. They're just populated by supernatural beings, many of them unlike anything you will have ever seen."

Daniel went to speak—he honestly tried to—but no words came out. His heart began to pound hard in his chest, and an oily slick worked through his gut.

His gaze drifted to Shannon's healed forehead. Then to Amadis and her now present wings.

"Okay, so you're the Keepers, and this World Tree is very

important. What are the risks to it?"

"Good question," Thrane said. "Without the World Tree here in the Mortalworld, this plane of existence would be cut off from the rest of the worlds. The people here would be cut off from their faiths. Any supernatural beings here when that happened would have free rein to take control of this world because no one could intercede to stop them. And there is one group of beings—we call them the Order —who have been trying to do just that for two thousand years."

"Let me get this right," Daniel said. "There's a tree that connects a bunch of different worlds, like heaven and hell, and then there's a group of bad guys—this Order—who are trying to kill the Tree so they can basically take over this world."

Amadis leaned forward. "Yes." Her glacial gaze held his. "But the Keepers have stood in their way for all these years. Continue to stand guard."

"You know this is hard to process, right?" Daniel asked as he folded his arms. "And what does that have to do with me ... and my mother?"

Amadis nibbled at her lip for a moment, then sighed. "Regarding your mother, well, my sire tells me she helped to save my life. And may have paid for that with her own."

What the hell? Daniel jumped to his feet.

15

Amadis swallowed the lump that rose in her throat as Daniel glared down at her.

"What? How the fuck did *my* mum save you?" Daniel asked.

How did his mother save her? And as though it had happened yesterday, not thirty years before, the memory of her rescue—and her capture prior to that—rushed back. The walls and ceiling bulged inward from every direction.

A shiver trickled down her neck. *Please, please go away.*

Blowing out a slow breath, she forced her gaze to the wall of windows, to the golden afternoon light streaming through them from over the lake.

And she breathed in. Out. In. Out. In ... Out ...

And then the bulging stopped, the shadows receded.

Finally, she rolled her shoulders, just a fraction. But even as she did, she tracked Daniel's eyes as he watched her movement. *Belar's breath*, did he realize how much she was affected still?

"Amadis, what are you hiding?" Daniel's eyes narrowed.

Gods, he did. "Nothing."

"Yeah, right. So you want me to trust you ... trust all this ... that you've dumped on me, but now you're hiding something. How does that work?"

Daniel needed to believe in her—otherwise, how would she ever get him to believe in her Task? And she was sure, so very, very sure, he was the one she was after.

She blurted out the truth. "I was kidnapped when I was ten years old. And it was only because of your mother that I escaped."

"What the fuck?" Daniel stiffened. "You were kidnapped? What happened?"

"I don't recall a lot of it. But what I know is that my mother and I were traveling from our home in the Kin lands to see her family in the Underworld. While we were on the road, two men attacked us. I must've been knocked unconscious in the fight because when I woke up, it was to pitch darkness. I ... I couldn't move my arms more than above my head or much higher than my face. I don't know how long it lasted. But I cried and screamed until my voice stopped working. I tore my hands and wings trying to get out."

The memory had a shiver trailing over her; the pain of torn wings and fingers and bruises all over her body sent a ball of fire to her throat. But she sat quietly, breathed in and out till she could swallow it away.

"What happened to your mother?" Daniel asked softly.

A lump rose in her throat. But she cleared her throat and swallowed the knot away like she had countless times before. "I found out afterward that they killed her and stole her magic—I presume they were going to kill me too when my mother's death magic waned and they needed more. Not that I had, or have, much to steal."

"Fuck," Daniel whispered. She met his eyes. Concern and sorrow shone through his gaze. "That must have been ... hell, I don't even have words. No wonder you're uncomfortable with confined spaces."

"It was awful." She shook off the memory. That path only led to fear—and she didn't need that affecting her Task. "And while I thank you for your care, you do not need to feel sorrow for me. The attack was then. And this is now— where we can stop other witches being killed and their magic—death magic—being used to hurt anyone else."

"Okay, got it. No more pity. So how did you escape?"

"Well, one moment there was only darkness, and the next, bright light hit my eyes. I'd been in a box of some kind, and when I could finally see again, a woman with long dark hair lifted me out."

Amadis blinked the memories away.

"And you think that was my mother? But my mother died when I was a little kid. Exactly how old are you?"

"I'm over four decades old. And I was ten years old when the incident happened. My body stopped aging from the moment I reached my immortality."

"What about you?" Daniel said to Thrane. "You're not twenty-ish. Are you immortal?"

"I am, yes. But I wasn't born that way. Aging only stops when our immortality sets in. For those like me, where it happened due to a specific event, the state my body was in then was how it stayed."

Amadis tentatively laid a hand on Daniel's arm. His muscles were tense; no surprise there.

"My father said that the Kin approached your mother and asked for her help to find me." She took a deep breath and repeated the rest of what Theron had said.

"Some fuckers killed her for helping you?" Daniel sank into the nearest seat.

"I am so sorry, Daniel." Amadis bit her lip. His pain made her want to reach out and stroke him. "If I could—"

"But why? And why the hell would the Angels go to *my* mother for help?"

"There might be one reason why," Shannon softly said. "One of your mother's strongest gifts was the ability to scry."

"Was she very good?" Amadis asked.

Shannon nodded. "She was. She could find anything, or anyone, when she put her mind to it."

"And scrying is ...?"

"It means to use supernatural ability—or magic—to find something. Or someone."

"And my mother was the only person who could do this scrying to find Amadis?"

"Well, I ... we ... know of one other at least." Thrane gestured between Nate, Moyarn and himself. "But she's in the Underworld. And that would be a bit of an issue, right?"

"That's putting it lightly," Moyarn said. "The beings of the Higherworld, especially older beings like the Angelkin, believe the Underworld is beneath them, and some even still believe it's a place of evil. There's a strict no-go code between them. So, if Amadis's family wanted to scry for her, they couldn't have asked for help from anyone in the Underworld. But a Mortalworld witch ... that would be palatable."

"That makes sense to me." Amadis slowly stood up. "Daniel, I know this is a lot to take in."

"You think?" He shook his head as if trying to clear it.

"But I wanted to be honest with you about your mother. Because you need to know I am also being honest about the World Tree. To be called as a Keeper to guard the Tree is an immense honor."

Daniel stared at her. Then his face tightened. "Amadis, you are out of your fu—out of your mind if you think I am ever going to join another war."

"But the Tree—"

"No. Not ever."

"But this is the World Tree." She froze, stared at him, dizzy in the face of his refusal. Her heart started to pound so hard it echoed through her ears.

How dare he? How dare he refuse the most honorable, noble duty anyone could ever be gifted?

And then her stomach dropped. She was going to fail her Task.

No. No, Daniel was a good man. She could convince him, if she could just show him the Tree, he'd see how important it was.

"Daniel." Thrane shifted in his seat. "If you really are who the World Tree is calling, then ..."

"What, you don't believe it's me?" he asked.

"Every other Keeper I have known—and over the centuries there's been a few—we've been called by the World Tree." Thrane spread his hands. "It comes to us in our dreams. Have you ever had a dream like that?"

"I don't dream."

"Ever?"

Daniel shook his head.

Amadis cut a look at Thrane; he stared harder than ever

at Daniel. Finally, the Keeper scowled, scrubbed a hand over his chin.

"Daniel, I think you should come to see the World Tree," Thrane said as if he was reading Amadis's mind. "I honestly don't know what the fu—what is going on here, either. But believe me in this. The World Tree is *the* most important being in our entire world. If you can help guard it, you are doing more good than you will ever know."

Daniel's nostrils flared, and Amadis instinctively knew he'd reached the end of his tether.

But her Task was clear. She had to keep trying. "Perhaps you should hear Thrane out. At least go to the Tree—"

Daniel pivoted to her, his eyes turbulent like an ocean crashing beneath a furious storm.

"No. I don't know how many times you people have to hear me say it. But flat out, no fucking way, no. N.O."

His eyes steadied, and everything about him stilled. His arms slowly dropped to his side, his legs tensed, and he stared at each of them.

"I'm having this 'chat' with you right now because of my mother, and for no other reason. And if you want to push this line with me, then you better be prepared for what happens when I have to back up my words with actions."

Amadis swallowed, the hairs on the back of her neck pricking. They'd pulled the tail of the tiger.

Thrane unfolded to his full height. But Daniel radiated a lethality that stole Amadis's breath.

Her mouth went dry, and deep in her belly, something warm and languorous coiled around and around.

She blinked. Gods, but this man made her body boil.

"All right, I think this conversation needs to simmer

down. Daniel, now you know what we are here to do. You also need to know that I found a soldier for the Order here at your property two nights ago. I killed him but given the attack this morning ... it looks like there may be more."

"What the fuck?" Daniel whirled to her. "Where? And where's the body?"

"It happened in the forest behind your lodge. And the remains have been returned to the universe. Now, I've been patrolling the grounds at night to ensure no others are here."

"Is that why you've been up every morning?" Daniel shook his head, eyes narrowing. "You haven't been rising early—you're heading to bed."

"Of course. I could not just sleep while danger may lurk in your forest."

"You should have told me."

"Why? You would not have understood, and I was able to handle the matter. And look, you know now."

"I could have helped."

"I don't know your skills in fighting, but these soldiers are trained with weapons that will kill you instantly. A sword or knife is hard to defend if you have no familiarity."

"You know I was in the army for a damned long time." He bared his teeth.

"This is not about the familiarity of wars. I do not know how your battles work here, but in our world, fights are close combat. Lack of proficiency will have you skewered on the point of a sword and dead as only mortals can be."

"And what, *you* have a lot of familiarity?"

Amadis raised her chin. "I have years of practice." As Daniel glared at her again, she hurried to distract him. "We need to discuss patrolling your grounds. Moyarn and I agreed earlier that he would take the first half of the evening and I the second. Nate, Thrane and India will guard the Tree from their side of the forest and help here as needed."

"So you're all going to be on patrol, without me, on my grounds? Remember, I was in the army for eighteen years. That's close to two decades of lived experience... versus"— he eyed her—"practice."

"Excuse me. My *practice* includes close to four decades of precision training, daily from sunrise."

He stared at her, her hands, her shoulders, back to her face. She'd seen that look on the face of Angels more than enough times to know what it meant. Her chin rose.

Finally, he replied, "I've worked with plenty of women in the field and know you can be as well trained and as determined as anyone else. But you don't exactly seem like a ..."

"A warrior?" she softly asked. She dropped her gaze, hid the fire that wanted to erupt at such a seemingly benign word.

"Exactly."

"I killed a soldier; you've seen me training. Yet still you question my skill?"

"No—it's just, how can *you* stop some kind of invasion?"

She erupted. All her life Amadis had been told she wasn't right for Tasks, not true enough, not good enough, not brave and courageous and skilled enough. Not *Angel* enough. Well, no more.

With a flare of her wings, and a bunch of her muscles, she leaped, somersaulting over Daniel's head. Behind him, she drew her swords and had them crossed in front of his throat before he could even look back.

Hovering midair, the tips of her toes just above the ground, she whispered into his ear, "I'm warrior enough to draw your blood right here."

Daniel stilled, then drew in one sharp breath. And his back brushed against her, and suddenly the fire of anger blurred, the edges igniting with a different heat.

Her nipples tightened and pressed against Daniel like this; he must have known.

She hissed, slid her swords clear, but with slow beats of her wings, she stayed aloft as Daniel turned. His gaze shifted to her swords as she smoothly sheathed them, then to her wings.

Then down her body.

Heat rushed through her cheeks; clearly, he had felt her breasts against him. But she didn't care. His back was to the rest of the group; no one saw where his gaze traveled.

And in his eyes, desire blazed too.

She licked her lips then shot to the second-level balcony. Called over her shoulder, "Don't doubt my ability again."

16

That night, Daniel's eyes snapped open to a pitch-black bedroom. He'd been getting up before dawn ever since he moved to Willow Grove, and his body had settled so comfortably into the routine, he didn't even have to set the alarm—although he had one set just in case something crazy happened and he slept in.

He snorted. Sure as shit something crazy had happened over the past few days, but apparently, even that hadn't been enough to affect his body clock.

Breathing out a curse, he braced for the predawn air, threw back the thick winter quilt, and headed into his bathroom. By the time he'd showered and dressed in jeans and a thick gray sweater, the sky had begun to lighten to the same color as his top.

Coffee. He needed that now.

The sun would begin to rise soon, and he had a second mug out, filled, and his feet taking him toward the lake before he knew it.

He pulled up short and stared at the two mugs. Great.

Three mornings in a row, and he was making Amadis another coffee in case she'd be there. No fucking doubt at all; she'd be looking out over the lake, probably without any gloves, watching the sunrise.

Daniel could always turn around, dump the second coffee in the sink, and head into the lounge instead. Watch the sunrise through the wall of windows. But damn, that's not what he wanted.

He snorted. Acknowledged the truth—at least to himself. What he wanted was to go out and enjoy the sunrise with A. Jones.

But hell, he was going to have to apologize. For two things. One of them was totally out of his control because, for some reason, his goddamn body lit up like a wildfire the moment he got near ... or even a whiff ... of Amadis. And when she'd gone all warrior-woman in the lodge, when her breasts had pressed into his back, no way could he have controlled his physical reaction. He'd had to turn around to make sure no one else in the room had seen his fucking tent pole of a dick.

But apologizing for his body seemed ... off. Because who wouldn't be attracted to someone as mesmerizing, as breath-taking as she was? Hell, just the memory of the tips of her breasts pressing into his back had him stiff again.

Was there any chance she was as into him as he was into her?

Their kiss by the lake and then in the kitchen replayed in his mind. His body grew warmer. Amadis didn't seem *not* into him.

And crap, was that even worse?

What if there were some rules about Angels, like a

mortal couldn't even touch them? And why on earth would she—an immortal warrior Angel who looked like a walking wet dream—even want him?

Hell, she hadn't met many mortals, so maybe she didn't know what—who—she was missing. She could be getting it on with the hottest of guys. Like movie star and billionaire hot.

But she'd landed—a smile cracked his lips, the first in a long time—in his neck of the woods. Had kissed *him*. Had seemed to be turned on by *him*. So hell yeah, he was going to take her out a coffee and enjoy the sunrise.

And apologize for the second thing because that had not been cool. Daniel didn't know her well enough to say whether she could take on an army or not. But she'd killed a soldier on her own. And that move with her swords had been one of the most impressive actions he'd seen. Better even than her sparring with Moyarn. He should never have questioned her skill. That had been pure douche.

And where was Moyarn? Was he also out with Amadis?

If he was, the Angel was getting his own bloody coffee. Daniel scowled as he eased the door open—hard with both hands holding mugs—and trudged around the building to the lakeshore.

Amadis was there. Alone. He kept his expression impassive, but anticipation made his heart pick up pace.

The sun was just beginning to crest the trees, and fine threads of fiery gold gilded Amadis's hair as a light breeze teased at the short ends. She tucked one strand behind her ear, highlighting the sweep of her jaw—that deceptively gentle jaw.

She turned and wariness entered her gaze, not the smile that had lit her face when he'd joined her on previous days.

His gut tightened. Damn.

"Here," he tried to gentle his voice, but it still came out gruff. Though Amadis just raised one eyebrow. "It's gonna be extra cold today. I grabbed these as well." Once she'd taken her mug, he fished into his pants pocket and withdrew a pair of gloves. "They're Shannon's, but she's going to be resting up today so won't need them."

"Thank you," Amadis murmured as she took the gloves. "How was she when you returned her home?"

"You mean when I drove her home? She was okay, and Mick, her husband, is going to look after her today. She wanted to come back up this evening and help out, but with the weather situation, she might be best to stay off the road today."

"What's the weather situation?"

"Looks like we might get some snow, at the very least sleet, later today." Daniel took a sip of his coffee.

Amadis still held the gloves in one hand, the coffee in her other.

"Do you want a hand putting them on?" Daniel gestured with his mug. "I can hold yours if you like?"

Amadis glanced down and blinked. "Thanks, but just so you know, I don't feel the cold like you. It's the opposite. I love the cold. How it zings along my skin."

She lifted her chin, and sure enough, a breeze must have carried across the lake just for her, playing with the ends of her hair.

And something inside him zinged too. But not cold. No, this zing was so fiery his dick throbbed.

He cleared his throat. "Sure, suit yourself. And hey, I wanted to have a word, if you can wait a moment before you head in."

Amadis watched him as she sipped her coffee. Steam swirled, momentarily hiding the crystalline aqua of her eyes.

Christ, his blood pumped harder. If she looked down now, she'd have no doubt about his reaction. But watching those lips. Inhaling her scent ... How the hell had he ever thought she was a human? He swallowed hard.

"Right, well, I wanted to say, that is, I wanted to apologize. For what I said yesterday. Clearly, you are capable. And I shouldn't have assumed you aren't because of your gender or your physical appearance."

Amadis slowly lowered her mug, then shifted on both feet and tilted her head. Considering him.

Finally, the corners of her lips curled upward. Just. "Thank you, Mr. O'Connor."

"Whoa, Mr. O'Connor?" He shook his head. "Where did that come from? It's Daniel. Just Daniel."

"Daniel."

"That means I'm forgiven?" He eyed her carefully, suddenly needing to know she was telling the truth.

"Yes. And thank you. What you said means a lot." Then she sighed. "And I must apologize too. For my behavior. I should not have lost my temper ... nor pulled my swords on you."

Some weird weight lifted off his chest, and his breath whooshed out.

"Nah, don't say sorry for that." He grinned. "I pissed you off; you have every right to lose your temper."

Amadis pursed her lips and shifted, gazing back over the lake. "But I am here to prove the Council wrong. I am a capable Angel. And that means not losing my temper."

"Why do you have something to prove?"

"Because I have to. I've always had to prove that I'm at least as capable as other Angels, if not more. Because I've always been considered … less."

"These Angels sound like dicks. You are the complete opposite of less. You are more with a giant fucking capital M."

"That is good of you to say." Her lips curved into a small smile. "But the Kin look down on half bloods like we are less perfect than them. Add to that my mother was from the Underworld, and that makes me as low as you can get in the eyes of the Kin. That's why I have to be in control all the time—and not let my temper loose."

"You're not allowed to get angry?"

"Correct." She gave him a tight smile. "Strong emotion leads to weakness. And an Angel cannot be weak. Ever."

"Well, yeah, there are times you need to be cool under pressure. I agree wholeheartedly. But you also need to have the moments where you *can* feel. Believe me, I know how important that is." He sighed and looked out over the lake as well. "Amadis, the other day you asked why I left the army?" He waited till she looked back at him. "Well, the truth is, it was because of my best friend, Ben. I joined the army straight out of high school, and we met in basic training. We hit it off from the start."

He blew out a slow breath. Fuck, this was hard to say.

Amadis turned to him fully, and he looked back at her.

Her clear gaze was strong, open. She didn't say a word,

but something triggered in his chest. He *wanted* to share this story.

"I haven't really told anyone else, and God knows why I'm telling you now. But Ben was badly injured about two years ago. We were ambushed out in the field, and Ben took several rounds. We, uh, managed to stabilize him, and he got medevaced to a hospital. But he lost part of his lower leg, and eventually, he was discharged from the army."

The oily coil in his gut tightened farther, and his heart began to pound.

"Were you injured?" Amadis asked, voice low.

"No, not even a scratch." A sharp laugh escaped him. "Again."

Images of Ben, bleeding, body torn, replayed through his mind.

"And you feel ... guilty?"

Daniel cut his gaze to Amadis. "Yeah. Of course. But that's not the end. You see, after Ben came home, he was ... different. He couldn't get back into the rhythm of civilian life. I don't know, maybe he didn't want to. But whatever, soon after he came home ..." Daniel swallowed the lump that lodged like a fucking mortar in his throat. "He, uh, committed suicide."

Daniel shook his head, turned back to the lake. To the gentle swells. Took a deep breath, tried to inhale the ease that normally came upon him standing right here. But the raw, grating edge of bile threatened to rise even farther.

His best mate, gone. Poor bloody Ben.

Then Amadis touched his shoulder.

It warmed him. And the tension inside him subsided.

Because for some who-the-fucking-hell-knew-why reason, Amadis moved something inside him.

"Thank you for telling me," she said, dropping her hand. "I should head in. But thank you."

Daniel kept his mouth shut. If he said another fucking word, it would be to plead with her to touch him again. Anywhere. Anytime.

As Amadis walked away, Daniel forced himself not to watch the curve of her backside; instead, he turned back to the lake. Alone, he inhaled Amadis's scent. Damn. He was never going to escape her.

And ... that was okay. Holy fuck. More than okay. He'd meant what he'd said about her being amazing. And given their kisses ... She wasn't averse to him either. Maybe she—he—could have something more together? Well, he was going to do everything in his power to make it happen.

The crunch of heavy footfalls on the gravel nearer the house carried in the now still air, and he tensed again, swiveling as Moyarn walked over.

Moyarn's hands were casually tucked in his long leather coat, and his hair was tied back in some kind of half-up, half-down man bun deal.

"May I join you?" the Angel asked.

"Sure, but the hot coffee's inside." Daniel forced a casual shrug and gestured with his mug.

"Good to know."

Daniel considered his newest houseguest for a beat. "So, what's up?"

"Up?" Moyarn tilted his head.

Bloody hell. These people ... were not really people. He inwardly grimaced. "It means, what do you want to talk about? Because I'm guessing you wouldn't be out here at sparrows without a reason."

"At sparrows? I have not heard that term before."

"It's a local saying, I guess. As in when the birds wake up. Sunrise."

"Ah. Well, what's up, indeed. I am here to see if you have any questions I can answer. And to talk about Amadis."

"What do you want to talk about Amadis for?" Daniel's hackles rose.

"Because I have never seen an Angel outside of the Fallen connect so strongly with the Mortalworld."

Daniel's protective instinct rose in line with his hackles. Amadis was amazing. No other word for it. She had a unique way of making an experience out of every interaction. Of finding good in everyone. But talking about her like this seemed ... off.

"She's pretty special," he murmured, leaving it that. Time to change the topic. "She called you an ex-Angel. How does that even work?" He gestured at Moyarn's back. "Do you have ... you know."

"Yes, of course. And I'll show them to you. Angels can reveal their wings to mortals whenever we choose—obviously, it's not something we go around doing all the time, though."

Daniel had to blink twice when Moyarn's wings suddenly appeared. "Holy fuck. But yours are silver. Is that because you're a Fallen?"

"No, Angels have differently colored wings just like humans have differently colored hair. And I am Fallen because I made the decision to leave my home, my family, the role that I'd undertaken for a thousand years because I knew I could do that job better not constrained by the rules that the Angelkin put on their kind."

"Whoa. That's pretty fucking intense."

"I feel intensely about it."

"So what—? Are you saying that Angels can be bad?" Daniel couldn't help but glance up toward where Amadis's corner room overlooked the lake. "Because that's not the vibe I'm getting from Amadis."

"Not at all. The Angelkin are given Tasks to help in the Mortalworld. Sometimes small, sometimes large, sometimes on a scale unimaginable. But the Task is always given with the aim of the Greater Good. That is the motto of the Kin."

"The who?"

"The Kin is short for the Angelkin. As you can see, not all Angels live with the Angelkin. When you choose to no longer serve their purpose and leave the control and order of the Angelkin, you are classified as an Ex. Sometimes we are also referred to as Fallen."

"Right. So why was Amadis all upset about losing her temper? She said before something about Angels not being allowed emotions, or some bullshit."

"Again, that is Kin methodology. Feel no emotion that may hinder in the achievement of the Greater Good."

"Why does that suddenly not sound good at all?"

Moyarn shifted on his feet, his silver eyes dulled. "Because in my experience, I can tell you the Greater Good was not always good for everyone."

Daniel slowly nodded. Years of battlefield experiences rushed back at him. Death and destruction that he'd believed was meant to be for the better, but inevitably someone ... innocent ... got taken apart.

Suddenly bile rushed back up his throat, and he spun back to the lake, inhaled evenly until his gut subsided.

"Yeah, I get what you mean," he eventually murmured.

"I can see that you do. And that is why I left the Kin. I still help. But I do it in a way that fits with the purpose *I* believe I was created for." Moyarn smiled. "Not what you were expecting to hear?"

"Well, you've totally rounded out the weirdness of the past few days." Daniel slowly shook his head. "First Amadis, then Shannon got attacked, India turns up and does some spell, then you're an Angel, and oh yeah, Amadis's dad turns up, and he's an Angel too. And throw in the local detective and some scary fucker called Thrane who guard a tree. I can safely say my life has been turned upside down, all in the space of four days."

"And you're handling it all ... exceptionally well."

"But ...?" Daniel waited till Moyarn glanced at him. "I get a sense there's a but coming."

"I don't know your purpose in life, Daniel O'Connor. But I do know this. You and Amadis obviously have a connection. It shimmers between you already. Be careful with her; she's new to your world, and while maybe your actual ages are not that different, her experiences have been well and truly sheltered by her overbearing father. And she's here on a Task—one that if she fails, she may never be given another, which would leave her trapped in the lands of the Kin, an Angel with no purpose. Unable to achieve the Greater Good."

Daniel's stomach clenched, and his eyes drifted back to her window. Connection? Shimmering? *Failure*? He swallowed the lump that suddenly thickened in this throat and swung back to Moyarn.

"What do you mean she won't get another go?"

Moyarn pursed his lips.

"Come on, man. What do you mean?" Daniel held his gaze.

"I don't know how much of this is my place to tell you. But you should know that if Amadis can't complete this Task, or if the Kin Council perceives any weakness, Amadis may be shunned. And while Amadis has not told me anything of her maternal lineage, my sense is that she is already looked down upon because she is not full-blooded."

Daniel nodded to himself. If Amadis hadn't told Moyarn about her mother, then Daniel wasn't going to say anything either.

"Let's head inside," was all he said. "I need a fresh coffee. And then you need to tell me more about this whole other fucking world that I don't know."

17

That afternoon, Daniel stalked to his woodworking shed as the sun began to bank over the forest, turning the canopy deep russet.

He wrenched the door open and checked out his zone. No one else had set up camp here, yet. Thank fuck for some peace and quiet. Between Angels, witches, cops and whatever Thrane was, who knew who'd turn up next—and where.

A flick of a switch had light filling the interior, and another had the heater whirring to life. Ah, the sweet scent of Victorian ash and cypress pine. Tension seeped from his shoulders, and his breathing exercises easily cleared his mind.

Daniel almost picked up a raw chunk from the carefully stacked timber, but the last piece he'd worked on, still on the bench, caught his attention. Dropping onto his stool, he wheeled over to it. The piece was golden pink under the shed lights. Why the fuck had he made this?

He made useful things. They were attractive, sure, with

sinuous lines of grain and stunning hues. But they were practical. Like joinery and fruit bowls or cheeseboards. But what was this meant to be?

Then a sweet, floral scent made his nose tingle. Was that ... lavender? He glanced around; sure as shit, he had no lavender here.

Then someone tapped on the door. He groaned.

Blowing out a slow breath, he was about to yell out "wait there" when the door opened, and Amadis stepped inside holding two mugs.

Daniel's mouth went dry. She must have just woken up, which made sense given she'd been up all night and only gone to bed after the sun had risen.

But now she was here, carrying two mugs with her bare hands.

Amadis smiled, and she stepped closer.

He swallowed, heart beginning to pound.

"You've brought me a warm drink each morning, so I'm returning the favor."

"Ah, thanks." Daniel automatically took a sip. Recoiled. "What the hell is this?"

Amadis raised her mug and took a sip. Memories of their coffee-flavored kiss funneled through him.

He bit back a groan.

"I added lavender sugar," she said. "You have been tense, which is understandable after everything, and the lavender will help you relax. India brought it yesterday—the herb comes from her garden."

Daniel wrenched his gaze from her lips. His pulse pounded harder. Holy fuck.

"Right. Well, thanks." He put the mug down ... far away

and forced himself to turn to the bench. He looked for something else, anything else, to focus on and picked up the thing he'd turned yesterday.

"Daniel, that is beautiful." Amadis leaned over his workbench and touched the carving. Her delicate warmth washed over him. Coffee and musk, and something else ... something fresh and beckoning, something all Amadis, infused his senses. "Why did you make a valknut?"

His dick hardened. His mind blanked. Every single sense fired up as her body brushed his.

"Ah." He cleared his throat. "A ... what?"

"Valknut. It is a symbol of the transition between this mortal life and the next stage of existence. My father—all the Kin—believe it to be a symbol for the power of God to bind and unbind all things."

Amadis reached out, ran one fingertip over the piece as if it were a piece of gold.

"It's just a chunk of wood."

"No," she whispered, eyes glued to the valk-thingy. "This is beautiful. And *you* made this?"

"Yeah. But it's just a bit of timber. I work with the stuff all the time. I do it to relax, that's all. I'll probably throw it out."

"You will do no such thing." She snatched the carving to her chest, her shoulders brushing his shoulders as she did.

His body roared to life, and the need for her obliterated every other thought.

Her scent, her presence. The press of her against him— ever so slight—and he was fucking ready to drag her onto his lap ...

Still leaning over the workbench, she turned back to

him, caught him staring like a man starved. But instead of jumping up, she placed the carving back on the bench.

"Mine," she whispered.

Fuck, he wished she was saying that about him and not the wood.

But then she stared right back at him. In the sudden silence, he swiveled his stool, the creak of the wheels turning on their castors grating over the concrete floor. He widened his legs, trapping her between him and the table.

The curve of her chest sharply rose.

Her gaze dipped to his lips. And his mouth fucking tingled like she'd kissed him. Because Christ, he knew her lips. Their silky, lush weight. Their taste.

His balls tightened. His body tensed. But he didn't shift forward. This next move was up to her.

EVERY NERVE INSIDE AMADIS IGNITED, screamed to get close. Closer. And he wanted her too. His glittering eyes homed in on her. Tension radiated from his massive frame.

And she wanted that. Wanted the mess of his desire to tangle with hers—the bite of need, raw and hot and forceful and consuming.

Amadis took another breath, dragged in more of his delicious scent of eucalypt and heat and spice.

And that spice—his spice—heated her blood. Sent her knees to jelly. More heat pooled low in her gut.

Some last remnants of reason made her consider her options: push his denim-clad legs aside and head back outside? Or step in closer to his broad chest. To the dark hooded sweater that couldn't hide the breadth of his muscles.

There was no option, really. Holding his gaze, Amadis pushed off the workbench and stepped into him.

Daniel's legs brushed hers. Tingles worked through her —met and gathered in her groin.

Her blood began to languidly heat, swirled molasses-heavy through her veins. She shifted closer again until his heat surrounded her.

She leaned forward, pressed her hands into his thighs for purchase. He hissed. His body tensed beneath her palms.

"Mr. O'Connor?" she murmured.

His gaze broke contact, dipped to her lips. She licked them reflexively. Delighted in the narrowing of his eyes. The tick in the vein at his neck.

"Daniel," she growled. She swallowed the lump that had lodged in her throat even as more heat flooded her. "Daniel, I want ..."

"Mm?" A red tint hit his high cheekbones.

"I want to kiss you."

His eyes flared. Cut back to hers. Their beautiful, glittering depths were awash with desire and need and ... something else. Something more. Something that made her heart pound.

"May I?" she asked, voice husky.

His lips curled upward, then his arms banded about her, pulled her onto his lap right as she launched into him. And his mouth crushed hers.

His tongue surged into her mouth, demanding hers. She

met it and hungrily followed him back. Tasted, demanded more of him.

The tips of her breasts tightened against his hard, hot chest. Gods, she wanted to be closer. She flared her wings, gave a tiny push—

The stool flipped and sent them tumbling into the pile of raw timber.

When everything was finally still, Amadis opened her eyes. Daniel was on top of her. Wood was everywhere. The stool was on its side, wheels spinning in the air.

"Fucking hell," Daniel groaned.

"*Belar's breath*," Amadis said at the same time.

"What happened?"

"I think I was too ... forceful, and I sent your stool, and us, into the woodpile." She tried to climb off the woodpile, but Daniel's arms were banded around her, and her motion only pushed her more into him.

Groin to groin.

"Amadis." Daniel hissed her name.

Something sharp jammed into her back, and she squirmed to get away from the hard point.

"Shit, wait a minute, Amadis. Let me up—"

"No, something's hurting. I need to get—"

"Here, I'll move first."

In a jumble of arms and legs, they detangled from each other and the pile of wood.

Amadis gingerly stood up, rubbing the sore spot on her lower back. Finally, she turned around and glared at the chunk of wood that had been stabbing her.

"Are you okay?" Daniel asked.

"Okay, yes. But your wood was stabbing me."

"The wood? Stabbing you?" Daniel's lips twitched.

"Why is that funny?"

He scrubbed his hand over his mouth. "Ah, no reason. None at all."

Something metallic laced the air, then a dribble of blood rolled down Daniel's forearm.

"You're injured," she said.

Daniel turned his arm over. A giant splinter pierced the skin, blood slowly leaking around it.

"Wow, that's a good one," he said.

"A good one?"

"Yep, a good one." Daniel inspected the wound. "You can't help but get splinters when you work with wood. This is just a bit ... bigger than usual."

"Right, well, would you like some help with it?"

Daniel stared at her. The glittering fire had subsided, but the spark that still shimmered in those indigo depths spoke to her of need banked but not forgotten.

"Yeah." His voice was husky as he stepped closer.

She deftly snagged the end protruding from his skin and pulled it clear.

"Ouch." He inspected the wound again. "That wasn't very gentle."

"I never said anything about gentle." She grinned and held his gaze.

Gods, this level of intimacy—both physical and emotional—was so unfamiliar. And why now? Why this man? Was it because he made her feel special? Valued? Feminine? Well, whatever the reason, she was going to make the most of her time with him.

As if he read her thoughts, the fire rekindled in Daniel's eyes, and he reached for her.

A knock hammered on the door a moment before it was yanked open.

"Hello, anyone there? Daniel?" Moyarn's voice echoed through the shed.

Daniel blew out a slow breath, and she released hers— unaware till then she'd even been holding it.

"Yeah, Moyarn, I'm here," Daniel said.

"Perfect. I'm getting hungry. What are we eating?"

18

The next morning, Daniel took two coffees and was out the front door to the lakeside well before sunrise. Icy puffs of air froze with every exhale, the tiny crystals suspended for a split second before they dissipated into the winter dawn.

Then his stomach fell. Amadis wasn't there.

Crap.

His heart picked up pace. Why wasn't she here? She'd been here every morning. And they had a ... thing. A moment, just the two of them. Amadis should have been here, he was sure.

She'd been on patrol the night before. When he'd been unable to sleep in the early hours of the morning, he'd gone out to spend some time with her, passing the dark hours with company instead of being alone, and he'd only gone in a couple of hours earlier. Had something happened since then? Had there been another attack and she'd been injured?

"Fuck." Tossing the contents of both mugs into the grass,

he spun around and ran around to the back door. He needed to wake everyone up, needed to contact India, and Thrane—

Then Amadis was there, practicing with her swords in the grass between the lodge and the woodshed. His breath whooshed out, and he skidded to a halt.

She wore black leggings beneath a loose white shirt held securely by the leather scabbard strapped around her body. He'd seen some shit-hot bondage stuff over his years, but those straps ... man, they were the hottest of all.

Her swords were out, silver tips barely visible in the gray, misty dawn as she went through a training routine. Again and again, her swords sliced through the air, and her body, all sinew and grace, followed, pivoting, sliding, weaving. More poetry than Daniel could find words to make.

And so goddamn beautiful. Not a soft beauty. A wicked, sharp beauty that would run you through and split you open and leave you begging for more.

Amadis threw her swords high, then flipped backward. The curve of her breasts, the line of her stomach crisply outlined in the morning light, followed by her legs whipping over. She landed on one knee in time to catch the swords as they fell beside her.

Daniel's heart stopped. Fucking poetry. And fuck did he want her. A growl worked up his throat, and she lifted her head.

Her eyes narrowed.

In a fluid motion, Amadis rose to her feet and secured her swords back in their sheath. She stilled for one moment, her chin tilted as she watched him. Then her shoulders straightened.

Was she going to come to him?

But no, she walked instead away from the lodge and toward the work shed. As she reached the building, she paused and looked back.

At him. Her lips curved before she opened the door and slipped into the darkened space.

His gut tightened. The shed. She'd gone into his shed. His heart began to beat hard and fucking painful against his ribs as his feet took him after her. Holy shit, he'd follow her anywhere.

The shed interior was dark, and he fumbled for a light switch.

Amadis sat on his stool, her scabbard and leather harness propped against the bench. Her loosely fitting white shirt was a beacon in the dark.

The beauty of her hit him like a fist in the gut, and his breath whooshed from him.

Then his blood began to heat. She held the valknut. Her small, capable, amazing hands cradled the golden timber, and her fingers swept over the rounded head, around and around.

His balls went tight. His dick began to throb. Oh shit, he wanted her hands like that on him. On his skin and flesh.

Mouth suddenly dry, he moistened his lips. But couldn't take his eyes off her.

She slowly placed the valknut back on the bench, her gaze following it.

"It's a beautiful piece, Daniel," she softly said. "But I think everything about you is beautiful."

Her low voice glided over his skin, goosebumps rising in its wake, and it took him a moment to recognize her words.

Even as his cheeks reddened, every goddamn part of him turned into one puddle of sensation.

AS AMADIS REPLACED the valknut on the bench, a new awareness shivered through her.

Her words were out now. She'd told Daniel he was beautiful because he was. And because she had to tell him. Had to connect with him somehow.

Because, from the moment he'd rounded the corner and found her training, her calm, inner peace had been fractured. And she hadn't even seen him.

But that hadn't mattered.

Of course, he'd come looking for her. And she'd wanted him to. Wanted him to want her enough to come and search her out.

And as he'd stood there, her heart had picked up pace, pounded harder, over and over, till she'd had no choice but to cut her practice short.

Finally, she'd looked at him.

His desire had been evident. The tension that screamed off his body. The tilt of his lips. The blaze in his eyes.

But he'd held back. Watching her. Was he waiting for her to make the first move? Well, she knew what she wanted.

Inside her, everything had lit up. She wanted him. He wanted her.

This didn't have to be complicated. In fact, this made more sense than anything she'd ever known. So, she'd led him into his workshop, and now here they were.

Back home, intimacy was not an easy thing ... She'd been isolated among the Kin. Her lovers had been infrequent—and none of the Kin saw her as a companion. Let alone wanted to combine their bloodlines in a permanent arrangement.

But here, none of that mattered. The only thing that mattered was that she could have a Mortalworld experience —and a real one. One that was for her, and for him.

She turned, meeting his gaze from where he stood in the doorway.

And everything inside her cheered. He was here. He'd followed *her*.

"It's cold," he murmured as he reached up to something mounted on the wall. "Here, let me turn the heater on."

She shook her head. "I told you, I don't feel the cold. But if you want it, of course."

Daniel slid her a look over his shoulder, a small smile curving his lips.

"Although," she continued, "I was hoping that maybe ... we could ..."

Daniel's gaze narrowed on her.

"Might we try to make our own ..." She spun around on the stool, her legs slowly parted over the seat.

"Our own ...?" He took one step toward her.

Her mouth went dry as he stalked another step closer. And another. Until his massive frame filled her vision.

She licked her lips, leaned back to meet his eyes. And found her voice. "Heat. Body heat."

His gaze dipped to her mouth. "Oh, baby. We could ignite an inferno." He stepped closer still. His thighs wedged between hers.

Everything in her clenched. Her nipples tightened. She leaned back, focused on his face. "Good."

He chuckled, and the sound had her lips curving.

"Amadis no-last-name, are you saying you want to make some ... body heat ... right here? Now?" He flicked a look over to the shed door. "Not in the house, in a comfortable big bed. With a condom. Lots of condoms."

Amadis laughed, a throaty sound that surprised even her. And her chest filled ... with a lightness she'd never felt before.

"Daniel, I absolutely want to make that heat with you." She slowly stood up. Rubbed herself up against his body. Moaned at the contact with his hot, hard frame. "But right here. Right now. And what is a condom?"

He groaned, and she stilled.

"Um, why was your groan one of pain?"

He dropped his forehead to hers and stared into her eyes. Something in that move made a different warmth rush through her. Not sexual ... but connecting. Intense. Powerful.

"Because I *am* in pain. How do you not know—oh hell. Okay, I guess you don't have these from wherever you come from. But here, a condom protects you from catching sexually transmitted diseases, as well as from getting pregnant."

"Oh." Staring into his eyes, Amadis's heart began to warm. "You are trying to protect me. But I am immortal—I cannot catch nor transmit your diseases. And pregnancy in Angels is very, very rare. So we have no need of these— condoms, you called them?—where I come from."

"So you're not like a virgin or anything? Because for a moment there, when you didn't know about condoms ..."

She couldn't contain a chuckle. "No, that I am not. So, any other questions? Or can we get back to ..." She leaned in and nipped his lower lip, then ran her tongue over it to say sorry. "This?"

He groaned, and a feminine thrill ricocheted to her core.

And then he cupped her jaw, and his lips caught hers. She captured him back. She wasn't the captive here, she was the captor. Or maybe they were catching each other.

Either way, she met his mouth. Hungry. Needing the contact.

And for long moments, their lips meshed, their tongues danced. And with every stroke, her heart pounded faster. The need in her gut coiled tighter.

Daniel crowded her back to the bench, his massive body hard against hers. But Amadis pushed into him right back. Pressed her breasts into his chest, stretched up on her toes, and wrapped her arms around his neck. Tried to get the pressure exactly where she needed it.

It wasn't close enough.

"Daniel. Closer."

His lips trailed to her ear, kissing and nipping over her skin. Fire trailed his nibbles, and she gasped, her breasts growing fuller. Her body aching for more of this male.

"Daniel," she demanded. "More."

Another chuckle reverberated through him, and without lifting his lips, he picked Amadis up and placed her on the workbench, spreading her thighs and stepping between them.

Finally. Pressure hit her right where she needed, and every nerve flared to life. She moaned and pulled his head back to hers. Fitted her mouth on his and plundered him.

Then he gasped and wrenched out of her arms.

Her body ached from the absence of touch, and she tried to grab Daniel, bring him back. But he chuckled, captured her hands. Amadis scowled.

"Whoa, slow down," he breathed.

"I don't want slow. I want *you*. Now. Fast."

His lips tightened, and his eyes glittered. Surely, he was going to come back—

He stripped off his outerwear, revealing a long-sleeved black T-shirt that molded to every ridged muscle over his stomach. Her mouth went dry. And then he drew that up and over his head.

Belar's breath. Daniel was beautiful. Rope after rope of gleaming muscle rippled over his wide chest. He was like some warrior of legend, built for battling hordes of invaders. Amadis's hands itched to touch him.

And then he removed the last of his clothes. His cock rose for her. Huge like the rest of him.

Every single part of her body clenched, needing that. *Him*.

"Oh. Oh yes, Mr. O'Connor."

"I think you can call me Daniel. And now you're way overdressed."

Delight twirled through her, making her head light. A laugh burst from her. "Well then, Daniel. Let me remedy that."

She pulled off her leggings and then reached for her shirt.

∽

As EVERY SINGLE piece of his world zeroed in on Amadis, Daniel forgot the cold. Forgot the timber. Forgot the messed-up world outside and drank in every fucking perfect inch of her.

Was this real? The most stunning, breathtaking person he'd ever known was stripping ... oh *fuuuck* ... it was.

Amadis tossed her top to the ground. Sleek, toned muscles. Gleaming silvery skin. Dusky nipples tipping gently curved breasts. Her shoulders were squared, her chin raised. And those glorious midnight arcs framed her perfect body.

His mouth went dry. His dick went rock-hard. "Why—" He cleared his throat. "Why do you look like you're daring me to do something?"

One of those perfectly arched eyebrows rose, and a smile fluttered about her mouth. Then she ran her hands up her torso, cupped her breasts. "Well, as good as my hands feel, they're not the ones I want on me right now."

His entire body went taut. Daniel lunged for her.

As soon as he had her sweet flesh in his grasp, a growl escaped him, and he dropped onto the stool, replacing one hand with his mouth.

Oh fuck, she was so perfect. He rolled his tongue over her nipple, groaning when it pressed into his tongue. Shivers worked up his spine, and his balls tightened. Everything in the room disappeared, the woman under his hands all that existed.

"Daniel." Amadis moaned his name; she grasped his head and pulled him to her. She was such a small thing, but Christ, she was sheer heaven beneath his hands. He let her nipple go with a pop and kissed his way to her other breast.

Her breaths became choppy as he sucked and pulled at her flesh.

"Daniel, now."

He swirled his tongue around her nipple again, delighted at the velvety nub of flesh against his tongue, but then her words registered.

"Baby, I am going to fuck you so hard, but first I want—need—this. Need this to be good for you."

Daniel swept an arm over the workbench, shoving things out of the way, then dumped his T-shirt and jacket on the cleared surface before he picked her up and set her down on his clothing. He rolled his stool between her thighs.

He met her gaze and licked his lips. Amadis fell back on her elbows. His body tightened, his dick more than ready to plunge into her. But then he grinned and dropped his gaze to her core.

He chafed his hands together then gripped her thighs. She was smooth and sleek, and he ran his palms higher up her silken skin. Higher still till his thumbs met at the curls covering her center. He rolled the stool in closer ... inhaled her feminine scent, then blew a long breath onto her delicate skin.

She moaned, and goosebumps rippled over her skin.

"I thought you didn't get cold?" Daniel said.

"That's not from the cold."

He blew on her skin again, chuckling as another shiver shook through her, but then she arched her back. Her breasts rose high, nipples flushed and tight, and a groan tore from him.

Christ, he needed more. Now.

He dipped his head and licked her up. The moment her taste hit his tongue, his head began to spin, and the instinct to feast roared through him. He growled, then stroked her flesh over and over.

Amadis's breathing grew choppy, and suddenly her hands clutched at his head, held him to her.

"Don't stop," she panted.

Another growl vibrated through him. Stop? Never. He plundered her with his tongue, drank her down, took her essence until she was all he could think and see and feel.

Then Daniel found the tight nub of flesh at the top of her sex and bit down.

"Yes! Daniel, yes!" Amadis gasped, her hips surged into his face and her body convulsed against him.

Christ, he had to move—had to slam high and hard and long into her—but no. Breathing through short, fast breaths, he shoved the urge to pound into her aside.

Blood humming through her veins, arcs of energy ricocheting around every nerve ending, somehow, Amadis raised her head as her orgasm subsided.

"Daniel, that was ... that was ..."

He licked his lips, and his stormy-ocean eyes flashed. Raw, masculine hunger shone from his gaze. Her heart did a flip in her chest—and she noticed, even while her body was still singing after her release, that he was the most fascinating, mesmerizing, addictive sight she'd ever seen.

"Amadis," he growled.

She pushed herself up on her elbows, drawn to the rough need in his voice.

"That was amazing. And I need more." She pushed off the bench, and in one smooth move, straddled his lap. "Is that okay with you?"

"Oh hell, yeah. I'm on board with this." He ran his hands down her torso to her hips.

Her breasts rubbed against his chest, her nipples tingled, and arcs of fire rocketed to her core.

His shaft brushed against her already sensitized flesh, and she moaned at the contact. Rubbed herself again and again over him.

"Fuck," he whispered. "Baby, I'm not gonna ..."

She wrapped her arms around his neck, then she settled over him. Enveloped him. Closed her eyes as everything in her devolved to focus on one thing. His hard, hot length filling her, stretching her. Hitting high inside her. She bit her lips as the sensation bordered on a fiery razor edge.

"Amadis," he rasped. "Holy fuck. You have the hottest, sleekest, tightest grasp."

A groan vibrated through him, and he cupped her jaw, his mouth slanted down on hers. She met his tongue stroke for stroke. And with every caress, every shared breath, her body gradually relaxed, adjusted to having him wholly inside her.

"Now," Daniel growled into her mouth as he surged upward.

An explosion of sensation burst through Amadis, and she bit his neck to avoid screaming.

A growl vibrated through him, and he lifted her again—

but this time he took his sweet, sweet time lowering her down over his hard, hot, shaft.

"Gods. Oh gods." She panted. She was so close. She scrambled to find a way to have him slam into her again. Tried to use her feet as leverage, but she couldn't find anything. She was totally at his mercy. And he wasn't moving *fast enough.*

"Daniel, I don't have ... I can't get any purchase." She looked around, a groan of frustration building. "And I need to move. I need you harder. Faster. But I can't—"

"What?" Daniel's eyes opened, and his lips pulled back in a feral grin. "Baby, I'm so close, I want to make this last."

"Next time we'll do slow." She gritted her teeth. "I promise. This time, I need you. Fast. Hard."

"Fuck, Amadis." His pupils dilated, and his jaw clenched. Then he launched to his feet. She wrapped her legs around his hips, refusing to let him go even for a second from her inner clasp.

Moments later, he slammed her back on the workbench.

"Hard?" His gaze bored into hers as he withdrew from her. "You got it."

He surged into her. Over and over, he plunged. Sensation rushed over every nerve ending as Amadis's body coiled tighter, tighter, tighter—until he surged so deep he was part of her, so filling that her body exploded, and a cry tore from her throat, mingling with his hoarse shouts, and then his body stiffened. And with one last shout, he came inside her, shuddering in her arms.

∾

DANIEL INHALED DEEPLY, sex and Amadis and eucalypt infusing his senses. And his dick rose for her again. Once was never going to be enough, and this need he had for her —it was a constant gnawing demand to bury himself inside her.

"I want to do this with you again," he whispered into the curve of her neck. "But I want you everywhere. I want you on the shore of the lake. In front of the fire in the great room. In the shower. Then right back here."

Her sigh swept over his skin, and he felt her smile against his chest.

"I would like that very much, especially the lakeshore, mayhap at sunrise."

Amadis slowly lifted her head, stared up at him through heavy eyelids. A tendril of warmth spiraled through him.

"You look like a sleepy kitten, ready for a nap."

She smiled and curled back against him. And something clicked inside him. She was sheer fucking perfection right there. Like his pecs were made for her head and no one else's.

"I am tired. Maybe we can have a nap first."

"You've been awake all night. Of course, you need a nap. No, not a nap. Sleep. Like a serious rest."

But his dick was getting harder by the second, still enveloped in her lush flesh.

Daniel forced himself to withdraw from her, but as he did, her body tightened on his, and she shivered in his arms.

"But you need to—"

"No, I need this." Amadis buried her face into his neck and scraped her teeth over his skin as she rose slowly, then glided back over him. "Slow, remember?"

Long, long minutes later, Amadis stirred in his arms. And his body stirred again too.

"Down, you," he muttered to the part of his body getting way too hard, way too fast. Amadis needed sleep ... and probably food. Not his too-eager prick again.

"Are you talking to anyone in particular?" she murmured into his neck.

"Just my dick. It can't get enough of you. But seriously, Amadis, let me feed you." Something primal inside him demanded more with her. Demanded he show her he was more than just good for sex. "I know you need sleep, but food's important too."

"Daniel, technically, I do not need sustenance to survive. But yes, for my energy resources, food is good."

He couldn't contain a grin. "Well, your energy resources have been well and truly worked this morning. So breakfast it is."

After they'd cleaned up and dressed again, Daniel led Amadis out of the shed and across the grass and ushered her into the kitchen.

"Right, have a seat, and let me feed you. Now"—he turned to the fridge—"I have eggs and can make a mean cheesy omelet on toast, and it will just take a few minutes. And I'll get you a juice now while you wait. Plus, you should have some fruit."

Daniel quickly grabbed apples, pears and kiwi fruit and after washing them, chopped them up and mixed them in a bowl. He slid the fruit salad across the table in front of her.

"Start with that."

Minutes later, he had the omelet ready, and he pushed that before Amadis as well. Her cheeks were lit with a warm glow, and her eyes were mellow. And having her at that table, eating his food, looking warm and satisfied from their time together ...

And his world shifted. Like an altered reality blasting his prior existence into pieces, his heart, his lungs, his brain— everything stopped ... lifted up ... slammed back down. And was irrevocably changed.

Because Amadis was fucking perfect right here. In *his* world. At *his* table.

Heart beating too fast, he quickly ducked back to the sink and washed his hands—didn't want her to see the panic that had to be rising in his expression. Oh fuck. She wasn't here forever. She was here for a few days—maybe less.

Maybe she could visit? Hell, could he even visit her?

Daniel put the doubts out of his mind. They had rocked together. And judging by her expression, she wasn't worried about the future. So maybe they could have a ... thing. Whatever that might be.

And Christ knew he'd had enough loss to know nothing was permanent. They could enjoy each other for now— make the most of whatever this was between them. And if they were both enjoying it after Amadis's Task was complete, then maybe somehow they could find a way to keep it going.

He quickly made a new batch of coffee and poured himself a mug before dropping into a seat opposite Amadis. She was eating her breakfast with the same fascination she'd approached every other meal.

"It's good?" Daniel asked.

"Good? It's all so ..." Amadis paused, took another

mouthful, chewed, swallowed. Smiled. "*Delicious*. I mean, of course, the Angelkin eat. But food is purely for energy, not for enjoyment. The way you prepare your food here—it's like my tongue is singing."

Damn, he was going to make her a fucking feast every night if that was the case.

19

L ong after the lunch dishes were cleared away, Daniel sat at the guest check-in desk in the great room, squinting at the computer screen.

A bed-and-breakfast beside a mountain ... He winced at the copy he'd just typed. Not exactly the kind of inspirational description to tempt someone to stay in a brand-new lodge in the middle of nowhere.

He deleted the line and hunched back over the keyboard. Timber creaked in the upstairs landing. His gaze darted to Amadis's door. Again. She'd had a few hours' sleep, but was that enough? Was she up? If she was, he could go up there—maybe check she'd had a good rest.

But maybe she'd still be in bed ... his blood began to heat. They really needed to try out a bed. And maybe some of those other locations too.

"Get much woodwork done today?" Moyarn asked, walking in from the kitchen.

Daniel cleared his throat and turned back to the computer.

"Yeah, sure." He eyed Moyarn. Where had that question come from? And Christ, he was a grown man. He was not going to be embarrassed.

"So, what is this you are doing now?" Moyarn sank into one of the couches as he nodded at the laptop.

"Work. Managing rooms and marketing-slash-advertising. My business plan was to take a couple of weeks to ease into things and get a feel for running a bed-and-breakfast, then focus on bringing some business in properly. But I've decided to shut the bookings down, for a few days anyway. Just doesn't seem right bringing customers out here given everything."

"So you don't need this business to make money? I thought money was essential for every mortal."

"Well, it certainly helps to have it. But I was a soldier for a long time, which basically meant not a lot of overhead and a good wage. And yeah, eventually, I'll need this place to turn a profit. It's just not that important. In fact, I can guarantee there are things more important than that."

"It is refreshing to hear those words from the mouth of a mortal."

"Yeah, well, I came here looking for peace and quiet." Daniel shrugged. "And to get away from the rest of the loco world. This was meant to be that place."

"Ah." Moyarn sat forward in his seat. "And now it is the very opposite. You must find that challenging to reconcile—provide your business with revenue, yet your guests are the embodiment of what you wished to avoid."

Daniel stared at Moyarn. The Angel had hit the fucking nail on the head. Christ. But before he could respond, a loud knock rapped at the front door, and the next moment it was pushed open.

India strode through, followed by two more vaguely familiar women. The first woman was on the short side, maybe late-seventies, with silvery hair and soft blue eyes. The second woman was much younger, maybe midtwenties, with a red braid hanging over one shoulder. She had a smattering of freckles over her up-turned nose. Then Shannon bustled through the door after them, carrying a large tote bag.

"Excellent, you're here, Daniel," she said.

His gut began to churn, and he slowly closed the laptop.

"Why do I get the feeling this visit isn't for a nice, quiet cup of coffee?" He stood up and walked out from behind the desk.

"Coffee?" India's eyes brightened. "Well, that would be a good start. But here, let me introduce you to my grandmother, Liz Jones; she has a property over in Hill End, and our very good friend, Sim Morris, who has the Grand Hotel in Warragul. You met Sim's partner, Nate, the other night."

Daniel made with the requisite pleasantries—why was he not surprised that Liz and Sim both knew Moyarn already?—then offered to make good on the coffee.

"No, no," Shannon said. "I'll get the coffee. You all take a seat."

Daniel hid a smile when Shannon gave Liz a hard stare before leaving them to it, then turned to his ... guests? He wiped his hands on his jeans and waited for everyone to sit down.

"So, what's up?" Daniel asked.

"Mr. O'Connor—" Liz began.

"Daniel is fine."

"Well, Daniel it is. I understand from India and Shannon that your mother was a witch, and apparently had a high level of skill with the tarot deck and that you're learning about this for the first time."

Daniel tried not to stiffen but couldn't contain his reaction entirely.

"Now, dear, it's never easy coming into knowledge of the craft in adulthood; however, you're not alone in that. Which is why we're here." Liz sat back in her seat, a wide smile over her face.

"Right. Well, that's good and all, but I don't need to know any more."

"Oh, well, if you're concerned with not having enough mental capacity to grasp the basic concepts, please don't worry as we can help you there too."

"Mental capacity? Do you mean I'm not smart enough?"

"Only if you're worried, that's all," Liz said, waving a hand through the air.

"Yeah, no. Can't say I'm worried about that."

"Excellent. In that case, we can begin, dear. Now, I believe I recall your mother, but to assist you with your craft, we should try to make some magic with you. I think if you try your mother's deck, that would be best. And I've brought Sim because she just discovered her witchcraft heritage, too. Plus India, just as an extra aid since we're not entirely sure of your heritage."

Fuck. Now *he* might be a witch? How was it possible to both want to run as far away as possible from these people as well as sit and hear every single thing they could tell him?

Before Daniel made his mind up either way, Shannon

came back from the kitchen wheeling the coffee trolley. She took one look at him—damn her for knowing him so well—and plonked down on the couch beside him.

He crossed his arms.

"Now, I told you a few days ago the Jones name was a familiar one," Shannon said, patting his knee. "Well, Liz belongs to the strongest witching family around these parts, plus she's India's grandmother, so is well acquainted with what's going on. I called Liz because, while you've never seemed to have any inkling of the craft, we both think you need to know more about your mother and her magic. And now Liz has come all the way from Hill End and Sim from Warragul—even farther afield. At least listen to them."

Christ, it didn't look like he had any other choice.

"I was just saying it might be useful for Daniel to try his mother's tarot deck," Liz said. "Perhaps the familial link to an object used for magic will help with your questions."

"Hold on. What questions?"

"Well," Shannon said, "you've been wondering about your mother, and I've been wondering just how much of your mother you have in you. And that's why I brought these over with me." Shannon stood up and grabbed her tote, then returned to the couch. She rummaged through the bag, finally producing a rectangular tin box, about the size of a deck of cards. She picked up Daniel's hand and placed the box in his palm.

A warm tingle shivered through his hand. He almost dropped the tin, but ... instead, he turned it over. The worn lid was covered in a celestial-type pattern in deep blue and silver. He traced the design with one finger.

"This was my mother's," he murmured. "I remember it.

She used to pull it out and play with the cards. Like all the time." He didn't mention that he used to sit with her, mesmerized by the beautiful designs.

"And this was hers, too." Shannon went back to the tote and produced a book. "This is a guide about reading the cards. I'll just leave it here for now." She placed it on the table beside the couch.

Daniel turned the tin over again in his hands before slowly removing the lid. And there they were—somehow, the colors were still as vibrant as decades earlier. He was about to take the cards out when timber creaked overhead, and footsteps echoed from the landing.

Amadis. His heart began to pound, but he forced himself to sit still.

"Why, hello again," Amadis called out from behind him a moment later.

Of course, they all knew each other.

"Right, then." Moyarn's voice boomed in Daniel's ear right before the Angel clapped him on the shoulder. "Now you know all about us, let's find out about your magic."

Daniel scowled, both at being torn out of the moment with Amadis and at the mention of magic and *him*. "Yeah, I don't have any of your ... magic."

"Actually," Amadis said. "I think you do. But it seems to be coming from you in surprising ways. I don't sense an overt magic—and witches know when we met another being with the craft. But I have another idea. May I try something?" Amadis smoothly withdrew one sword and held the blade out as if ready to attack.

"Sure." Daniel eyed the blade. "But why do you look like you're going to attack?"

"Because that is what I am going to do, though I plan only a shallow slice. Do not move, however, I would hate for the strike to be worse than I plan. Please lift your sleeve and hold out your arm."

"You're going to cut me? Is this really necessary?"

"I believe this strike is vital. Now watch my sword."

"Fine. But try not to make me bleed too much." Daniel rolled up his left sleeve—if she was going to cut him, he wasn't going to use his preferred hand—and held out his arm.

"Ah, Amadis, do you know what you're doing?" India asked, standing up and peering over at Daniel.

"Yes, I do. But please, everyone, stand back. I do not want to cause any injuries."

"Except to me, right?" Daniel muttered. He cut her a look, then lowered his voice. "This better not be some weird Angelic mating ritual that I'm only finding out about now."

Amadis's lips curved, but her eyes stayed serious.

Daniel kept his gaze on Amadis as she slowly lowered the blade. But at the last moment, the sword twisted and swung wide.

"Phew, I thought you were really trying to cut me then." Daniel dropped his arm.

"I was."

"What?" Moyarn leaned in. "Amadis, are you saying ...?"

Amadis pursed her lips and then drew her second sword. "Please raise your arm again, Daniel. And do not roll your eyes at me. Remember, vital. And Moyarn—everyone —stand back. Please."

His gut tightened as her actions—and his history—came together. Fuck—if she was right ... He stared at Amadis—

determination pouring from her gaze. "You're serious about this, aren't you?"

"Yes, I am. Now let me really try."

"Fine, here you go. But go hard this time."

He ignored everyone else and, this time, locked his gaze on the swords as Amadis sliced the two blades down at his arm. Again, they swung wide at the last moment.

His breath whooshed out. Holy fuck.

"Ha. I knew it!" Amadis's eyes flew to his, and she swiftly sheathed her swords.

"Dear lord," Moyarn breathed.

"Can someone fill me in?" Shannon shoved her hands on her hips.

"Daniel cannot be injured." Amadis's eyes grew round, and she turned to Liz and India. "Have you heard of such magic before? Could it be a spell?"

"Wait." A sinking sensation dropped in his gut. "Am I—am I like immortal or something, like you?"

"I cannot speak for immortality. However, you appear to have aged past your mid-second decade, which is when immortality usually sets in."

So this was why he'd never been injured after all these years. He absently picked the tin back up and flicked the lid open, shut. Open, shut. Open, shut ...

His mother's face swam into view. "Don't play with the box, sweetie." She firmly closed the lid and then laid out a card on the table. "Now, my boy, let's do this again. This card means ..."

"Daniel ... Daniel ..." His arm being shaken and his name being called brought him back to the room.

"Daniel, can you hear me?" Amadis said.

"Yeah, sure, I was just ... thinking." Remembering more

like. But he scrubbed a hand over his jaw and swallowed the lump lodged in his throat. "What did you say?"

Amadis stared at him, concern clear in her expression. "Liz and India have never heard of such magic."

Then the tin in his hands began to heat. It grew hotter and hotter until he almost dropped the box—and at the last second, he transferred it into his other hand and ended up playing hot potato with the bloody thing.

Shannon frowned at him. "Be careful with that."

"It's not me. The tin got hot all of a sudden. And it's getting hotter." He tried to place it gently on the table, only it slid from his fingertips and dropped lid-down onto the timber. The tarot cards within the tin slid out, one of them faceup. The card had a stone tower, like something out of a medieval story.

Someone knocked hard and fast on the front door. Daniel stared at the cards for another second before brushing his palms on his jeans.

The knock rapped again, louder.

"Coming," he called out, standing up.

"Ah, Daniel, are you expecting anyone?" India asked as she stood up.

"Other than you all? No."

20

Amadis eyed India. The witch-Keeper was slowly rubbing her knuckles over her chest as Daniel walked toward the lodge entry.

Then Shannon pointed at the table and shot to her feet. "Daniel," Shannon whispered, "you turned over the tower. That's not a good card. It can mean danger—sometimes imminent."

But Daniel was already opening the door.

"Hi, welcome to the Angel's Lakeside Lodge," Daniel said.

"Hey," a rough masculine voice replied. "We're looking for accommodation and heard you might have rooms available."

Amadis silently stepped to the window nearest the entry. The angle wasn't perfect, but there was enough room to make out two figures, one behind the other, opposite Daniel.

"Sorry, guys, I'm fully booked," Daniel was saying. "But if

you head into town, the hotel on the other side of the lake might have a room."

"Damn, we were looking for somewhere out of the way, you know."

"Yeah, certainly know what you mean there. But if you're back in the region again, check us out."

"Thanks. Can we take a look at the lake while we're here? We spotted it as we drove up, but it looks like we have to walk through your property to get there."

"Sure thing. Let me show you around." Daniel stepped outside and pulled the door closed behind him.

Amadis shared a look with Moyarn and India. Their grim faces echoed her concern. Heart beginning to race, Amadis mouthed to Moyarn, "The back door."

Moyarn dipped his head once and silently strode through to the kitchen. Good, he'd keep their backs protected in case this was an attack.

Then she held India's gaze and nodded at the three women still sitting on the couches. India nodded back.

"India," Amadis whispered. "I'm going to keep an eye on Daniel—just in case. We don't know the limits of whatever power keeps him from getting hurt. Can you stay here and watch the front door? The Order are hunting witches—and there are three of you right here."

"Of course. But Amadis"— India grabbed her arm—"I'm getting a message from the World Tree. Something bad is coming. And the timing with those two turning up is too much of a coincidence. I can fight—but you're right, one of us needs to stay here in case there are more coming. And I need to let Thrane know to be vigilant at the Tree."

"We can help, too. We may not be fighters," Liz said, "but we can use our magic to assist."

"Thank you, Liz. I'll go out the back in case they're watching."

Amadis quickly filled Moyarn in. His silver eyes flashed, but he agreed to stay at the kitchen entry to ensure no one could get to the women that way.

With the afternoon sun warming her skin and a soothing breeze rolling in from the forest, Amadis snuck around the outside of the building.

"—and as you can see, the lake." Daniel's voice echoed from up ahead, and as she peeked around the last corner, sure enough, there he was, standing between two men on the grassy shoreline, a good way down from where Amadis and he took in the sunrise.

They all had their backs to Amadis, facing the water.

The two men were dressed in baggy trousers and jackets. One had long dark hair, the other short blond hair. At first glance, they looked casual, their legs were set an equal distance apart, and their arms held loosely at their sides.

But their stances also had an air of preparing to fight. Instinctively, she tightened her wings to her back and made sure they were clear in case she needed her weapons.

At the lake's edge, the man farthest from Amadis pointed out over the water. Daniel followed his line of sight. And the other man reached one hand behind him.

Belar's breath. She'd never get to Daniel in time. She had to act now.

"Daniel," she called, "here you are."

Daniel spun, his eyes narrowing on her as she strode across the grass toward him.

The man who had been reaching behind his back paused, turned side-on, but kept one hand hidden.

"Ama—Ammy, what are you doing out here?" Daniel said through gritted teeth. His expression was calm, but his body was tense, and she only had a moment to appreciate that he hadn't used her full name before he clapped one of the men on the shoulder.

"So, this is the lake. And absolutely, you should come back again when I've got rooms available. Just check the website."

The man who Daniel had clapped slowly straightened, his gaze locking on Amadis. He cut his friend a look, nodded toward Amadis.

The other man turned to her, and his eyes widened.

"Ammy, you said?" The first man asked. He held out his hand. "Nice to meet you."

Amadis opened her sight and looked for the man's aura. He was telling the truth; he was happy to see her. Why?

"Ammy's just a guest," Daniel said, stepping forward and blocking the man's outstretched arm.

"But I am willing to greet you in your customary manner and shake your hand," Amadis said.

Daniel hissed.

The first man frowned but kept his arm outstretched. The second man, she would call him Short Hair, maneuvered to stand behind her. But Amadis yanked Long Hair around so that she was standing beside Daniel. And they were now facing the two strangers together.

Her palm tingled as magic met magic. But his magic had a decaying taint that left an acidic burn on her skin. Death magic, right here. Ice flew through her veins.

"Witch," Long Hair breathed. "Get her."

Short Hair gasped and withdrew a knife from his back.

Still holding Long Hair's hand, Amadis spun around and hauled him off his feet, then pushed him into his friend.

"Daniel, get behind me."

"Fuck off," Daniel shouted. He grabbed Long Hair's shirt and punched the man in the face.

But Long Hair just shook his jaw and regained his feet easily.

"Daniel, please, these men have been fed death magic. They are not normal mortals."

"That's right, witch. We're not normal. But we are going to take you."

Her lips curved. "Oh? You and the army that I do not see?"

"It's meant to be, you and what army," Daniel said, bringing his fists up again.

"You mortals have such odd patterns of speech." Amadis shrugged. "No matter, for I do not see the army, and therefore, I have no fear that you will have the capability to take my magic."

Long Hair and Short Hair exchanged glances, expressions puzzled.

"Yeah, boys, I know the feeling," Daniel said.

Amadis cut him a look. What did that mean?

"But here's the thing," Daniel continued, "she's right. You can leave now, and no one gets hurt. Or you can stay and fight, and *you'll* be the ones getting hurt."

"Thank you for the support, Mr. O'Connor; however, that's not entirely correct," Amadis added, keeping her gaze on Long Hair and Short Hair. "You should know that if you stay and fight, neither of you will survive this day."

"Enough chitchat, witch. The bloke might be big, but he's no match for these." Long Hair withdrew a gun and knife from his jacket.

"Or this." Short Hair waved his knife in the air. His grasp of the knife hilt was odd, not the traditional hold for a fighter; instead, he held it like a sword.

But Long Hair had his Mortalworld weapon and knife gripped correctly for combat.

"Remember, we need the witch alive," Long Hair said to Short Hair. "Wound only. We'll get rid of the bloke. No magic there. And then check the rest of the building—where there's one witch, there's more."

"I gave you fair warning, so be it." Amadis reached back and withdrew *Daudhi* and *Dagr*. The blades hummed as they kissed when crossing over her head, then glinted in the winter sun. "Meet Death and Day. Even your stolen magic cannot stand up to them. They shall be the last thing you see in this world."

"Watch this, bitch." Long Hair swung the gun toward Daniel and pulled the trigger, but as he did, his feet slipped, and the bullet tracked wide.

A sharp retort cracked from the gun and echoed around the lake. An acrid smell tainted the air as a burning weight punched into her arm. She dropped *Daudhi* as her arm fell to her side, but gritting her teeth against the pain, she kept *Dagr* steady and drove it through Long Hair's chest.

The soldier's eyes widened, locked on *Dagr* as she pulled it back. His mouth dropped open, and he sank to his knees.

Blood fountained from the wound in the center of his chest, more bubbled at his lips, and then he collapsed to his side.

"Behind you—!" Daniel's voice rang out, and she whirled as the other fighter came in with his knife. But her sword was on the wrong side. Instinctively, she blocked with her arm. A cut there may at worst sever her limb, but that was survivable.

And then Daniel was between her and Short Hair. He body checked the other fighter, ramming the man's knife arm with two hands, sending the weapon high.

But Short Hair spun fast back into Daniel, knife blade whipping through the air.

Not fast enough, though. Amadis spun and freed her sword, swung *Dagr* in a low arc, striking Short Hair from low to high. His arm froze for a split second, then his grip on the knife hilt loosened, the blade dropped to the ground. His body followed.

Heart hammering, Amadis raised *Dagr* and turned, making sure no one else was around.

"Holy fuck," Daniel whispered, chest heaving. His eyes were bright, his jaw tight.

Adrenaline raced through her, but she forced her breathing to even out and nodded at Daniel's sentiment even as she kept her gaze on the bodies.

"There's blood everywhere. Are—are you hurt?" Amadis asked him.

"Can't be—remember?" He cut her a look before stepping between the larger pools of blood, knelt at each of the soldiers and checked them over.

"They're dead," Daniel said over his shoulder. "What the fuck was this all about?"

Then he turned to where her sword lay on the ground. His eyes narrowed and tracked to the blood dripping down her hand and over her fingers. He leaped to his feet and was at her side in a flash.

"You're bleeding," he said through gritted teeth.

"I know." *Belar's breath.* As if Amadis's acknowledgment had caused the wound, suddenly fire arced through her arm, but she kept *Dagr* raised, just in case. "Gods, it hurts."

"Let me see."

"No, I need to keep watch in case there are other Order soldiers around."

"I think we're good now," Daniel said, his voice oddly gentle. "We've got a good hundred feet between us and the forest, and if anyone was out there, we'd have plenty of warning before they got to us. And up this end of the lake, there's no one else around. See? So come on now, just rest your sword on the ground, and I'll check your wound. Where is it? Is it near your wings?"

Amadis scanned the forest's edge, then finally nodded. But she couldn't leave *Daudhi* on the grass, so cradling her injured arm to her chest, she picked her sword up from where it had fallen. The blade was clean, so she quickly laid *Dagr* in the grass, hilt toward her so she could grasp it quickly if needed, and then sheathed *Daudhi*.

"Can I look now?" Daniel asked. "But your wings—where are they?"

"The wound is through the top of my arm. I lost my ability to grip *Daudhi,* so the bone may be shattered. But my wing is moving freely, so no damage there."

"Good news about the wing. Okay, let me see what you've got." He gently took her elbow.

Fire pulsed, radiated from the wound up through her shoulder, but she exhaled hard through her nose.

"It's a bullet wound," he said flatly.

"I have never been stuck by one of those before. Slices and stabs, yes. Bullets, no."

Daniel stopped. Stared at her face.

"What?" she said. But he just shook his head and went back to looking at her arm. "Is the bullet still inside the wound?"

"I need to see the other side but don't want to move you more than necessary."

"Do what you need."

She couldn't contain a hiss as he maneuvered her arm.

"Fuck, sorry." His lips tightened. "Good news. Looks like the bullet went right through, so it's not still in your arm. You need to get rid of your shirt so I can see the full extent of the injury, though. But fucking hell, the bullet hit *you*." He eased her arm back to her chest, then he stepped back. "Fuck!"

His jaw clenched, and he whirled to face the lake.

"Hey, Daniel. Daniel—look at me." She waited until he turned back to her. "I am fine. This wound will mend. I am an Angel; this cannot stop me. In fact, bullets are far less dangerous than swords."

"But the bullet was aimed at me. Me. Yet somehow, it hit you instead."

"He slipped as he went to shoot you."

"But remember back in the lodge, you tried to hurt me, but you couldn't ..." Daniel's face went white.

"What? Daniel, what's wrong?" She grabbed his arm.

"Wrong? Fuck yeah, something's wrong. All these years,

what if there were more bullets meant for me and somehow they ended up in other people instead? I'm your worst fucking nightmare."

"Daniel, no, you are not. I don't know why you can't be injured, but regardless, that does not make you my—or anyone's—nightmare. You just took on an armed Order soldier without a single weapon; how is that a nightmare?"

"Because you got injured. You got shot, Amadis."

"Yes, I can see that. And feel it." She craned her neck to see the damage on the back of her arm. Pain ricocheted through her. "*Great Belar,*" she hissed, aborting the movement.

"Ah, hell. Here, let's get you inside. Sorry, this isn't the time. We need to get your wound looked at, although it's not bleeding anymore. How much pain are you in? Do you need me to carry you?"

"No, thank you. I do not need you to carry me; I can walk perfectly fine, see? And, of course it's stopped bleeding. Angel, remember? Even if only half. I am immortal, and the wound began to heal the moment the injury was caused. And I will show you, just as soon as I can take my top off and get to the wound."

"Fine." Grim-faced, Daniel eyed her arm before finally nodding. "Let's head inside."

"That is a good idea. I also need to see India and have her arrange for the salt to remove the remains and release the souls."

"I have no fucking clue what you mean, but sure. Can I take your sword for you?"

"I need to clean it."

"You need to do that now?"

"Yes. Yes, it's a ritual—*Dagr* and *Daudhi* may never be sheathed in the blood of my enemy. That would be disrespectful to the elements that are *Dagr*, and to my mother's family who mined the ore for these blades in Underworld."

"Okay, I can see it's important. I've got it." Daniel took the sword to the lake and cleaned the blood off in the crystal waters. Then he shrugged out of his jacket and used the material to dry the blade. "Here you go."

At that moment, the sun broke through the clouds; its rays caught *Dagr* as Daniel passed it to her.

She paused, searched his eyes as he held the blade. He was giving her a sword. And on the shores of the lake, that motion was the most special, significant moment she'd ever had. It bettered the blinding light of the coffin lid being lifted in her tenth year. It bettered coming to the Mortalworld and seeing the World Tree. It bettered—barely—the sex they'd had that day.

It was perfect. And Daniel was perfect. He was going to make an amazing Keeper once she convinced him of his purpose.

"Thank you," she said. "Thank you for honoring *Dagr*."

"No worries." Daniel cleared his throat. "Now, can we get you inside and look at that wound?"

21

Daniel shouldered the back door open and held it for Amadis as she eased into the kitchen. Moyarn stood at the window, expression grave, so he must have seen them walk past.

"Sit at the table," he directed Amadis.

Her face was pale, and her lips set. But while she carried herself stiffly, she didn't say anything, just nodded.

But shit, with the wings, she wouldn't exactly be comfortable in his timber-backed chairs. He swiftly turned one of the chairs around so its back was to Amadis's uninjured side, allowing her wings to be unimpeded. She shot him a small smile as she sank into the seat.

His heart filled as if he were some goddamn hero at getting that smile.

Daniel shoved the feeling away.

"I heard a gunshot—" Moyarn said.

"Amadis got shot."

"What the hell?" Moyarn strode over to Amadis, gaze roving over her.

"Don't yell at her. And don't touch her either," Daniel said when Moyarn reached out for Amadis's shoulder.

Something uncomfortable jumped inside Daniel. Moyarn needed to back the fuck off. Amadis was Daniel's to look after.

Except, no. She wasn't really. And what did he care if another guy helped her?

Moyarn halted; his gaze swung to Daniel. But the fucker did lower his arm, avoiding contact with Amadis as he searched Daniel's face. "Oh hell," Moyarn breathed. He shot a look at the ceiling. "This is a clusterfuck, isn't it?"

"What is a cluster of fucks?" Amadis asked.

"It's an army term for when things go from bad to very bad." Daniel cut a look at Moyarn; although, as the Angel backed away from Amadis, something in him eased. "Thought you were an Angel. How do you know that term?"

"I've studied mortals for millennia. I know how you talk, especially those from the army. And trust me, this qualifies as one of those times."

"Care to share?" Daniel found the kitchen scissors.

"Not while you have those in your hands."

Daniel frowned. But then shrugged off the Angel's comments. He had more important things to see to.

"Moyarn, Daniel is concerned about my wound," Amadis said. "Perhaps he needs to see for himself that it will be of no consequence to me. However, would you inform India and her guests that the men have been dispatched?"

"This isn't about me." Daniel rolled his eyes. "This is about checking your *bullet wound*, remember? Are you okay if I cut the material?"

"Dispatched?" Moyarn's gaze sharpened.

"Of course, cut away," Amadis said to him. Then she turned in her seat and called after Moyarn as he left the kitchen, "Tell India we will need her salt."

"Hold still," Daniel muttered.

He carefully sliced through the fabric of her top and opened up the sleeve from her neck to arm. He was just about to peel the fabric away from the wound when the kitchen filled up with Shannon, India and the others.

"Amadis, what happened?" India demanded, taking a seat beside her. The other women all took seats too. Moyarn went back to stand at the window.

Suddenly, the usually spacious kitchen was over-crowded. An itch grew between Daniel's shoulder blades at being closed in with all these people.

And he swore that Amadis stiffened too.

Drawn to comfort her, he rested a hand on her good shoulder. Sure enough, a fine vibration trembled through her frame.

He squeezed her and didn't let go. After a moment, she covered his with hers.

And while all around them questions were thrown and answers tossed back about the men and the fight, he and Amadis stayed that way. Connection flowing from where they touched. Slowly, Amadis's shoulder relaxed.

She gave Daniel's hand a squeeze and let him go. Inside his chest, something that had been tight released.

"I said, let me look, Daniel," Shannon muttered as she pulled her chair around to Amadis's injured side.

He glanced at Shannon. When had she even stood up? Fuck, he'd been so focused on Amadis he'd entirely missed

Shannon beside him. "Uh, sure. Here, I was just getting to the wound."

"Does it hurt?" India asked. "I can try a spell to reduce your pain, but it tends to take away all feeling."

"No, not needed, but thank you." Amadis shook her head. "You all know my injury will heal. This is for Daniel's benefit. To show him I am okay."

Daniel cut Amadis a look. "Your version of okay and mine differ. A lot. Your arm is covered in blood, and fine, it's not bleeding now. But it was, so you must have lost a lot. And trust me, I've seen battlefield wounds enough"—he ignored the oily slick that greased through his stomach—"to know that blood loss alone can be a killer. But sure, humor me and let me look for my sake."

"Amadis is telling you the truth, Daniel," India said. "Her immortality means her wound will mend without any assistance."

"Okay, Amadis, I'm getting the medical kit and will wash you up," Shannon said from where she stood. "I take it you don't need stitches then?"

"Of course she will," Daniel said, finally pushing away the cloth. The ragged puncture hole in Amadis's arm was messy and gory with blood and bone fragments.

"Moyarn," Amadis called out loudly, "can you please wet a cloth so I can clean away the blood?"

"At least," Shannon said, "let me get the disinfectant wipes—"

"Not needed, but thank you, Shannon. Now Moyarn, please—the wet towel. And Daniel, watch as I clean this."

"No," Daniel said, "if you're going to be all stubborn

about this, then I'm going to be stubborn and say let me—us—clean the bloody thing."

"Fine." Amadis snorted and threw the wet towel at him. "While you clean that, I need to talk to India. The sooner we take care of the bodies, the better. What if someone stops by and sees them?"

Daniel traded a look with Shannon. Everyone seemed certain the wound would heal. But Amadis could talk tough for as long as she wanted, and fine, she was immortal, so this injury might not be the worst thing ever, but her pain was evident—at least to him. And he hated putting her through more.

Shannon nodded, and with her help holding Amadis's arm, he gently cleaned the blood away. At least her conversation with India was keeping her attention off what he was doing. Although she did flinch when he ran the cloth over the edges of the grape-sized fucking hole in her arm.

The ragged edges that at that moment began to smooth out, and the gouge where muscle and flesh and bone had all been mangled, filled in.

"Holy fuck," he breathed, rocking back on his feet.

He looked up. Everyone else was watching him with varying degrees of amusement and impatience. Amadis was on the impatient side, one eyebrow raised.

"Okay, okay. So it's not life-threatening," Daniel muttered. "I'm still making sure it's taken care of." He went to say *that you're taken care of*, but he slammed his mouth shut. This feeling shit had to stop. The physical, yeah, he was on board with that, but Amadis was leaving. He needed to get a grip on his feelings.

"And I thank you for that," Amadis said, voice softening.

"Uh, right. So I'll just get rid of this." He stood up and went to toss the towel away when a thought struck. He whirled back to Amadis. "Any issues with your blood being in the rubbish here, or should I get rid of it permanently, like in the fire or something?"

"Permanently is safest for Amadis," Moyarn answered. "There are trackers who trace beings through blood, even old blood, and if anyone from the Order gets a hold of it, that would be bad for Amadis if she returns to Mortalworld."

Amadis stiffened and darted a look at Moyarn. "I didn't know that."

"You should have been taught that before being sent on your first Task," Moyarn said, frowning.

"Yes, well, I get the sense this Task was as much of a surprise to the Kin as it was to me. Freya visited my sire and ordered him and the Council to send me on the mission." She shrugged her good shoulder. "Otherwise, I doubt they would have called upon me."

"Why not?" Daniel said. "You were amazing out there with your swords."

Amadis's eyes widened, and her cheeks tinted a peachy red before she sighed. "Thank you. But I said that because the Council haven't called me before, and I reached my immortality two decades ago."

"Okay, then let's get rid of this towel now," Daniel said. "And then we need to work out a plan because those two men said they wanted to take Amadis with them to have her magic stolen. I'm guessing the Order will have more soldiers looking for other witches, too."

"You're right, Daniel, although it's not just witches that

are in danger," India said softly, her eyes glowing with a mysterious green fire. "The Order need death magic so they have enough power to attack the World Tree. And you know what happens if the Tree falls."

Daniel stared at Amadis. Her face was grim and resolute as she regarded him back.

"Okay," he said into the silence. "Let's regroup. Alerting Thrane and Nate about the Tree's warning to India is our number one priority. Getting rid of the bodies and burning Amadis's blood comes next."

"I'll get onto Thrane now," India replied.

"Thanks. Then we need to find out what brought those two men here—did they find us by accident? Or do others know they're here, which means we should expect more ... visitors? Or were they reconnaissance, scouting the area?"

"Did they drive up?" India asked.

"Not that I could see," Daniel said. "But if not, how did they get here? And how did they find us? Can they track magic? They seemed surprised that Amadis was a witch. I'm going to take a look around now, see what I can find."

IT WAS WELL over an hour later when Daniel wrapped up his recon of the town and turned his SUV onto the dirt road that led to his lodge. Another vehicle, a large 4x4 utility truck, followed him. Through his rearview mirror, Daniel made out Nate in the driver's seat.

Daniel parked in the garage and trudged over to Nate as he hopped out of his vehicle.

"Hey," Daniel said, rubbing his hands together to find some warmth.

"Hi. Sorry it took me so long to get here." Nate went around to the bed of his truck and hefted a bucket over the side.

"That's the salt?"

"Yep, I just brought enough for what we need."

Daniel nodded but couldn't completely hide his unease.

"Talk about a crash course in a whole new world, huh?" Nate said, whacking him on the back. "We can get into the details later, but right now, I want to see Sim and Liz. I almost, hell, not almost, I totally lost my shit when I heard there were Order soldiers here."

"Yeah, when I found out what they do ... what they wanted to do to Amadis, and would've done to Shannon, everyone ..." Daniel couldn't help but clench his fists at this side. Those assholes had been going to kill the people he ... cared about. And he hadn't hesitated to help deliver them to their maker when he'd realized that. Even though it went against everything he'd vowed to himself.

"Here, I'll take this around the back," he muttered, forcing his fists to unclench. "I can see you're antsy to head in. I'll meet you there soon."

"Thanks," Nate said before jogging toward the lodge.

Daniel took his time and had cleared his mind by the time he reached the back door.

He walked into the kitchen right as Amadis came in from the lounge. Her hair was still wet like she'd just hopped out of the shower. She wore a long-sleeved black tee with skintight denim jeans. Her wings were once more folded tightly at her back, and the harness for her scabbard and swords wrapped around her torso, under the elegant curve of her breasts and over her shoulders.

His mouth went dry. Holy hell, she was hot. And so very, very not from this world.

"Is that it?" Amadis asked.

"Huh?" He blinked and stared at his hands. "Oh. The bucket. Yep, that's what we need."

Amadis stilled, and then she squared her shoulders as if steeling herself for something.

"Hey, what's wrong? You wanted this, right?"

"Yes, of course."

"Is your arm hurting?"

"No. Daniel, no. It's just ... I know what must come next."

"If it's bad, I can do it. I'll get Nate to tell me, and you wait inside."

"No, I took their lives—it should be me who sees them into their next life."

"I have no fucking clue what you mean. But you're very serious, so okay. Let's do this thing. I'll let Nate know first, though. He might want to see the bodies beforehand."

By the lake a few minutes later, Nate whistled as he took in Amadis's death strike in the Order soldier's chest. He gave Amadis a cool, approving look and stood up and turned to Daniel.

"What did you find out in the village?" he asked.

"I sussed out the pub—Jenny, behind the bar, mentioned two men had been after accommodation earlier this morning. As she's full, she mentioned a few places, including mine. Jenny saw the men head off on foot around the lake. I took a slow drive along Main Street but couldn't see anything out of the ordinary."

"So they weren't targeting you—us—here."

"Doesn't seem like it."

"But still, they were here. And they had death magic. Fuck. I need to get back to the farm. We need to watch out for Tara—she's been targeted before by the Order—and the Tree." He glanced at Amadis. "Thrane said you know what to do next?"

Amadis nodded.

"Okay, I'll take Sim and Liz with me now. We'll keep close to Tara and the Tree from our side of the forest." Nate met Daniel's gaze and nodded once toward the lake.

Daniel eyed the other man for a moment before carefully stepping around the bodies and following him until it was just the two of them at the lake's edge. "What's up?"

"I know what it's like to have the World Tree call you but not be ready to accept that call," Nate said. "It came to me in my dreams for years before I saw why the Tree and becoming a Keeper is so important."

Daniel blew out a hard breath. "Your Tree hasn't called me. And I don't want to go to war—ever again. The idea of joining an immortal war—fighting every day for the rest of my endless existence? Nah, that's not me. But those guys came onto my property and would've hurt the people I care most about. So yeah, I'll help now. But that's it."

"Amadis believes you're the reason she's here." Nate cut a glance over Daniel's shoulder. "At least hear her out. I've got to go, but we need to get together and work out what the hell is going on."

As everyone said their goodbyes, Daniel stood back from the group. Even Shannon had been brought into the fold, with her and Liz exchanging promises to meet up to talk business, whatever the hell that meant.

But Amadis stood apart, her gaze also on everyone else. She wasn't favoring her arm now, so it must have completed healing. That, or she was hiding any discomfort. And she seemed so set on being the strong, capable Angel; hiding any pain was a real possibility.

Her expression was calm, but there was something ... a kind of wistfulness in her eyes. Then she stared at the bodies.

Ah, hell. She'd taken a life. Lives. And it might not be her first, but she was still so new at this.

Before he knew it, Daniel was standing behind her to keep the wind from hitting her injured arm—just in case. She shifted on her heels until her wings touched his chest.

And while he wanted to wrap his arms around her and bring her even closer, he stayed exactly as he was, content to be right here in that moment with her—for her—until everyone had left. Moyarn had ushered Shannon inside until it was only Daniel and Amadis.

With a sigh, Amadis knelt beside the bodies.

"Can I help?" he murmured. Speaking loud seemed ... wrong. Even the trees had stilled as if the wind recognized what they were doing.

"Just watch," Amadis said, glancing at him, her face somber.

The silvery stuff coated the remains, and bit by bit, the bodies dissolved into nothing.

Still on her knees, Amadis's gaze rose to the sky.

"Is it happening?" Daniel asked.

"Yes, their souls are leaving them now. You cannot see

them," she murmured, "but I do. The life force that sustained these physical shells is departing now. The remnants of stolen magic with it."

And then the wind picked up, the trees around the lake rustling and swaying in the growing breeze.

"I think a storm's coming in," Daniel said.

22

A winter storm had swept in by the time Amadis, Moyarn, Shannon and Daniel sat down to eat dinner in the dining room. With a sigh of appreciation, Amadis finished her last mouthful of the pasta and meat dish Daniel had called lasagna—another first in her culinary experience.

"That was delicious, Daniel. Thank you," Amadis said. "It will be perfect to keep my energy levels high for the night ahead. I'll take the first shift to watch the lodge tonight."

Then a yawn caught her by surprise, rolling through her to the point she couldn't keep her eyes open. When she could see again, Daniel, Moyarn and Shannon all stared at her.

"Hold on, did you just say you'd take patrol again, as in tonight?" Daniel said, dropping his spoon into his empty bowl. "After that injury?"

"Yes, of course." Amadis frowned. "I am healed as you saw this afternoon, and as there will only be three of us, we need to take turns. I can take first shift."

"Right." Daniel rocked back in his seat, one eyebrow high, and folded his arms. "So, the yawn that just about knocked you off your chair and the fact that you're almost asleep at the table don't mean anything?"

"No. And it's only because your meal has warmed my stomach that my body is yawning." She didn't mention how much Daniel's food had also filled her heart—as if preparing her such an enriching meal had also deepened their connection.

"Mm." Daniel leaned forward and started to fiddle with his bowl. "Catch this, then." He threw the spoon at her forehead.

"Ouch." She rubbed the spot where the utensil had hit her. "What did you do that for?"

"Daniel, what are you doing?" Moyarn said.

"Daniel!" Shannon jumped up and rested a hand on Amadis's arm. "Here, honey, let me look. Oh."

"Shit, sorry. Are you okay?" Daniel asked.

"What? Did it cut me?" Amadis felt around the sore spot. "I do not feel anything."

"No, it's not cut. Just red." Shannon glared at Daniel. "Why did you just throw your spoon at this poor girl?"

Poor girl? "Shannon, I thank you for your concern, but I am fine. And I am not a poor girl. I am a warrior Angel." Daniel cut her a look, rolling his eyes, and she scowled as she met his gaze. "But yes, Daniel, why *did* you do that?"

"Because your reaction speed is off—I didn't realize how much, though. You would have stopped that spoon otherwise. You're not giving yourself enough time to deal with the blood loss that your body has been through. Yes, you might be immortal, and yes, you are a fu—fierce fighter, but your body still needs to recuperate." Daniel turned to Moyarn. "Am I right?"

"You are correct about the recuperating part. Not sure I can approve of your methods of determining that, though."

"Yeah, sorry about that part." Daniel shrugged, but his eyes did crinkle at the edges. "But there you go. And I'm not saying you shouldn't be out on patrol, just that you should make sure you're in the best condition first. Plus, you've got Moyarn and me here, and we can also take shifts."

"And I'll keep watch as well," Shannon said. "I might not be the kind of fighter you all are, but I can help too before I head home."

"Actually," Daniel said. "This storm's pretty bad, and I don't think anyone should be out on the roads right now. Why don't you stay tonight?"

Shannon turned to the window. "You're right, it's blowing a gale still. And heaven knows we've got the rooms free."

"Okay, so that's sorted," Daniel said, turning to Amadis. "So?"

Amadis sighed as they all eyed her squarely. Damn it, Daniel was right. She was off if she couldn't stop a spoon from connecting with her head. How would she be up against a sword?

"Fine. I shall take the second shift." She dropped her gaze to her shirt, smoothed a hand over the material.

"Hey, don't look so dejected," Daniel said. "You'll still have your turn. But how about third? Moyarn and I will cover first and second; that way, none of us will be too fatigued to be useful if there is a problem."

"And I'll take first watch," Moyarn said. "I'll head out

now. Daniel, I also give you my thanks for a good meal." And with that, Moyarn unfolded his towering frame from the table and left the room.

"Sure," Daniel said. "I'll be out to take over at ten o'clock."

"In that case, I'll get the dishes done," Shannon said and started to pick up dishes and utensils from the table.

"I can help you there," Amadis offered.

"No, I think you should just get that rest." Shannon paused, her nose kind of wrinkling. "And maybe have another shower?"

"A shower?" Amadis blinked.

Daniel coughed—a sound that sounded suspiciously like a laugh—but when she swung to him, he just looked at her.

"What?" he said, spreading his hands. "I was just going to say that's a great idea. A shower. I know you cleaned up after the attack—but sometimes a nice, hot shower, even if you don't feel the cold, helps you relax. And can get rid of the last ... remnants of action, you know?"

Amadis cut a look between Shannon and Daniel. They eyed each other once, their expressions ... odd. As if they were colluding on something that she was unaware of. She turned her head and deeply inhaled.

Overlaying the scent of the meal, and the house, and Daniel, a whiff of something ... metallic tingled in her nose.

"Oh. You mean I smell," she said, laughing. "Well, in that case, yes, I will take another of your showers. It may be that my wings need a more thorough clean. The washroom you have provided is a little on the small side to fit my wings in, you see. But I thank you for telling me I stink."

"I didn't say you stink." Daniel winced.

"Well, you should have. There are some from the supernatural world who can scent blood on the wind, and even a trace may provide insight into my position when I am trying to hide."

Daniel stared at her, then finally shook his head. "The first time I've ever been told to tell someone that. So anyway, would you like to use my bathroom? I have a tub there that should be big enough for you."

"That would be lovely. Thank you."

After helping Shannon clear the table—Amadis was completely unable to not help at least with that task—Amadis followed Daniel into his bedroom.

"I got the bath started while you were helping Shannon, so it should be ready soon," Daniel said over his shoulder.

Curiosity zinged through her—what would Daniel's personal space be like? It overrode the heightened awareness of the walls and ceiling as they boxed her in.

He flicked the switch for the light, and the room lit up.

A massive timber-framed bed flanked by two small tables, each with lamps, sat opposite a large window seat. The curtains were closed, but given the room faced the forest, what a stunning view that would be to wake up to. Another darkened doorway was beyond the bed.

"You can come in. Shit, is it the confined space thing again?"

"No—I mean yes, that will always be with me. I was just taking everything in."

"Got it. Well, when you're ready, the bath is through here," Daniel murmured, leading her into the darkened space. "I'll keep the lights on low."

She focused on Daniel, and the walls and ceiling closing-in sensation receded as she followed him into a dimly lit bathing room, easily large enough for her to spread her wings. A mix of warm-hued tile and timber covered the walls and floor, and at the far end, a large tub sat in front of an arched window, water streaming from a faucet into the bath.

"It's ready." Daniel walked over and turned a handle, bringing the water to a stop.

Amadis couldn't help but spin around and take it all in, run a hand over the beautiful cabinetry.

"Daniel, this is wonderful. It's such a tactile thing, warm, alive almost."

"Thanks, I, uh, made the vanity." Standing up, Daniel dipped his head toward the counter. "Most of the timberwork here is mine."

Amadis eyed him as she caressed the rest of the counter. "You have a gift, Daniel. It must be lovely to bathe here."

"Yeah, well, it was therapy, you know?" Daniel cleared his throat, his cheeks red as he brushed past her. "I'll leave you to it."

Amadis paused and glanced back over her shoulder. Daniel hunched against the doorway, hands in his pockets.

"Therapy?" she asked.

"I'll grab you a towel." Daniel practically raced through the door.

Amadis bit back the urge to ask him more. Clearly, he hadn't wanted to discuss the topic, so she would not push him. Instead, she turned back to the mirror above the counter and unfurled her wings. As her muscles stretched, a sigh of relief slipped from her lips, and the usual shiver shimmied through her. *Belar's breath,* but that was good.

Amadis slipped out of her clothing and stepped into the tub. Daniel had closed the view of the forest in his bedroom, but from here, the trees standing as nights sentinels were visible through the window. She lowered into hot, steaming water.

A sigh escaped her. And with every silent swish and sway of the tree limbs, her body relaxed a fraction more.

"You know Moyarn is out there, right?" Daniel said from the doorway.

"He should be. He is on patrol," Amadis said. "You may come in, you know. And you don't have to avert your gaze."

"I didn't want to stare, in case it made you uncomfortable." He dropped two fluffy towels on the small stool beside the bath.

She considered him for a moment. He was a very special male. Was it because he was human? Or was it something other than that—was he a product of his environment as much as she was?

"What?" Daniel said, cutting her a look.

"You are very considerate. But you have no need to worry about my feelings. I am comfortable in my body. And Moyarn is an Angel—he would be used to those from Higherworld in their skin as much as anyone."

"I thought Angels were too uptight to walk around naked."

"Well, we don't walk around naked all the time. But if we need to be naked? Of course we do. We are flesh and blood, Daniel. There is no shame in being what we are. When we must be naked, we are." Amadis shrugged. "Do you mind?"

Daniel shook his head, the light in his gaze deepening. "No. No, I definitely don't mind. Just didn't think the Angelkin, or whatever you call them, wouldn't either."

MIND HER BEING NAKED? That would be no. Hell, no. Daniel's dick had been stiff from the moment he'd led her into his bedroom—all he could picture was Amadis splayed out over his quilt. Her body a feast just for him.

And then in the bathroom, more images poured into his mind. Amadis in the shower, bent over the vanity. In the tub.

That had to be why he'd slipped up and mentioned the therapy. He didn't usually talk about that. Not that he was hiding that he'd needed help—he just didn't like it when people delved into the abyss of his psyche.

"Would you mind?" Amadis said, turning to face the window. "I could use a second set of eyes to help check my wings?"

His breath whooshed from him. *Her wings.*

"Uh, yeah. Sure." Heart hammering, body stiffer than the timber bench, Daniel sat on the stool beside the tub. The sweeping arcs of her wings filled his vision. At first, they'd appeared like the deepest midnight, but up close, each feather was a dark rainbow of the deepest green and reds and blues and purples, the hues just visible from the black, and only as she shifted under the gleaming bathroom lights.

"Your wings ..."

"Yes?" she said over her shoulder.

"Beautiful. They're beautiful," he whispered.

She slowly lifted one arc of feathers, her shoulder rising as one with the movement, and she stretched the stunning span out wide. Water dripped from the lower ends.

"They can get wet?" Daniel said.

"Mm." She soaked a washcloth in the bath and ran it over the midnight-rainbow tips. "Here, would you?"

"You want me to wash your ... wings?"

"Yes, if you do not mind."

Daniel slowly reached out and took the cloth, stared at it for a heartbeat. Then he dipped it into the water beside her and brought it back up. Ran it down from the top feathers— the longest, widest, down to their tips. Then he gave in to temptation and smoothed the cloth over the delicate, outer-most end of her wings.

Her breath hitched, and a shiver ran down Amadis's spine.

"Is that ticklish?" he asked.

"Not ticklish. Sensitive. And ..."

"And?" He leaned into her.

"Hot. As in sexually hot. Your touch makes my body want more of you."

Heat exploded inside Daniel. His dick went from stiff to ramrod, his balls so fucking tight they tingled. His hands clenched on the washcloth. Hot? He was fucking dying inside with want for her—and she'd found his touch hot? He could kiss his way across the arcs of her wings, over to where the feathers gave in to supple skin and the muscles of her back—

"Why have you stopped?"

Amadis's voice permeated the fog of want. One by one, he unclenched his fingers from the washcloth, slowly dipped it back into the bathwater, then set about thoroughly washing her other wing.

Focus, Daniel. On anything *other* than the naked Angel in his tub.

"So listen," he said, voice rougher than he'd expected. "Sorry about the spoon at dinner. I didn't think it would hit you—more like you'd bat it away in your normal faster-than-the-eye-can-see pace."

"Yes, well, perhaps I was more tired than I realized. Thank you."

"For?"

"For recognizing I was not at my peak and therefore ensuring the safety of this house until I am recovered. And for the compliment about my speed. I have trained hard to be the best warrior I can be."

"No worries. Can I, uh, ask a question, though? It's about the whole warrior thing."

She glanced at him over her shoulder, expression curious. "You can ask me anything you like."

"Earlier today, you said you'd never been shot before, but you've had plenty of stabs and slices." Daniel studiously ran the cloth over her feathers. "That seems pretty harsh."

"Harsh ..." Amadis sighed and, for a moment, dipped lower into the water. "We do not think it harsh. But it is the Kin way. When I was a child, Fate decreed me to be a warrior. Therefore, my instruction began early. And to make sure I was the best warrior I could be, my instructors never held back."

"Fate *decreed* it? When you were a kid?" Daniel had to unclench his fists and somehow kept his hands steady while he continued to wash her feathers.

"That is our way, although usually our path is not recorded in the Book of Fate until we are much older. But for me, I was grateful to have the path identified early. It gave me a purpose among our people."

"Really? That's how you feel about it?"

"Yes. And as my father brought warriors from all the worlds to help my training, I have met beings from places I would never have otherwise."

"You certainly have a way of looking at the world that makes me ... envious, to tell you the truth."

"Of me?" She looked back over her shoulder again. This time her eyes were wide.

"Yeah, you." Daniel ran the cloth over the feathers at the farthest span of her wings. "You have such purpose. You know who you are. Where you're going. You are amazing. And now your beautiful wings are clean."

Still facing away from him, Amadis stood up, water sliding over her gleaming skin. His palms itched to cup the delicious curve of her butt.

His body went tight. His mouth dried up. She was a walking wet dream. He rose to his feet too, wincing as his dick jammed against the zipper in his pants. Somehow, he draped the cloth over the faucet and turned on the overhead shower.

"Rinse," he said hoarsely, unable to make any more words come out.

Amadis shifted beneath the spray, and then she turned around. Her nipples were tight buds, her skin flushed. Her eyes gleamed.

"Oh fuck." Turned out he did have more words. But then

his brain lost all power as every drop of blood went to his dick.

"I think that is exactly what we should do." Amadis turned the shower off and then stepped over the edge of the tub.

AMADIS STRAIGHTENED her shoulders and held Daniel's turbulent gaze. "Look all you want, but you can touch too," she said as she moved past him.

A growl rumbled from Daniel and then he grabbed her, pulled her close until her breasts grazed his shirt. His hands curved around to wrap her backside. His fingers clenching on her skin.

He dropped to his knees and parted the curls at the apex of her thighs. Expression rapt on her core.

"Ever since this morning, I can't get your sweet taste out of my head; I need you. Need this." And then his tongue slid along her slit.

"Yes, Daniel. Yes. Right there." Amadis's head dropped back, and she fumbled to grab the edge of the vanity. Shivers exploded where his tongue traced her sensitive skin. Her legs fell wide, and he lifted one of her thighs over his shoulder.

And his tongue speared into her.

A cry tore from her throat as coils of pressure twined and curled and exploded inside her.

"That was—that was—" She struggled to lift her head.

"The fastest orgasm ever?" he said with a feral grin. "And only the start."

He surged to his feet and undid his jeans, dragging them down. Ripped his shirt over his head. Ropes of golden muscles gleamed under the overhead lights, and she ran a hand over his warm, vital skin.

And then Daniel flipped her around. Through the mirror, his eyes gleamed, and he trailed his fingers down her spine. Goosebumps followed in the wake of his touch, and then he swept back up, over the sensitive flesh where her wings met his chest.

Amadis gasped, and in the mirror, his gaze went to her nipples, the peaks tight and flushed.

"You like that?" he murmured. Then he did it again.

More shivers coursed through her, all the way to her core. Her hips shifted, looking for pressure to ease the ache growing inside.

"*Belar's breath*. If you keep doing that, I shall have another orgasm. But I would rather you be inside me this time."

She reached around and grabbed his cock, ran her hand up the length and over the slit at the top. The thick length pulsed in her grip, and in the mirror, Daniel's lips pulled back, baring his teeth as a guttural groan tore from him.

"A bed." He grunted. "We need to do this in a goddamn bed."

"Really?" She laughed as he surged into her grip again. "But fine." Amadis shifted forward and spun around. Pressing a hard, fast kiss to his lips, she ducked under his arm. "I am calling dibs—that is the term, is it not?" she called over her shoulder as she darted into his bedroom. She leaped onto the bed, spreading her wings against the fabric headboard.

"Amadis, you are going to fucking kill me."

"From sex? I did not know that was possible."

He laughed, his face a mix of delight and desire as he gazed at her. "Maybe not. But it'd be a hell of a way to go out." Then he stalked around the bed. "So, you called dibs, huh? In that case, you call the shots. How do you want me?"

Amadis drank in his body. His tree-trunk thighs, those indents at his hips, the ridged muscles along his stomach, and that powerful chest.

His arms were loose at his sides, and his tone casual. But the vein at his neck pounded. His stormy-ocean eyes were bright, and a flush tinged his cheeks.

And his cock was thick and straight.

Warmth pooled in her core.

"On your back, please, Mr. O'Connor." This male was all hers—even if just for a few hours. She licked her lips.

"If you insist." Daniel grinned, and he stretched out beside her. "I'm at your disposal."

"Oh, yes, you are." A laugh burst from her, and she pounced on top of him.

23

With Amadis tucked into his side, her head on his chest, every curve of her body flush to every plane of his, Daniel inhaled, breathed Amadis's scent in so deep it would be fused with every memory he ever had. Because that's how amazing she was. He might have no fucking clue about their future, but he never wanted to forget the perfection of her.

Hell, he never wanted to move, period.

"Is it time?" she murmured.

"My alarm hasn't gone off, so not yet." But he picked up his phone anyway. "I've got a few minutes. Will you be all right to take over four hours after that?"

"Yes." Amadis smiled into his chest. Then she wrapped her arm around him, curved one wing over him too.

Daniel couldn't help but tighten her to him and pressed a kiss to her head. "I've got to tell you; I love your hair. Not that I've ever thought about it, but I guess I envisioned Angels as being more ... long, shiny locks, you know?"

"You are the only one who does like it." Amadis sighed.

"I wanted to blend in for my first Task, so cut the length myself just before I left. The Angelkin, however, were not impressed—they expressed their displeasure via the Council before I departed."

"What, no hairdressers in the Higherworld? Mind you, I think people pay good money to get cuts like what you've managed."

"I am glad you like it." Amadis curled back into him.

"Tell me about where you're from. The Angelkin?" Daniel asked. "When you first came here, I remember you said you had a fear of small spaces—and I get that now, with what happened to you as a kid. But you quickly changed that to discomfort instead of fear. Why?"

"You remembered I said that? From when we'd just met?"

"Amadis, I think I will remember everything about you. Forever."

"Thank you, Daniel. That means ... well, it is something no one has ever said to me before. And so, I will be honest. The Kin are tough. For my entire life—and yes, I'm older than you—I've been taught that Angels are perfect. Perfect at weaponry, perfect at achieving Tasks, perfect at managing emotions. Even sex is perfect."

"Let me guess, fear is a no-go?"

"Perfection means zero fear." Amadis shrugged one shoulder, her wing brushing his bicep. "But I started having nightmares almost as soon as I was home after the ... incident. It took me a long time just to stay inside the long-houses where the Kin live. And still, today, when I'm in small places ... my entire body seizes up. I ground myself, force myself to focus on what's around me until I can control my body again. And that's another reason I'm not perfect."

"You know, I still struggle with something similar," Daniel murmured into her hair. "Flashbacks, I guess you'd say, from my days in the army. Sometimes, I can be doing something totally normal, like walking down the road, and one little thing will click in my brain, and all I can see and smell and hear, and even fucking feel, is bombs going off, and people being ..." He shook his head. "Anyway, because I know it's not reality, I have this thing I do that brings me out of it."

"Oh, Daniel." Amadis tightened her arms around him, and she burrowed her cheek into his chest. The warmth of her seeped through his skin, through to his heart. "Both with our rituals. Both with our past still swaying our present. We are a pair, are we not?"

"Yeah, you could say that."

He ran a hand over her shoulder, down her spine between her wings. Her body shivered, and he couldn't hold back a low chuckle.

Then she rolled farther into his side, and the leading edge of her wing brushed right between his mouth and nose. He laughed and swatted her away, but the deep black of her inner feathers caught his attention.

"Your feathers here, they're a different color," he said.

"Those feathers are matt, and they angle so that they pull in light. That way, if anyone looks up when I'm overhead, they won't see me in the night sky."

"Handy."

"Stealth does have its benefits. Do you know I believe I would make a fine Keeper?"

The odd note in Amadis's voice made him look closer at her. "Is that possible?"

"I wish that it could be. But no, the World Tree calls its Keepers, not the other way around."

"But you're here, looking for a Keeper, right? Surely—"

"No, usually the Keeper is called *by* the Tree—except in the case of my Task. And it is the highest honor a being can have."

"Yeah, well, I can't say going to war is an *honor*."

"Daniel," Amadis said. She tilted her face up toward him. He met her gaze evenly, but fuck, he knew what was coming. "To safeguard the continuance of this world—and all of its people—that *is* the honor."

"I know you think I'm this person you're after. But I'm not. I can help, sure, you're here now, and no way do I want to see you or Shannon or anyone else hurt. But becoming something that lives just to fight ..." He blew out a hard breath. "I can't. Not again."

"But that's exactly what will happen if the World Tree falls. Everyone you care about will be at risk."

"Amadis, you're not hearing me. I can't. I promised myself a year ago, when Ben died for fucking nothing, that I wasn't ever going back. I can't renege on that promise. It'd be ... letting Ben down. And me."

Amadis stiffened in his arms, then she rolled over and rose to her knees. Her midnight wings draping down her back and over the bed. Her aqua eyes dulled as she stared at him. "You're serious, aren't you?" she whispered.

"I've been saying it all along. You—everyone—just haven't been listening."

"But this is the World Tree. I would give anything to be

called as a Keeper. You will have a place—a purpose—in all the worlds more important than everything else. You said you were envious of mine. Well, I am envious of you—of what you can have right now."

"Then you go and make it happen." Daniel pushed himself up till he was sitting against the headboard and folded his arms. "You're an amazing fighter. You want to do this. So do it."

"It's not like that. I told you—only the Tree can call a Keeper into duty. Of course I'll help. Any way and every way I can. But the Keepers have a reason they're called, Daniel. There's something about you that only you have. Otherwise, the Tree wouldn't have called you."

"You don't even know it's me."

"Actually, I have never been more certain. For some reason, you don't dream—and that's how the Tree calls a Keeper into duty. So that's why it needs help to get you to hear its message. And you can't be wounded. And you're a fighter. Believe me, you are the perfect Keeper."

Daniel tightened his arms. She just wasn't listening to him.

And then the alarm on his phone dinged. His turn to keep an eye out. Fuck, he hadn't done guard duty in a long time.

Rubbing a hand over his hair, he met Amadis's gaze. Her eyes were narrowed, and something like disbelief shone back at him.

His gut clenched, but he couldn't give her what she wanted. "Listen, I have to get dressed. Stay here and sleep. I'll see you in four hours."

S<small>PEECHLESS</small>, Amadis knelt in the middle of Daniel's bed as he donned outerwear and prepared himself for the winter night. At least the rain had stopped, so he wouldn't be drenched while on guard outside.

Lastly, he jerked on a black jacket and flicked the hood over his head. He looked dangerous. Capable. And yet he wasn't accepting the call. He may be the most important Keeper ever to protect the Tree. But he wasn't accepting the call.

Amadis's stomach knotted even farther.

"Amadis ..." Daniel paused at the bedroom door. He opened his mouth as if to speak, but no words came out. Then he shook his head, flicked a switch to turn the light off, and walked out.

Belar's breath. She'd failed. Her Task was to find the next Keeper—but as of yet, the Keeper had not been found because Daniel wouldn't. Accept. The *call.*

She doubled over, unable to catch her breath.

And then the walls of the room began to bulge inward; the ceiling edged lower ... lower ... Heart pounding, Amadis jumped off the bed and raced to the window, shoved the blind aside. The tops of the trees were barely visible, black silhouettes against the charcoal sky. But their movement stood out, the wind pushing their mighty forms back and forth.

Back and forth. Sway and rush.

Finally, she got a breath in. She held it in for a count of five, then exhaled. Pulled another in. Out.

Daniel was saying no. And after what he'd explained

about his past, how resolute he was ... he wasn't going to change his mind.

Her gaze lowered from the trees until it was only her naked reflection staring back at her. Amadis lifted her wings high. Angelkin wings. Warrior wings. Except, she wasn't fit to be called Angelkin. She had failed her calling. The Council would never give her another Task now.

And rightly so.

She had gotten involved with Daniel—had grasped at the opportunity to be wanted for herself—when all along, she should have been focused on making Daniel see he was the next Keeper.

Her father would be furious. The Council would be disgusted. What would they do?

She looked away, unable to stand looking at herself any longer.

Clothes. She needed clothing. She stumbled back to the bathroom and gathered up her garments from the floor. The bathroom lights gleamed brightly. Too brightly for her grim heart.

Amadis flicked the switch off and got dressed in the dark, then padded back into Daniel's bedroom.

The bedcovers were everywhere, pillows dented from their heads. Her gut clenched. *Great Belar,* what a fool she'd been. She raced through the lodge, up the timber steps, and down the landing to her room.

But she left the lights off. Just sat on the bed. Outside, the trees bent this way and that in the icy winds.

Magic thrummed through Ri'Anit's veins. She sat up in the bed, the cessation of the rain that had poured all night rousing her from her sated state. Her soldiers lay spent around her, their will bent to hers, and her power strong. But it would not last.

Leaving the tangle of bodies, she shrugged on a robe. The lightweight fabric did naught to stave off the cold, but with magic coursing through her, she had no need for protection from the elements. But the slide of the silk made her body hum, so she wore it for her own pleasure.

Perhaps Ri'Anit would get one for Irrika and present it as a tribute with the heads of the Keepers wrapped up inside.

A smile curved her lips. What a delightful image.

Stepping over yet more soldiers on the ground—some groaning, some still coming around after their sexual gathering—Ri'Anit strode through the pathetic little house. But this would not be her abode for long.

Provided she had more witches—exactly what her fourth follower was meant to be providing.

"Fourth," she called out. She waited in the silence of the night. "Fourth!"

Ri'Anit strode back to the bedroom. Her soldiers were rousing, but none were her fourth follower.

"Rise," she ordered her soldiers. "Second, you will take a team and locate Fourth. Everyone else—your task now is to locate the Keepers. But do not engage. Not yet. We are close, my pets. Very, very close."

In under an hour, her second returned and bowed low at the waist, her long braid swinging. With the house empty, Ri'Anit took her second, one of the few others here who knew the truth of their magic, into the sitting room of the farmhouse. She sat on the shabby armchair and nodded for her second to take a seat as well.

"What have you to report?" Ri'Anit asked.

"Fourth and one of the newest recruits were last seen in a village up toward the mountain range that guards this valley. They were to undertake reconnaissance and locate local witches, but neither met the team to check back in."

"Would Fourth and this other have left us?" Ri'Anit drummed her fingers on the arm of the chair.

"No. They were fully in control—both believing the witches to be evil and fed enough stolen magic to keep their bodies fast and able to withstand minor injury."

A vision played in Ri'Anit's mind of her dismembering her soldiers' worthless bodies. But death was not good enough for any soldier of hers that had allowed themselves to be taken—or removed.

Ri'Anit's hands clenched on the arms of the chair until her knuckles were white.

"Call in every soldier," she bit out. "I want every one of our Chapters on the ground. I want leaders out in these pathetic towns. I want every witch remaining brought with us and made ready to sacrifice as and when we need their power."

She waited for her second to lower her eyes and nod.

"You may leave me now. I will update our god shortly; however, one last thing. Direct your search teams to be on the lookout for Keepers and witches both. Only someone with power could have stopped Fourth from returning to us. I need answers before the sun rises. Otherwise, our god may recall us all—or order all of our deaths."

25

C old for the first time in her existence, Amadis hugged her arms to her chest as she slipped through the side door into the predawn night.

Daniel sat on an old tree stump near the woodshed, almost obscured by nighttime shadows.

But even had the dark hidden him completely, she'd have known where he was. As soon as his gaze focused on her, goosebumps prickled over her as surely as if it were his hands roving over her skin.

Belar's breath, but he had a way with her.

"You sure you want to be out now?" he asked.

"Yes," she replied, rubbing her hands up and down her arms.

"Thought you didn't feel the cold."

"I'm not cold." She refused to let on that the chill racking through her had nothing to do with the chill in the air. She took a deep breath and forced the question she was terrified of the answer to past her lips. "Have you ... thought any more about the Tree?"

Daniel slowly appeared from the shadows.

"I don't want to hurt you," he said. "And I can see this does. I get it—you're here to find this Keeper person who you think is me. But I'm not that person. I told you. I can't be."

"There is nothing I can say?" she asked. "What if you just come with me to the Tree?"

"No, Amadis." He shook his head. Sadness tugged at his features, but the resolution was still there, visible even in the starlight.

No sight of truth needed to know Daniel meant what he said. Her heart sank.

"Well, you have made your mind up." She blew out a long breath and nodded. "I shall see this shift out and then find Thrane. I need to see what help I can provide to the Tree before I return home."

"Return? As in ... now?"

"As in today, yes. Though not immediately. I will not see the Tree in danger. But I have to report back to the Kin Council about my Task." Somehow, she kept her voice steady when everything inside her wanted to crumble. "I'm going to patrol the grounds—you head inside. No need to stay out here in the cold."

Daniel hopped off the stump and touched her arm. "I can stay—"

"No. No, you've done your shift. And you'll need to be alert when I head to the Tree. You should really get some rest now."

She swallowed the lump that rose in her throat. But she needed him gone. Needed not to face her failure for one second more because she was going to lose her composure.

The most un-Angelic trait. But *Belar's breath*, who cared if she transgressed again? She was already the biggest failure the Council had ever sent on a Task. What was one more transgression among the many?

Daniel stared at her, but she held his gaze. Then his lips tightened, and he nodded once before he turned and strode inside.

The kitchen door slammed behind him, the crack echoing into the night.

With a flare of her wings, Amadis launched into the sky and landed squarely on the roof of the lodge. She sat on the highest point, surrounded by the lake and forest, a piece of paradise in this mortal land. Where, not more than a fast flight into the forest, the World Tree waited for its next Keeper.

Who wasn't coming.

And now she had to return to the Kin lands and lay out her shame before the Council. Deal with the consequences of her failure.

FOUR HOURS LATER, the velvet symphony of stars were dimming as the coming day turned black skies to charcoal, and the sounds of someone moving inside echoed from within the house. It was time. Amadis dropped to the ground outside of the kitchen.

Moyarn emerged a moment later. "Good morning."

"It is the morn." Amadis nodded but couldn't bring herself to smile. There was nothing good about this start to the day.

"No, *good morning*. It is a common greeting here in the Mortalworld."

"I know what you meant."

"Ah." Moyarn exhaled heavily, the pale mist of his breath hovering in the air. "Is it the mortal? Or is it your Task?"

"They are one and the same."

"You know, sometimes it does not matter what we say or do, we can't make the outcome we wish."

"Is that why you left the Kin?"

"No, more that I did not feel the Kin were always right in their pursuit of the Greater Good. Sometimes, mortals need … the opportunity to do the right thing."

"Well, I understand Daniel's motivation—his past is impacting his present. And I can't say it's not the same for me. I guess I'll just have to accept this is the way it is to be."

Moyarn rested a hand on her shoulder. "Sometimes, that is the right course of action. But you never know—you have put information to your mortal he has never had previously. Who knows how that will shape the present for others—or the future for Daniel. Even you."

"Well, I know one way it will shape *my* future." Amadis snorted in a most un-Angelic way. "The Kin Council will never select me for another Task."

Moyarn sighed but didn't disagree. Which told her more than any words would have. He knew the Kin. He had been with them from the start.

Her gut tightened, but she took a steadying breath.

"What do you need from me?" Moyarn asked.

"Will you stay here with Daniel and keep watch while I see the Keepers? They are meeting at the Tree shortly."

"Of course. But will you break your fast with me first?

Plus, the Keepers will need time to come together." Moyarn led the way inside before he turned around, stopped. "Amadis, there's something I need to say ..."

"Belar's breath," she said with a sigh. "Why do you look even more serious? What else is there you can possibly say that is worse than what I have just told you?"

"Your mortal ..." Moyarn grimaced.

"You mean Daniel?"

"Yes, *Daniel*. You and he have become close. That is apparent."

"I guess you could say that, yes. At least until our argument last night."

"Be wary with your heart, Amadis. When an immortal being bonds with someone, the nature of our existence makes that bond ..." His expression tightened. "Irrevocable. And it matters not if that person is mortal, or not from our world, or even if they feel the same bond."

The pain in his face made her stomach clench. And her sight of truth supported Moyarn's statement.

"You speak from personal experience?" Amadis asked.

"Yes. In my case, the bond is one way only. But I think your mortal has feelings for you, too. I just want you to be careful."

"I am sorry to hear about your connection." She stepped back to him, and drawn to comfort him, touched his arm. "But thank you for caring."

And then Daniel walked into the kitchen, and a current of tension zapped through the room.

"Caring for who?" Daniel softly asked. He folded his arms, a dangerous glow lighting his eyes as they locked on where she was touching Moyarn.

Amadis patted Moyarn one last time and steeled herself against the warmth coiling low in her gut. The same reaction she'd been having to Daniel from the moment she'd seen him.

"For me," she said coolly. "If you must know. Now, I am glad you're here."

"Hold on. He *cares* for you? What the fuck does that mean?"

"How do you not know what care means?" She stared hard at Daniel's granite expression. She whirled to Moyarn. "Does care mean something different in this world?"

"No, it means the exact same thing." Moyarn's lips twitched, but then he backed away until he was near the exterior door. "And before Daniel reverts to his ancestral cave dweller roots, I'm going to head out and take a walk around. I'll be back to eat shortly. I suggest you two ... work it out."

"Okay." Amadis could only blink as Moyarn disappeared outside. She spun back to Daniel. "Why do you make it seem that caring is a bad thing?"

Daniel cursed under his breath. Damn, what did it matter if Moyarn cared for Amadis? That was a good thing, right? Except, something nasty roiled in his gut, and when he'd seen Amadis touching the smoking hot motherfucker, he'd wanted to punch the guy in the face.

Which was totally wrong. Moyarn was a good motherfucker. Daniel knew it. There was just this irrational ...

stupid-ass urge inside him to keep Moyarn far, far away from Amadis.

But no way was he going to be a slave to the ugly thing inside him. So he forced his muscles to unkink.

"Sorry," he muttered. "I was ..." He blew out a slow breath.

"You were ...?"

"Jealous," he blurted. "Jealous, okay? You were touching him, and he was all like, 'I care for you.' And I know I've let you down with my choice, but—"

"Daniel, no. No, please stop right there. You have not let me down. I—I should have worked harder at my Task and not gotten sidetracked by other ... matters. But that's on me. And right now, I have a favor to ask. Would you contact India via your telephone?"

"Uh, yeah, sure. Here." He fished around in his back pocket and thumbed his phone open. "It's still early, though—do you think she'll be up?"

"This is about the World Tree. I can't imagine she would want me to wait."

"Okay." He dialed India's phone, and sure enough, it picked up almost immediately.

The conversation was swift between Amadis and India, with Amadis's full attention on the call. She mentioned Daniel just once, but as soon as she did, a sense of awkwardness stole through him. He couldn't just stand there and eavesdrop.

But it was almost five o'clock, so he could at least make breakfast. And that was perfect—it'd keep him busy while Amadis made her plans. Plans that did not involve him.

Plans that would see her leave the lodge, the area—hell,

not even the country, but to a whole other world. And fuck if he was ready for that to happen. Because no matter that she was pushing for something he was unwilling to give, Daniel was goddamn happy to have her around. No, not just happy. Content. It was as if his chest filled up, and his body loosened, and his heartbeat settled.

The acrid smell of burned toast made his nose tingle.

"Fuck!" He flicked the toggle on the toaster. Hell—had he toasted it twice? Based on the blackened, rock-hard mess, he must have.

Hell, his mind was batshit right now.

He blew out a surreptitious breath and tuned into Amadis's conversation right as she said, "See you in an hour," and then he fumbled for some fresh bread and tried to make toast again.

"Um, is that for breakfast?" Amadis asked from behind him.

"Yeah, no. Not anymore anyway. I'm making new stuff now. The toaster ... overtoasted."

"Right, well, I will join you for the ... toast, and then depart."

"What about your bags?"

"Bags?"

"Yeah, you know, the stuff you arrived with. Remember all those bags you made me carry up to your room when you first got here?" The day when the sun had shone on her silvery hair and her aqua eyes had somehow captured his heart in that very fucking moment. He cleared his throat, forced his mind back to the toast. *Don't burn it again.*

"Oh. Those bags. Well, they were goods that India helped me purchase for my Task as I was not attired suitably for the Mortalworld. But I have no need of them when I return home—all I require are my swords and my scabbard. Is there someone in your town who could use the garments? Most of them are barely worn, some never."

"Yeah, there will be. Shannon will know someone, no doubt." The toast popped, and he quickly grabbed it and tossed the hot slices onto a plate.

"Perfect. I would not want them to go to waste. I shall repack them and place them in the bags they came in. And that toast looks much better."

"Do you want eggs or anything? Or will this do?" He got out the butter, blackberry jam and Vegemite and placed them all on the table beside the toast.

"This is fine. Thank you."

"Right." He buried the hollow ache that gnawed in his chest. *Stay out of it, Daniel. Stay out of it.*

26

Daniel sat at the kitchen table, staring at his coffee cup when Moyarn reentered.

"Is it safe to come inside now?" he asked.

"Yep." Daniel swallowed the last dregs of his coffee. "You saw her off?"

"I did. Although I don't know why you would not?"

Because he didn't want to have to watch her fly off into the sunrise when this time of day had been so ... special. And fuck, didn't he sound like a sap?

"I said goodbye earlier," was all Daniel said before standing up and rinsing his mug in the sink. Through the kitchen window, the treetops were cast in gold.

"Do you know why I left," Moyarn murmured, "when you first came into the kitchen and saw Amadis and I talking?"

"No fucking clue," Daniel said as he dried his hands on a dish towel. He slowly turned around and leaned back against the sink. "But I get the feeling you're going to tell me."

"You'd be right." Moyarn pulled out the seat Amadis had been in earlier, sat side-on, just like Amadis had been sitting, and grabbed the last piece of toast off the table.

"That'll be stone-cold by now," Daniel pointed out.

"Don't care. It's food."

"Well, hell. You're a paying guest—my only one right now—at least let me make you some goddamn hot toast."

"And coffee?"

Daniel sighed. "And coffee."

A few minutes later, Daniel took a seat opposite Moyarn with a freshly brewed pot of coffee and poured them both a mug. He managed not to burn the toast this time.

"Okay, hit me," Daniel said after one sip. "Why did you leave the room earlier?"

"Because you and Amadis have connected. And when connections are so new, you are still settling into it. No one —male or female—would be comfortable with the one they have connected with being physical, or close to, another they perceived as competition."

"Competition?" Daniel snorted. "Sure of yourself much?"

"Like I said. Connected."

"You're shitting me, right?"

"No." Moyarn shrugged. "I'm telling the truth."

"And what, Angels can't lie?"

"Not at all. But I am not lying. Not that it matters. I'm just telling you the answer to the question I know you have been pondering. And now Amadis has gone. Your heart must be ... breaking."

"What the fuck? No way. We barely know each other. It's

been, what, a week? No way you can get to know someone—really know, as in their past—in that time."

"Knowing each other's history isn't the important part," Moyarn said. "What matters is that your soul recognized something in Amadis's that no one else in this universe has. And so you have connected. And I fear Amadis is the same."

"Fear? Even if it was true, which I am not agreeing to, by the way, why is that scary?"

"Amadis is immortal, Daniel. She will never connect with another being. And one day, you will pass from this world—your physical form anyway—and Amadis will never know that you felt the same way about her. I fear for her heart for the rest of her existence."

Daniel rocked back in his seat and stared at Moyarn as the Angel casually munched on his toast.

In his gut, a churning sensation gathered, whirled harder, heavier. Amadis—immortal—never knowing he, what, cared for her? Fuck, of course, he *cared* for her. About her. If he didn't, deciding to say no to the Keeper thing wouldn't have meant jack shit. But it had been a tough call —not because of the Tree. Because of Amadis.

Oh fuck. After she met with India and Thrane and Nate, she was leaving. And if the Council never gave her another Task or quest or whatever the hell they were called, she'd never be back, so he could never say how much he ... cared.

"I have to go." Daniel leaped to his feet, heart pounding.

"She's halfway to the Tree by now. It'll be slow with the two of us, but I could fly you ..."

"Thanks, but Shannon's here; she'll probably wake up soon. I need you to stay here and keep an eye on the place in case more Order soldiers turn up. Can you take them on if you need to?"

Moyarn recoiled, insult flashing over his features. "I am the Angel whose sword techniques are still taught to this day in the Kin lands. Of course, I can."

"Sheesh, don't get your knickers in a knot. I was just asking. But cool with that. And, no, not by foot. I'll drive. Thrane said he has a property in Hill End, right? I'll drive there now and call India on my way. She has to keep Amadis from leaving until I can get there."

"And then?"

"And then ... then I'll tell her I care too. You're right, I should've told her that. It might change nothing else, but she deserves to know."

Daniel grabbed his keys and was halfway to the garage when he backtracked to the woodshed. He picked up one thing, shoving it into his jacket pocket, before running to his SUV. He connected his phone to the vehicle's speaker system, then took off.

As soon as he was on the dirt road into town, he hit redial on his phone.

Come on. Come on. Come on. The words spun in his mind as the phone rang and rang and rang, all the way around the lake and into the village.

India didn't pick up. And he had no idea where to go. Daniel pulled the SUV up sharply—ignored the hand gestures from the woman in the vehicle behind him—and turned into the car park in front of the local hotel.

Fuck. He whacked the hell out of his hand on the steering wheel. What to do next?

Ignoring the curious looks of the townsfolk walking past

his SUV, Daniel racked his mind for all the details Amadis's crew had divulged. Sim was a publican over in Warragul. Nate was a cop—and a Keeper. Liz Jones had a farm near Thrane.

That was the key. He used voice command to get his phone to look up Liz Jones—there were a lot of Joneses in the region, but only one Elizabeth who lived in Hill End. And her farm had a phone number listed. Perfect.

He dialed that number next, and within moments, Liz answered. Daniel explained he was meeting Amadis at Thrane's—left out the part about Amadis and Thrane not being aware he was coming—and got Thrane's address.

With that piece of the puzzle worked out, he started the SUV and drove north out of Willow Grove toward the rural farmlands of Hill End, with the state forest closing in around him.

When Daniel reached the address Liz had directed him to, he pulled over onto the verge. Wow, this was some place. He'd expected a farmhouse, maybe some kind of garden even. But this property ... fucking hell. An old stone wall bordered the road, with a sturdy modern-looking black gate. Tall pencil-like trees lined the driveway as it wound off toward buildings in the distance.

Fuck, Daniel couldn't just open that gate and drive up to the house.

So be it. He was on foot from here. He locked his SUV, and with an easy jump, swung himself over the fence and onto Thrane's land.

As soon as his feet hit the gravel, a weird hum sang up through his feet and legs. Out of nowhere, a breeze kicked up and pushed him sideways onto the grass beside the driveway.

"What the fuck?" he whispered, swinging around. That wind had pushed so hard there might as well have been someone right there, shoving him toward the forest.

He stepped back on the gravel, but the wind pushed at him again. He jumped back onto the grass. The wind dropped. What the hell? This was no normal wind.

He tried one more time. Same result.

"Okay! Okay. I get it. Stay off the gravel." Daniel turned around in a circle and considered his options. The grass would still lead him up to the house, so he took off in that direction.

The wind returned. This time it buffeted him chest-on, side-on, *and* at his back. There was only one direction the wind wasn't coming at him from. The forest.

No one had mentioned anything about the freaking wind being part of this whole World Tree thing.

He tried one last time. Once again, the wind stopped him in his tracks and finished with a nudge—more like shove—toward the forest. As if it had lost patience with him.

Daniel jammed his hands on his hips. What the fuck was he meant to do now?

As if aware of his indecision, the wind ripped around his legs in a swirl, picking up leaves to spin around and around him.

Daniel raised his hands, palms up. "Fine. Fine. I'll go into the forest. You better not be pushing me into something bad."

The lawn soon met low-lying shrubs, and within

minutes, Daniel had to pick his way between ferns, little trees and rocks.

He grabbed his phone and tried India again. Still nothing. But he wasn't giving up. It rang and rang and rang, and all the while, the wind shoved at his back. He hung up when he reached India's voicemail and redialed. It rang and rang and—

"Daniel?" India's voice was a whisper through his phone.

"India. Thank fu—ah … thanks for answering. Listen, I'm at Thrane's. Kind of. I need to find Amadis, and I know she was coming to you."

"What? Where? Do you mean at the house?"

"Why are you whispering?" Instinctively, he dropped his voice too. "And I was at the house, well, at the front gates. Now I'm in the forest out back of his place."

"You're in the forest? At Thrane's?" Her voice rose to an incredulous whisper. "Wait. How did you get to Thrane's?"

"I drove here. And, yes, at Thrane's place. Or, I would be if this fricking wind would let me get up to the house."

"There's a wind?"

"Yeah, it's odd." Which was putting it mildly. "It's pushing me toward the forest. But is Amadis with you?"

"And it's pushing you *into* the forest?"

"Again, yes, but that's not important. I'm looking for Amadis. Is she with you?"

"Actually, this is very important. And yes, Amadis is here. Beside me. Here, I'll put her on."

"Finally." Daniel's gut unclenched, and a buzzing roared through his ears. And when Amadis's voice came through the phone, his heart pounded. "Amadis, where are you? I need to see you."

"Daniel?"

"Listen, I need to speak with you. I'm coming to you. I'm guessing this Tree that's so fricking special is pretty deep into the forest?"

"Yes, but Daniel, this is important—did anyone follow you?"

"Into the forest? No. No way. There was no one else around at all."

In the background, India's voice echoed as she said something to Amadis. Daniel stayed silent while they spoke, but he kept walking, the wind still insistent at his back.

"Daniel?" Amadis said.

"Still here."

"India wants you to think very carefully about your drive here. Did you see any other vehicles—cars—on the road?"

"Well, yeah, a few cars and trucks. And yes, before India asks, some of them were traveling in the same direction as me."

In the background of the call, multiple voices cursed.

"Anyway, I'm trying to get through this forest," he said through gritted teeth as he pushed through the wind to walk around a large rocky outcropping. This was batshit. He stopped. Shoved one hand on his hip. "Listen up, wind. I'm going in the bloody direction you want me to. But see that rock? I can't get over it. So let up, and I'll go around it and get back on track."

"What?" Amadis said. "Uh, Daniel, who are you talking to?"

Finally, the wind let up.

"Thank you," he muttered. "Just the wind," he said to Amadis. "So anyway, as I was saying, I've been walking for about fifteen minutes, and I can see larger trees ahead. Any idea where I am?"

"Hold on. India's communicating with the Tree."

"The Tree talks?"

"Oh no. But it does communicate."

Of course it did. Well, the wind might've let up on making him walk straight over rocks, but it hadn't paused its continuous push forward. Daniel had to keep going, picking his way between ferns and scrub and rocks and trees. Funny, after eighteen years in the army, and too many deployments to count, he'd thought he knew every environment of the world.

But he'd never been here. And this forest was ... different. Awareness coursed through him on a level that could only be completely internal, yet the hairs on the back of his neck rose. Was it the land? The trees? The magic wind?

Daniel wanted to pause and turn around, soak in this beautiful, rough, fucking special place, but the wind kept at his back. So he kept on walking.

Finally, India's voice murmuring in the background echoed through the phone.

"Daniel, India thinks you are due southwest of us. Perhaps halfway between Thrane's property and the Tree and heading straight for us."

Thank fuck, he was heading to Amadis. And huh, that meant the Tree they were hell-bent on protecting had to be somewhere between Thrane and Daniel's properties. "Is it you doing the wind thing?"

"You keep saying that, but there is no wind here. Hold on. India and Nate are both speaking to me."

"Sure."

"Daniel, apparently the Tree can use the elements to communicate. India and Nate both suggest you do exactly as the wind pushes you to do."

He rolled his eyes. Not like he had any choice there.

"Oh, and Daniel, Thrane has asked us to be silent so we can pinpoint you. And just in case there are others around, we are all going to stay and guard the Tree."

"Yeah, well, I'm already on the move. This wind is an insistent fucker."

"Funny. The Keepers all claim the Tree to be very stubborn, although their terminology was not quite as ... colorful ... as yours."

27

R i'Anit stared at the SUV driving away until her eyes burned. Exultation coursed through her, but she kept it restrained as she had done from the moment this mortal had mentioned the World Tree.

She had been surveying the townsfolk in front of the Willow Grove pub when the SUV had suddenly swerved across the traffic and pulled up in front of her. Within moments of stopping, the mortal driving the vehicle had said, *the World Tree*. Words she would have heard even had he whispered them on the wind from the Underworld.

All their hard work had paid off.

The driver of the vehicle was heading to her target. Ri'Anit's army was ready to launch their attack. This was meant to be.

"Second," she murmured to the woman at her side, "have two of your soldiers follow that SUV now and report back their progress and location."

Her second gave the necessary orders then turned back to Ri'Anit. "It is done, my first. Your next command?"

"How many witches do we have left?"

"Three."

"That will have to be enough. Bring them with us. We will follow the vehicle at a distance. Once we know where the Tree is, sacrifice two of the witch-folk and transfer their power to our mortal soldiers. Bring the last to me."

"Yes, my first."

Ri'Anit nodded but didn't say that if the attack was prolonged, she wanted another source of death magic to see out this fight.

"The Keepers have no idea that we are close or that we will soon know their precious Tree's location. Gather the Chapters. Today, we will take down the Keepers. We will steal their magic. And finally, *we* shall destroy the Tree."

She forced her hands to remain steady as her second obeyed the command. By all that was holy, Irrika would have Mortalworld this day. And Ri'Anit would have her glory.

And her vengeance.

28

Amadis's stomach churned over and over and over. Daniel was coming here, to the World Tree. Why? Had he changed his mind about joining the Keepers? Hope crashed inside her chest. Her heart picked up pace to pound so hard it thrummed in her ears.

She'd said her goodbyes back at the lodge. Had held in her tears until she'd been aloft, and then let the wind wick them away. But *Great Belar*, she was happy to see him again, whether it was for one heartbeat or a million.

A distant crack and swoosh echoed through the forest. In the clearing, tension arrowed between the Keepers and her.

They all stilled—holding even their breaths.

A twig snapped. Footsteps crunched through the leaf litter. And then a figure appeared, moved in and out of the trees in the distance, wide shoulders and long legs moving smoothly through the scrub.

"*Daniel.*" Amadis breathed his name as he reached the edge of the clearing. The urge to run to him surged through her, but she tamped it down. No loud sounds. Nothing to give away their position in case there were others out here.

Across the clearing, Daniel's gaze locked on her.

Why *was* he here? Butterflies took flight in her belly. And then her palms tingled. Reflexively, Amadis rubbed her hands together, but the tingling grew. And then an enormous force wrenched her gaze away from Daniel. To the Tree.

Beside her, India gasped. Nate swore. They both pivoted to the Tree, too. And the ground beneath their feet trembled.

The force released her gaze, and she spun around as Order soldiers ran between the trees toward the clearing.

There were so *many*. Amadis's gut tightened, then adrenaline flooded her system.

"Daniel," Amadis shouted as she whipped her swords free, "run to the Tree!"

He ran.

"Keepers, surround the Tree," Thrane cried as he raised his sword. "Amadis, you take the other side. India and Nate, between us. Daniel, stay near the boiler."

Daniel threw a fast glance at Amadis.

"Trunk. That's the trunk," she yelled at him as she raced to the other side. *Belar's breath*. More Order soldiers wove through the forest from all directions.

"Six to the north," Amadis called over her shoulder. "Some well trained, some less so. My swords are up to the task."

"Maybe ten on my side," India yelled. "I've got magic that can take them out, but I have to be in contact."

"Same here," Nate shouted back. "My magic can slow

them down, but it will be hard to take them all out together."

"Six coming from the east." Thrane nodded toward the trees in his direction. "Same mix of skill. But I've got them. Watch for their leader, though—whoever the hell it is. They'll be directing the foot soldiers."

"Suggestion," Amadis called out. "Thrane, you and I take the skilled fighters. India and Nate, watch our backs and slow or stop the soldiers from getting to the Tree."

"I can fight too," Daniel said.

"You may need to." Amadis swallowed the lump threatening to lodge in her throat. "But for now, stay close to the Tree. You might be our last resort." She lowered her voice. "Remember, they can't hurt you. But they don't know that."

"Watch for witch-fire," Thrane yelled. "If they have magic, we can't let them get close enough to launch it at the Tree."

"We will guard it, Thrane. At all costs," Amadis promised. "But let me try to reason first."

Amadis ignored the looks she felt the Keepers and Daniel throw at her. Instead, she focused on the soldiers—men and women—closing in on them. She waited till they entered the clearing surrounding the Tree.

"Hold," she yelled. Allowing her wings to be seen, she flared them wide. Then she leaped into the air and circled the Tree.

The soldiers faltered. Ha. They hadn't expected *that*.

Behind them, another compact figure, female, slipped between the trees, circling behind the fighters. Was this their leader?

"All of you, know this," Amadis continued as she spun through the air, tracking the furtive woman with her peripheral vision. "If you pursue this fight and threaten the World Tree, you threaten everyone mortal in this world. Mortals who are your family. Your community. And we cannot let you do that. Therefore, you will be cut down in this clearing. Our swords and our magics are too strong for you to survive, no matter what lies you have been told. But you don't have to do this."

The soldiers encircling them didn't budge.

"You don't have to be the enemy in this fight." Amadis tried one more time. "We will give you one chance to leave. All of you. Now."

"Don't think they got the message," Daniel called out.

"I really don't want their deaths this day." Amadis swept back to her side of the Tree, landed squarely on the leaf-strewn ground, and furled her wings. She swiveled *Daudhi* and *Dagr* in the air. "But that must come if they do not heed me."

"Don't listen to her." The female figure circling behind the soldiers spat. She had two swords strapped to her back and daggers at her thighs. "The *witch* is the one who feeds you lies. Look at her. Look at the form of one so evil she needs to be wiped from the face of the earth. You have the magic. You have the strength. We have the numbers. And we have our orders."

"Thank you, Second." A new feminine voice rang out from the forest.

Amadis cut a glance in that direction. Another shadowy female figure wove between the trees. But a sharp tingle cut across Amadis's palms.

"One more," Amadis murmured. "My side. Behind all the others. Too far away to make out any details."

"Take them all," the newcomer yelled. "And then take the Tree."

As one, the soldiers jolted like they'd been hit with a bolt of electricity, and then they charged.

From her left, Nate sent a bolt of red-tinged energy through the air at the incoming soldiers—forcing them to duck the blast. On her right, India hurled wind through the clearing, knocking soldiers off their feet. Behind her, the ring and screech of sword on sword echoed in her ears as Thrane battled the Order.

This was her purpose. Amadis calmed her breathing. Calmed her pulse. Spreading her stance to find solid purchase, she raised *Dagr* and *Daudhi*.

"Come, then," she called to the advancing soldiers. "This will indeed be your death day."

The most skilled fighter, wielding two swords like hers, pushed two others ahead. They didn't pause. Raising their weapons, they rushed at her, wildly slashing. Amadis jumped back, avoided the clumsy attack, then stepped in and took down first one, then the other in rapid strikes.

Blood splattered. The soldiers cried out. But she didn't stop to see them fall as the next soldiers were on her.

"They're in ranks," Daniel shouted. "They're holding their best fighters back."

"Got it," Amadis called out, ducking beneath an incoming knife and slashing high with *Dagr*, straight across the soldier's chest. More blood flowed. The soldier fell.

Another raced in. He came at her in a flurry of strikes

while another soldier rushed at her from the side, trying to get around her.

"Not happening," she muttered and flared her wings, thrust backward to Daniel. The space gave her room to swing her swords wide, and she took both soldiers down in precise strikes.

Daniel was right; they were improving in their skill. She eyed the next fighters carefully.

The closest held a sword and a knife in a practiced grip. He had to go.

She darted in low at the knife-man and dispatched him first in two thrusts and parries. Then she spun in the blood-stained leaf litter, whipped *Daudhi* and *Dagr* low to high to take out the next.

"Three remaining to the east," Daniel called out. "Thrane, two coming around your side. Nate, India, can you hold back the ones facing you? Keep funneling them into Amadis and Thrane. And watch out for the two not fighting. One is circling the clearing, the other—maybe the leader—still hidden deeper into the forest. I can't get a good look at her."

Thrane grunted, Nate and India called out their acknowledgments.

"Soon to be two to the east," Amadis replied, and with a flare of her wings, she swept into the man facing her.

And then a burst of golden flames surged at the Tree between India and Amadis.

"Witch-fire!" India shouted.

Heat scorched over Amadis's back, and she cried out, stumbled in her attack, fell to the ground.

"Amadis!" Daniel shouted her name.

The soldier above her swung his swords. She furled her wings tight, screaming as furious white-hot fire raced over her.

Glinting metal sliced the air above her face. She rolled away, the sword biting into the ground where her head had been.

Amadis spared one second to turn to the Tree—witch-fire had hit one of the large roots rising from the ground but hadn't taken hold, and Daniel had taken off his jacket, was using it to smother the flames.

Another burst of witch-fire flew at the Tree, this time from a different direction. But then a pulse of green-lit energy surged through the clearing and smashed into the golden flames.

India. *Great Belar*, India was combating the witch-fire.

"Daniel, I need to watch India's back," Amadis shouted. "Tell me if the leaders approach this side. Thrane, which direction is the witch-fire coming from?"

"On the move. Deeper into the trees. Once I get rid of this one"—Thrane grunted, a scream and wet choke followed—"I'll hunt down who's throwing the witch-fire. Nate, can you work with Amadis to handle the remaining soldiers and the leader we *can* see?"

"We've got them." Nate bit out, and a burst of fiery energy surged from his hands, searing the last soldier. The injured man staggered toward India, sword wavering.

"Stand down," Amadis snarled, stepping in front of him. But the soldier kept coming, his hate-filled eyes locked on her instead. "So be it." She struck both swords, then leaped over his body.

The next soldier hesitated—looked over his shoulder

into the woods once before he turned and raced at Amadis, striking her swords hard with blow after heavy blow. Shock waves thundered through her arms.

He pressed her harder, forcing her back beneath the weight of his strikes. *Belar's breath,* but he was strong. She couldn't let him through to India. As the soldier's next blow swung at her, Amadis darted inside his strike range, spun and whipped under his arms, running *Daudhi* through his side.

Then a scream echoed through the surrounding forest. Amadis halted. *Belar's breath,* where had that come from? Was it Thrane's work? Something else?

A shiver shook through Amadis. This fight wasn't over yet.

"Fire's out on the Tree," Daniel called. "And apart from whoever's throwing those fucking volleys of flame, there's only four more, including the woman hanging back at the edge of the clearing."

Pain blazing across her back and wings, Amadis pivoted. Bodies covered the ground. Too many to count.

DANIEL IGNORED the stinging burns on his palms. He ignored the metallic scent tainting the air. Ignored the urge to run to Amadis and stop her from putting herself into fucking danger.

Instead, his focus zoned in on the battlefield. Because that's what the fuck this was. Combat.

The World Tree was at his back, but he couldn't see the

other side unless he had x-ray vision. But that was one superpower that had eluded him. So far, anyway.

A burst of golden fire from ahead caught his eyes.

"More witch-flames—fire, whatever the hell it is," he shouted. "My side."

India ran around to him, got there just in time to close her eyes, and then that batshit-crazy green energy of hers surged through the clearing and took out the witch-fire before the flames could reach them.

Another volley of flame came in. Closer. Closer. Almost to Amadis.

"Uh, India—" he muttered.

India let loose another pulse of whatever she was doing. Surges of power and fire collided. A shower of gold and green sparks rained down on them.

Amadis pirouetted in the leaf litter beneath the deluge of sparks, her swords slicing through the air as she took down another soldier, her charred wings whirling with her.

Just like the magic that had surged through the clearing, fiery anger flashed through him. Fucking hell, Amadis must hurt so much. These bastards had to go. He needed a weapon. Needed to take them all out—

Except no, anger and rushing meant dead. This was combat. He needed calm. Precision, automation. Strategy. Strategy won wars too.

Ice and pure, absolute focus replaced anger.

"Two left, Amadis. Coming at you now," he bit out. "Nate, how's your side?"

"Need India now. Witch-fire!" Nate cried.

India hauled in a broken breath—her face pale as she ran to the other side of the Tree. Fuck, she looked almost spent. If she ran out, they were in serious fubar. And then India stumbled over one of the Tree's massive roots. Daniel darted to her side and picked her up.

"You good?"

"Yep," she said through gritted teeth. "Just can't stop. Daniel, if witch-fire gets into the heart of the Tree, only magic will put it out. But if they get through us, and we're not here to stop it, then they can hold the Tree long enough to kill it."

"Got it. Amadis has this side, and I have her back. I promise."

Lips tight, she nodded and took off, disappearing around the trunk. The next moment, another shower of green and gold sparks lit up the clearing.

But how many of these Order assholes were out there?

He spun back to Amadis. She had two fighters on her now.

"Last two on this side!" he yelled at her. "The leader is over with Nate and India. And who-the-fuck-ever is throwing that witch-fire is still free." Amadis nodded but didn't speak. He left it at that—she needed all her concentration on the two soldiers.

These two were strong and fast—they had Amadis entirely engaged. She was holding her own, but as quick as she was, they were fast too, and she couldn't get a break between their combined hammering blows on her swords. And with her wings damaged, could she maneuver like she was used to?

A stone of fucking ice lodged in Daniel's gut, and he tensed—his muscles prepping as if to pounce and somehow help. But he reined in the urge and let Amadis do what she was clearly born to do. Because somehow, she kept meeting each of their strikes.

And not just meeting ... every blow of theirs she defended, she added in one of her own. Her swords whipped faster. Harder.

"Death. Day." Amadis whispered. Over and over, she chanted the words with every strike of her twin blades.

The smaller of the two soldiers faltered, his swords not fast enough to keep up with her.

Like lightning striking from a storm, Amadis spun into him, and as his swords went high, she struck with both of hers through his chest. Blood sprayed. The soldier cried out, but then Amadis pivoted again, the soldier still on the end of her sword, and pushed him into the other.

The larger soldier stumbled back, and Amadis spun the other way, whipped her swords free and slashed him from groin to neck as she spun like a fucking ballerina on stage.

"Holy fuck," Daniel breathed. She was magnificent. She was stunning. She was bloody and gore-covered and the most amazing being he had ever seen. And he couldn't take his eyes off her.

"Any more?" Amadis called out, the rapid rise and fall of her chest the only sign of her exertion.

"No, they're all gone. Nate, India?"

"Done. We're coming round to you."

"India! Nate!" Thrane's voice echoed through the clearing as he emerged from between the trees carrying a limp body in his arms.

Daniel leaped over the giant roots and helped Thrane lower the person to the ground. It was a woman, covered in bruises and blood, her forehead mangled and cut open.

"What happened to her?" Daniel said, trying to find a pulse in her throat. Finally, a faint beat met his fingertips. He rocked back on his feet.

"The Order happened to her," Amadis said from behind him.

"Thrane!" India came running around the Tree, Nate hot on her heels. "How bad?"

"Injured, but alive. Can you help her?"

"We can try." India dropped to her knees and looked up at Nate. "I'm close to tapped out. Can we work together?"

"Yep," Nate replied. Together, they placed their hands on the woman's chest. "Keep away, Daniel, not sure how this is going to go."

He staggered to his feet and slowly backed away, step by step, until his legs hit the giant trunk.

"Here goes," India said, and then she and Nate closed their eyes, murmuring something over and over.

"So pathetic," a cool voice called out from within the trees.

Daniel whirled as a new woman, this one had long pale hair, stalked into the clearing.

On the other side of the Tree, Amadis and Thrane spun, too.

"Of course, you would give up your advantage to look after a witch."

Oh fuck. Daniel backed up tighter to the Tree. Spread his arms as far as he could over the trunk.

His heart slowed. Ice chilled his blood. Amadis had been right. He was all that stood between the Tree and destruction. But they worked as a team, and if he could keep this woman distracted, Thrane and Amadis could take her out.

"And who are the fuck are you?" He curled his top lip.

"Call me Ri'Anit, or Master, given that by the end of this day, my god shall rule this world," the woman purred.

"Well, Ri-whoever, you'll have to get through me first."

But she just smiled, rubbed her hands together, spoke a tangle of words in an unfamiliar language, and then a golden flame erupted in one hand.

"Witch-fire!" Thrane cried out.

29

Daniel widened his stance against the Tree, bark pressing into his back. He held the woman's gaze as she stepped closer. "Told you," he said, sneering, "you'll have to get through me."

"Oh, that is special. So very, very special." Ri'Anit laughed. "Charred mortal, my favorite dish." She drew back one hand and threw the witch-fire at his chest, but her feet slipped in the bloody leaves, and her throw went high.

Scrambling back to her feet, she rubbed her hands together again, this time shouted the words of her spell—or whatever the fuck it was—and drew another flame in her palm.

From the clearing, Thrane let out a massive roar and ran at the woman, his sword raised. The woman spun, altered her aim, and threw the fire at Thrane.

The Keeper skidded, grunted, and the stink of charred flesh overlaid the metallic scent of blood before Thrane rolled to the ground.

"Thrane!" India screamed. She leaped up, shouted at

Nate, "Hold the healing spell with her!" and ran to Thrane, dropping to his side.

Daniel swallowed a surge of bile.

"More like that?" The woman advanced on the fallen Keeper, drawing two wicked-looking blades from sheaths strapped around her thighs. She spun the blades in her hands as she stalked closer to Thrane and India.

India crouched over Thrane, one hand on his chest, but then she spun, facing the knife-wielding woman. "You will not get him," India hissed, "or the Tree."

"Oh, yes, I will. I will have you all." The woman laughed.

Hell. Was Thrane badly injured? Daniel's mind raced. How could he keep the woman off Thrane and India?

All *he* had was himself. But they also had Amadis. And she was a deadly weapon in her own right. He just needed to stall.

"Now I see why you needed the fire," Daniel drawled as loudly as he could. "You have no idea how to use those little knives." Fuck, where was Amadis? But he didn't risk looking for her—instead kept his gaze locked on the woman. "Want me to show you how?"

The woman stilled, pivoted toward him instead. Her chin tilted at an angle as she surveyed him with those eerie eyes. Fuck, she was ... scary. And not in a good way.

"Come on," he taunted. "Bet you have to be right on top of someone to use those tiny things."

"You dare talk to me? *You?* A useless, pathetic mass of skin and bones? Time to say goodbye, mortal." The woman's hands shot out, and her knives spun through the air toward Daniel. But just before they stabbed into his chest, their arc changed, and they crashed into each other, falling to the ground at his feet.

"Who are you, mortal?" The woman snarled, stalking closer. "Never mind, you shall burn just as this Tree shall." Once again, she rubbed her hands together, yelling her spell as she did. The largest flame yet erupted in her hand, and she heaved the witch-fire at him—the flame expanding as it got closer, closer. And then a gust of wind swirled through the clearing, catching the witch-fire, sending it careening off into the canopy.

"Who are you?" she screamed again, her face distorting with her shout.

"His name is Daniel," Amadis said through gritted teeth as she dropped in from the canopy, hovering above the ground behind the woman, her magnificent wings tattered and burned but holding her aloft. Face bloody, her lips pulled tight, she brought her swords down over the woman and stared at Daniel. Determination glittering in her aqua gaze. "And his is the last face you shall see on your death day."

Amadis crossed her swords in front of the woman's neck.

"No!" the woman screamed.

Amadis struck. Blade sang along blade, metal ringing high and pure. The woman's mouth dropped wide—then her head toppled to the ground. Her body followed.

Above them, golden streams of sunlight shone through the canopy, gilding Amadis's hair as she furled her wings and dropped to the ground on one knee. Head bent forward, she completed the arc of her swords and brought them to rest behind her.

AMADIS'S BREATH SAWED IN, out. In, out. Visible in the icy air. The singing of *Daudhi* and *Dagr* rang in her ears.

Gradually, the clearing quieted. And then Daniel was there, sinking to his knees on the bloody ground.

She drank him in. His face that would fill her dreams for the rest of her existence. His stormy-ocean eyes, his hard jaw, his frown tugging at his brow.

And then he crushed his mouth to hers.

Yes. His taste. His scent. His heat. She moaned into their kiss, went to wrap her arms around him. Fire lanced through her wings, stabbed through her shoulders. She gasped and let him go.

"Fuck." He jerked back. "How bad are your wings? How were you even flying?"

"Well, they hurt. A lot." Amadis clenched her jaw as she gingerly brought one around. The burns were along her primary feathers and shoulders. No wonder it had been agony to be aloft. She let them settle back and stared at the body and head on the ground. "But they worked well enough to do the job."

"You certainly did the job." Daniel rose to his feet. "Here." He offered her his hand, and she took it gladly.

"Thank you," she murmured.

"Will she ... uh, heal?" Daniel asked. "Isn't immortality like not being able to be dead?"

"Not always," Thrane muttered from behind them. He limped over, India propping him up on one side, his other side blackened and charred from waist to head. "Immortality means you don't need mortal stuff to live, like air or food, and that you regenerate from wounds. But losing your head is the end of the game for most of us."

"Fuck, man, how are you even walking?" Daniel darted to Thrane's side. "Here, India, you look like you're about to drop. Let me help." He looked around Thrane to where Nate still knelt beside the injured witch on the ground. She was trying to sit up.

"Thanks," India whispered. Her face was pale, her eyes glassy. "I used a lot of ... energy to hold back the witch-fire. Is that her?" she asked, leaning over the woman's head. "Holy crap." India jumped back.

"What?" Amadis said.

"It's the witch who was after Tara. Nate! She's dead. Like *dead* dead!"

Nate staggered over, face as pale as India's, eyes a wild blue as he knelt beside the head.

"Well, thank fuck for that," he breathed out. His shoulders dropped like he'd been carrying around a tremendous weight and it had only just now released. "It's over. Really over." He whirled and grabbed Amadis. "Thank you. Thank you. Thank you!"

Amadis stiffened, bit back a hiss.

"Whoa, there, Nate—hands off Amadis," Daniel said. "Her wings took a fucking big hit of that witch-fire."

"Oh shit. Sorry. Are you okay?" Nate said.

Amadis nodded and kept her expression blank when all she wanted to do was scream. Thankfully, Nate let her go. She cut Daniel a glance. *Belar's breath,* but she wished she could embrace him and thank him for his care of her. For her. But she wouldn't. She'd already shown enough weakness.

The Order was gone. The threat—for now—to the Tree had passed. Which meant she had to return to the Kin and face the Council.

Instead, she dipped her head once in thanks. Daniel nodded grimly in reply.

Amadis blew out a hard breath, then swiveled her swords. Blood covered the blades, along with her hands and arms. No doubt her entire body was stained red. In fact, they all were. But she needed something to clean her blades before she sheathed them.

"Hey, Nate, can you help Thrane for a sec?" Daniel asked. "Amadis, I've got something." Daniel came back from the charred root and held the jacket out to her.

"I used it to put out the fire," Daniel murmured, "but it's the only cloth here that's not covered in blood. You can wipe your swords with it—they won't do any more damage than the fire already has. Those swords saved us all here today. They deserve the respect of being put away clean."

Amadis's heart stopped. Damn him. Why did he have to be so good? She swallowed the lump that lodged in her throat and wordlessly took the jacket. She wiped *Daudhi* and *Dagr* clean, the jacket bunching around the blades. Once they were both back securely in her scabbard, she gripped the jacket tightly.

"Thank you," she whispered. Gods, her eyes were stinging. She bent her head and blinked until the sting went away. She thrust the jacket out. "That was ... very good of you. Sorry about the blood." She faced the rest of the Keepers. "Thank you, all. I have never felt so privileged as to work alongside you all to protect the Tree. But now I have to go."

"What? Now?" Daniel said.

"I have a responsibility to return to the Kin, to inform them of my Task's ... outcome. While the Tree was in danger, there was a reason for me to stay. But that danger has passed now."

"Do you have to leave right away?" India asked softly.

"I do, unless you still need me to protect the Tree?"

India opened her mouth, but a greenish haze had already gathered around her eyes. India's face fell. "You can tell if I lie, right? Crap."

"Yes." Amadis nodded. A tiny bloom of genuine joy had her lips curve. "But thank you for trying. And thank you for helping me so much on my Task. I do not think I would have been able to manage even the start of this mission without your support."

"Stop, you're going to make me cry," India said. "And here, I need a hug. I'll stay clear of your wings, promise."

Amadis didn't have a chance to stiffen before India leaned down and hugged her. And once again, she found her eyes stinging. Damn these Mortalworld beings—how did they cause her to leak so much?

Nate helped Thrane hobble closer, and they both said goodbye before turning back to see the injured young witch. India flicked a glance at Daniel and then, after squeezing Amadis's arm, followed them.

A heavy weight burned in her chest, but holding her breath, Amadis turned to Daniel. She'd said goodbye to him earlier that day. But now ... *Great Belar*, why was this so hard?

"I truly thank you for your hospitality, Daniel O'Connor. Even if this Task did not work out the way I had hoped, I have enjoyed my time here more than words will ever express." And she wished more than all the words in all the universe that she could stay. But that was not to be. She turned to the Tree.

"Amadis—hold up." Daniel's face tightened, and something burned in his gaze.

The Tree awaited ahead—just a few steps, and she'd be on her way home. With her back to him, somehow, she forced a casual expression, when in truth, she wanted to run to him and wrap her arms and wings around him and never let him go. *Not an option, Amadis.* She took a deep breath—and turned to face him.

"You don't need to say anything more," she whispered. "I will not try to change your mind. I understand why you feel the way you do about going to war."

"No, I mean yes, I've made my mind up. But no, that's not what I wanted to say. You see, I, uh, have something for you." Daniel turned his hand over, and there in his palm was the valknut.

"For me?" She darted a look up at his eyes. They were locked on hers.

"Yeah." His voice lowered as if his words were for her only, and he pressed the carving into her hands. "This is for you. Because I ... I care for you. And I want you to know that. No matter what happened here or what happens in the future."

Amadis couldn't help but trace a finger over the grain that swept around the carving. The tears she had tried so hard to hold back stung her eyes.

"You care for me?" She glanced up at him, but he was looking at the carving, too, not her.

"Yeah, of course." Daniel jammed his hands into his back pockets.

"Daughter!" Her father's trembling voice called from the Tree.

Amadis stiffened. *Belar's breath*. This was the last thing she wanted. The very last person she wanted to see her tears —or her failure. But he was going to find out about the failure soon enough. She swallowed back the ache in her throat and slowly turned around. "Father."

Theron swooped to her side, hands gently turning her wings.

"It is not too bad," she said stiffly.

"Yes, I can see by the burns and damage that is the case." He cut Daniel a glance, and once again, his mouth turned down in displeasure. Although, of course, her father's manners were too perfect for him to do anything other than nod in acknowledgment.

"Hey," Daniel said back.

Amadis bit back a grin. Theron would hate that casual greeting. Had Daniel done it on purpose? Something about the glint in his eyes told her perhaps he had.

Theron greeted the Keepers a little more warmly and then turned back to her. "I had come prepared to render aid to the Tree, though I can see that is no longer needed. So I can only ask regarding your Task, how does it progress?"

Heavy coils tightened in Amadis's stomach. She'd known this moment would come. Well, here it was. She lifted her chin and stared at her father—the Warden of the Angelkin.

"I have news to deliver to the Council. We should leave now."

Theron grimaced, but then without a word, he pivoted and returned to the Tree—one hand on the mighty trunk, and he disappeared.

The coils tightened farther, rose higher through her chest until they clamped so hard she couldn't breathe. And then the valknut tingled in her hands, the sensation breaking through the vise. She squeezed in a breath.

"Thank you," she whispered to Daniel, gripping the carving for everything she was worth, and she followed Theron to the Tree. A tingling—not unlike the valknut in her hands—pierced her back all the way until she touched the Tree and left the Mortalworld.

30

Daniel stared at the Tree so long his eyes burned. Fucking hell. She was gone.

Thrane and Nate came over. Nate was now supporting the witch, and Thrane was already on the mend.

"Daniel, this is Jodie, a witch from a few towns over," Thrane said, making the introductions. "We need to get her to a hospital. And I need to get the salt. Will you wait here with India while we do that? We can't leave all these bodies alone like this."

"Yeah, yeah, of course." Daniel rubbed his arms as a sudden chill chased over him.

"You okay? I know this has been a lot to take in."

"Yeah," he repeated. His gaze tracked around the clearing, passed over body after body, broken, bloody, torn. But the thing that made his gut churn was that Amadis wasn't there. "I'm okay. Just cold."

After Thrane, Nate and the witch had left, Daniel turned back to the Tree.

Amadis had gone. Like really fucking gone.

India stalked over to Daniel and punched him in the arm. Except she missed and did an air swing.

"Hey." He pivoted toward her, held up his hands. "What was that for? And careful you don't hurt yourself."

"You need to be punched in the arm. I can't believe what you said to Amadis."

"Huh?"

"You care? You *care*? Daniel, what the hell was that? You told her you *cared* about her. Well crap, *I* care about her. Thrane and Nate care about her."

"What?" He crossed his arms over his chest. "I told her the truth."

India stared at him, crossing her arms, too.

"What the hell do you want me to say?" An itch prickled behind Daniel's shoulders. The same itch that had started the day Amadis had first arrived at the B and B. And at the same time as that itch had prickled, something else in him had ... eased. For all her kookiness, he'd relaxed around her in a way that even dead bodies and revelations about his mother and an entire other world hadn't been able to wipe out. And it was because of Amadis. She was in your face. She was sexy. She was beautiful. Beautifully lethal. She was funny. She was special. She was way too fucking good for him.

And he didn't just care about her.

"Well?" India said, her mouth tightening. One foot started to tap.

"Man, you're stubborn." Daniel threw his arms up in the air. "Fine. Should I have told her I'm in love with her and don't want her to leave? She's an Angel in case you didn't notice. And she has a whole other life—in a whole other fricking world."

"Yes, Daniel. That's exactly what you should've told her. Don't know if you need the effing part. But hey, that's up to you." India's expression softened a fraction. "And just because she's an Angel doesn't mean you can't love her. If you ever get the chance again, don't waste it."

He blew out a hard breath. Amadis had gone home. Getting that chance wasn't an option.

Fucking hell, he'd blown it. Daniel staggered backward until something hard hit his back. He looked up. The giant limbs and canopy of the World Tree soared above him.

The winter sun lit the long, fine leaves in a vivid green. Leaves that were turning toward him, their tips curling over and over, like fingers beckoning him to come closer. Then the branches turned too, the smaller stems shifting, creaking.

"Ah, India?" he said, gaze locked on the Tree.

"Yeah?" she replied.

"Am I imagining this, or is the Tree bending toward me?"

"Holy crap. Nope, you're not imagining it."

"Why is it doing that?" Daniel asked.

"The only way to know is to touch the Tree—with your hand. With your bare skin."

The leaves rustled, still in that steady rhythm, tips curling, unfurling, curling upward again.

"What's it going to do to me?"

"It won't hurt you if that's what you mean. But the choice is yours, Daniel."

The choice. The choice to do what? To stop more innocents

like Jodie the witch, like Shannon, like Amadis and her mother, like *his* mother, being targeted for their magic? He slowly turned around, and his gaze dropped until the dark trunk dominated his view. Daniel reached out a hand and touched it.

The ground beneath his feet, the metal-heavy air, the greens and browns and charcoals of the forest, they all faded. Disappeared. Until it was only the World Tree and him, purely meeting mind to mind.

Because, of course, the World Tree had a mind. And that consciousness touched him like leaves swaying gently beneath a breeze. Like soothing waves lapping at the lakeshore. Like the rhythm of turning wood over and over until it gleamed.

It was comforting. It was solid. As peaceful as a sunrise. As vital as taking a breath.

And then a vision played through his mind: torrential, fiery rain decimating the Tree. The forest being incinerated. The lake burning. Billions of people crying out as their bodies exploded, their screams ringing in his ears.

And then the vision changed.

Timber being polished. Swaying leaves. The lapping waters of the lake. And Daniel, standing guard on the edge of the forest. A last stand that no one could get through, to protect the Tree. And the world as it should be. As it would be—as long as the Tree existed.

"Of course," he whispered. The life Daniel had sought—peace and calm and quiet—was *his* choice. But everyone deserved to have the life they chose. And if he didn't do his part, no one would have it.

∾

AFTER WASHING AWAY the remnants of the battle, both on herself and from her garments, Amadis returned to her space in the family lodge, carefully folded her mortal clothes, and tucked them into an oak box. Then she laid the valknut on top of them.

"Amadis," Theron's voice echoed from the other side of the screen that separated her personal area. "The Council are meeting in the inner sanctum. However, we will see you outside if you would prefer."

"Nay, Father. I will see the Council in the chamber." Amadis traced a finger over the carving. For seven days, she'd lived like a mortal—and this one piece would remind her of that for the rest of her existence.

On the other side of the screen, Theron's silence spoke volumes. After one last touch to the valknut, she closed the box lid. Latched it. Her new life would begin right now. Amadis would face the Kin as the accomplished warrior she was—fear of small places and all. Her fear did not make her less. Her fear made her stronger for overcoming it every time she entered an enclosed space.

"I will see you there shortly, Father," she firmly called out and then donned the traditional wear of the Kin: tunic and leggings with her scabbard belt wrapping around her torso. She squared her shoulders, furled her healing wings, and stepped out into the lush land the Kin called home.

The longhouses that housed each Angelic family were set in a circle into the natural slope of the earth at the foot of a giant mountain range. At a distance, the structures blended into the surroundings.

The Council met in the largest longhouse, with an inner chamber that was dug into the rise of the earth behind it.

Amadis took a deep breath and entered. The hairs on the back of her neck prickled, but she kept walking until she reached the inner doors. She could do this.

The doors swung open. Her stomach clenched. Now came the hard part.

Torchlight lit the chamber, illuminating rounded walls of bare earth to remind Angels of their simple existence. Five senior Angels sat on stools lined up across the room, including her father, the Warden, in the center.

"Amadis, daughter of Theron, welcome to the Council," the Angel on the end called out.

"Thank you, Council, for seeing me."

"Of course we would see you. We are the Council for all Angels."

Amadis blinked, bit back a laugh. The Council had never seen her before—in fact, most Angels pretended she did not even exist. Her stomach began to churn. What by the gods was going on here? She cut her father a glance.

Theron's expression was relaxed—more than she had ever seen it in her presence. Okay, something was not right. But there was no time to dwell on what that was. Instead, she focused her gaze on the back wall. Recalled the words she wanted to say.

"I am here ..." She cleared her throat, tried again. "I am here to report on my failure with my first Task. I understand this means I will not be given the privilege of assuming another."

"You did not fail, Daughter," Theron said.

"However, for the honor of attempting this Task, I wish to the thank ..." Amadis stopped. Had her ears misheard?

"Nay, Father—Warden. I failed. The World Tree was unable to call the next Keeper."

"You are wrong. However, I understand you may not have had time to hear the news. You are now an accomplished member of the Angelkin, Amadis. You may receive future Tasks, although not immediately. Your wings have to heal, and you have to review this first mission, see where you might improve for your next—"

"Wait." Her wings flared, but she ignored the pain. "Are you saying Daniel is a Keeper—?"

"I am *saying*," Theron said between suddenly clenched teeth, "that you succeeded in your Task. That the *mortal* you located accepted the call. He is now a Keeper. But do not question me again on this, Daughter."

Amadis heard no more. Daniel had received the Tree's call. And had accepted it. Her heart almost burst for him— but then a chill washed through her. Why? He had been so set on not becoming a Keeper. What had changed?

Gods, what if he'd done so because of her? What if he'd gone back on everything he ever wanted because he knew the impact his actions would have on her?

And while yes, there was no question the World Tree and the purpose of the Keepers was the most important role of any in the three worlds, that was only with free choice. Never forced into it. *Belar's breath*. Was this what Moyarn had meant? The Greater Good was not always the greater outcome.

And she had caused it to happen. Daniel had gone back on his vow thanks to *her*. This was beyond wrong—it was a terrible injustice to him. And what about her? All this time,

Amadis had been the one to push fighting for the Tree, but she'd left it. To join the people who had never wanted her—and had only accepted her now because she'd proven herself.

When all she'd proven to herself was that she wasn't one of them.

"Daughter? Daughter? Did you hear me?"

"I have to go." Amadis spun and raced from the chamber.

"What? Daughter?" Theron's voice echoed after her.

But she didn't stop, just ran back to her family's long-house and threw open the lid on the box.

"Daughter, what are you doing?"

Of course Theron had followed her. Amadis carefully took out the valknut and closed the lid before turning to her father.

"I am returning to the Mortalworld."

"You are an Angel, Amadis. All the Kin will recognize you now. You cannot just leave at will. You will have Tasks to undertake, the Greater Good to achieve."

"Father, not long ago, I would have given anything to have that be the case. But now, I ... I will never really be an Angel of the Kin."

"Amadis, of course, you're an Angel," Theron whispered. But his gaze dropped.

"In truth?" She stared at him until he met her eyes. "Because I don't feel like one. And that's the problem. I *feel*. I cry. Get angry. Get scared. I *dream* of being a Keeper—of fighting to protect the World Tree above all else. I love. In fact, I love—"

"Don't say it!" Theron held up a hand.

A smile curved her lips for the first time that day.

"Father, I love you. And I love Daniel. And that is why I am going to leave the Kin lands. I may not know where my place in these worlds *is*, but I know it's not here and that the only way I can find it is to look for myself. I want to visit my mother's people. See the Mortalworld. Tell Daniel how I feel. And protect the World Tree, Keeper or not."

"But, the dangers—"

"For almost four decades, you have had me trained as a warrior, Father. And you had me trained well. I am more than capable of protecting myself—and those I care for. I proved that this morning in the Mortalworld. Mayhap that's why Fate called me so early—my fighting skills are far more useful for the Greater Good out there—in the worlds—than right here."

Theron's face fell, his shoulders dropped. "You are set on this, aren't you?"

"Yes, I am. And finally, I find myself ... at peace with who I am." Amadis took his hands and squeezed them. "Look at me, Father. Look at me. You can see my truth. This is the right call. And I finally know that. And, I think, you will too."

Theron inhaled sharply, but his gaze roved over her from head to toe and back again. And then he nodded. "Aye, Daughter. I see you."

"Good. Then you know this is the right move. But before I go, I have two questions for you."

31

The sun was setting over the other side of the lodge when Amadis arrived back in the Mortalworld. Running her thumb over and over the carved valknut, butterflies taking flight in her stomach, Amadis took a deep breath and opened the front door. A long, low creak resonated through the building.

"Hello?" Amadis called out, stepping over the threshold.

Silence greeted her. Dust motes hung in the air, suspended in the ray of sun streaming through the windows. Where was everyone?

A sound echoed from the kitchen, and then Daniel appeared in the doorway. He wore his customary jeans and long-sleeved sweater that brought out the indigo in his eyes. But tight lines bracketed his mouth. His cheeks were pale.

"Amadis. What the—why are—" Daniel's mouth dropped open, and for a second, all he did was stare.

"Hello," she whispered, drinking him in. Had it been only hours since she'd seen him?

"You're here?" Daniel shook his head. "You're here."

"Yes, here I am."

"But, why? You left. I mean, I thought you left. Fuck, that didn't come out right. Oh hell, did they kick you out? They mustn't know. Amadis, I have to tell you something."

"No, wait, please, Daniel. I have to tell you something." She thrust the valknut in front of her. "Please, you gave me this—have given me so much. But all I have done is take from you. Now I need to give you something. That is why I returned."

"You want to give me that back?"

"No!" She yanked the carving back to her chest. "I was using it as an example of everything you have given me. No, the thing I have to give you is in words."

"*Words*." He regarded her strangely, his eyes narrowing.

Through the windows, the lake waters glittered gold beneath the setting sun. *Belar's breath*, he was angry. Understandable, given the choice he'd been forced to make.

"Could we speak out there?" Amadis had been prepared for his resentment but seeing it ... hearing it ... her gut tightened. Maybe being outside surrounded by the trees and the lake, with the sun on her skin, she'd get through this without breaking down.

Daniel led the way back through the front door and around the side of the lodge, eventually stopping on the grassy bank, hunching his shoulders. He jammed his hands into his pockets.

"Okay, we're here," Daniel said. "What's this thing you want to say—give—whatever the hell you mean?"

Amadis blew out a steadying breath. He was angry. But he deserved to know what she was here to tell him.

"Do you remember the night I killed that first Order soldier?"

"Yeah, I thought something was out there in the woods but couldn't see anything. After we'd been at the pub, right?"

"That was the night. Well, after the ... death, I went to the World Tree. I wanted to connect with it. See for myself why all this death and destruction was happening. And while I was there, the Tree showed me an image of myself as a child—it was after the kidnapping, and I was being returned to my father by a woman.

"The Tree also showed me something I had not seen as I crossed home. My father gave the woman a small glass bottle. Today, I asked Theron what that was for."

"Your father gave my mother something? Is that why you're here?" Daniel's eyes narrowed, and he spun away from her.

"Wait." Amadis grabbed his arm and didn't let go, even when his muscles tensed beneath her grip. "Please, please, I have to tell you this. You know your mother was a witch. So you likely carry the gene for witchcraft, but I sense nothing in you. In fact, all of my senses are clouded when it comes to you."

"What do you mean?"

"I don't have many Angelic traits. And yes, obviously the wings—but even my sight of truth disappears with you. And I think I know why."

"And it's got to do with what your father gave my mother?"

"Yes. That bottle was a very special spell. In his efforts to find me, my father had reached out to every contact he had—even my mother's people in Underworld—and had procured a spell for protection. He gave it to your mother to help keep her safe from those who would want revenge for helping rescue me. She was meant to take it for herself. But ..."

"Fuck." Daniel stiffened. "You think she gave it to me?"

"Yes. Yes, I do." Amadis dropped his arm. "Your mother obviously loved you more than life itself, and she was a good woman, Daniel. The kind of woman who saved an unfamiliar child. I wanted you to know that about her. And now, hopefully, you understand yourself better. You are not a monster, Daniel. You are a gift. A gift from the love of your mother, the kindness of her heart."

Daniel's eyes gleamed, and he spun to the lake, silently staring over the waters. And then suddenly, his hands shot out and grabbed hers, and he pulled her into him, his arms tightening around her. Amadis wrapped hers around him, too, held him as his massive frame shook.

A gentle breeze rolled in across the lake, rustling the treetops, carrying the scent of the lake and the forest.

Eventually, Daniel stilled. His breathing evened out; his head turned so his cheek rested on her head as he faced the water.

"Thank you," he whispered into her hair. "Thank you for telling me that."

"You are welcome," she whispered into his chest. "But you shouldn't be thanking me. I am the one who is thanking you. And I feel so bad, terrible truthfully, for forcing you into becoming a Keeper."

Daniel gripped her arms and eased back. "Hey, I didn't

do it for you. And fuck, that didn't come out nicely. But it's the truth."

"Then what did make you change your mind?" She carefully took in his tight features, the pale skin. "And why do you look so ... devastated?"

"Listen, yeah, it was you who pushed me to see the Tree. But I didn't choose to become a Keeper because of your Task. After you left, I realized I've been hiding out here. Hiding from the world, from who I am. And the fact is I want to help—I don't want to sit back and let awful shit happen when I can help stop it. So when I touched the Tree, well, it spoke to me. And I saw exactly who and what I wanted to be. I don't want to go to war. I don't *want* to be a fighter. But I won't see innocents die when I can stop it."

"So you did this, became a Keeper, for you?"

"For myself, for the Tree. For the Mortalworld and everyone here who deserves to live their life however the hell they want."

"So you're not angry at me?"

"Angry? No. No way. In fact, I've got something to tell you." A scowl tugged at his features. But his glittering gaze was locked on her. Something deeper—deeper than any meaning she knew—lurked in the stormy ocean depths of his eyes.

"Okay." Amadis shifted her arms until he was holding her hands. "You can tell me."

"I don't gel with people, you know?"

"Gel?" She cut him a look. Gel ... gel ... what in the worlds did gel mean?

"Get on with, like, just be comfortable to be around them."

"Oh, I see. *Gel.*" She filed that use away. "So you don't gel with people. Is this what you want to tell me?"

Daniel's lips twitched, and he rolled his eyes.

"You do that a lot, you know." She nodded at him. "Roll your eyes. But please, continue."

"Amadis, I'm trying to tell you something important. Because yes, I don't *gel* with people. Except something rare happened. Maybe it was all those sunrise chats, who knows? But I grew comfortable. *With you.*"

"And being comfortable with someone is rare?" she asked.

"So rare it's still mooing."

"How can rare moo?" Amadis stared at him.

"That's not the point. What I'm trying to say is there's something special about *you,* Amadis No-Last-Name."

"Oh." Amadis's heart flipped in her chest. "Me? You think I'm special?"

"Hell, yes." Daniel laughed. "So special I'm in the middle of packing up stuff here so I could figure out a way to get to the Higherworld—and you."

"You were coming to me?" The pressure in her chest grew. He had been coming to *her!* "Then it's just as well I caught you before you began your journey. You see, I've left."

"I thought they must have kicked you out?" He frowned, those beautiful eyes darkening. "You *left*? As in ...?"

"As in left the Kin. Moyarn gave me much to think about while he was here."

"Moyarn. Right."

"I have followed in his footsteps and will find my purpose outside the lands and control of the Kin. And to start, I'm heading to the Underworld to see my mother's family. Then I will return to fight for the Tree. At best, I'm a mediocre witch, and an Angel by blood and wing with no traits to make me one of them, nor the desire to bend myself so. But what I am is a fighter. A warrior. And I will be that for the Tree and any other who needs my help. *That* is who I am."

"Holy fuck." Daniel's mouth dropped wide again.

"That is a good summation. But I need a room until I can work out the right approach in the Underworld—I'm hoping Moyarn can help me there—it might be a few nights. And then, afterward, I will make Mortalworld my permanent home. I might not be a Keeper, but I will be of use."

Daniel's mouth closed with a snap, and his eyes lit up. "That is the best decision ever."

"Do you really think so?"

"Yes. Hell, yes. You are an amazing fighter, Amadis. And you're right. You don't have to be a Keeper to protect the Tree. Look at what you did this morning—Christ, was that only this morning? You did all of that just as you are now. The Tree is lucky to have you."

"You mean that, don't you?"

"I think ... Amadis, I think there's something very fucking special about you." He cleared his throat. "So, you're looking for somewhere to stay?"

"Until I travel to the Underworld, yes. And later, when I come back here—well, I will work that out when the time is right. But I was wondering ... hoping ... you might have a room I could stay in for a few days?"

"You know, I've got a lot of bookings, and all the rooms are full ..."

"Oh. Well, that is wonderful for your business, of course."

"Yeah. But there is one option. At least to try for a few days."

"Oh?"

"It's my room. I can always sleep out here—but if you don't mind staying in my space, then yeah. You can stay."

"Daniel, why by all the stars would I want you to sleep out here when I am in your room—in your bed?"

"So you're saying you'd want me in there with you?"

"Oh yes. If you do."

"A. Jones, I would love nothing more than to be sleeping in the same bed as you. For as long as you want. And I know this sounds batshit after just a week. But I think—hell, I *know*. I love you."

"Batshit means ...?"

"Insane. Mad as a hatter. But I think you're missing the point here. I said I love you."

"No, you said the notion that you think you love me sounds insane. I think it sounds perfect. Because I am the same, Daniel O'Connor. I love you."

THE NEXT MORNING, sitting on a rug on the grassy bank, as the trees stood once more silent sentinels to the break of dawn, and glimmers of gold spread across the lake, Daniel pulled Amadis into his side and wrapped the end of the blanket around her bare shoulder.

"Remember, I don't get cold," she murmured into his chest as she leaned into him, one wing wrapping around him. Warming him more than any blanket ever could. "But if you want to generate some heat, I'm all for working up some steam. Again."

Daniel pressed his mouth to hers, their lips caressed in a long, languid kiss. His body tightened. Fucking hell, they'd already made love right here on the blanket as the sun rose. And he was ready to go again. But more than just his body, his heart was packed full of pure, fucking, bliss.

"You know I was lying yesterday. What I said about having no rooms?" Daniel said between their kisses.

"Yes, I did notice there were no other guests around."

"I just wanted you in my bed. Or on my blanket. But you can have a room of your own here for as long as you want. I'll reopen soon, and then maybe we can add on an extension and make a space where you can spread your wings."

"You would do that for me?"

"I would do anything for you," he whispered against her lips.

"Thank you, but I am happy right here. By the lake with you. I don't need more."

"This here? Sunrise by the lake. This is everything I want too. How about we start our own morning ritual? Every day you and I are here together, we share this moment."

"The sex part too? As a Keeper, you're immortal now. There will be a lot of sunrises. And sex."

He laughed into their kiss. "Oh yeah, that too."

EPILOGUE

In her remote Underworld castle, Irrika turned away from the bag of flesh that had been her Second follower.

"Remove him from my hall before he bleeds all over these hallowed floors." Not that they were hallowed enough. Nothing would be enough until she had dominion over an entire world. Not a tiny corner cut from her sire's lands.

Irrika flicked her tongue over her lips as the Followers still standing backed away from her dais, genuflecting so low their weak noses were almost at the floor.

They were fortunate she had left any standing after delivering the news about her First's failure.

At the end of the room, an underling skidded into the hall, expression bordering on terrified. "My god, you have a visit—"

"I can announce myself," a cool, masculine voice called out. And then a tall figure strolled into her hall. "Daughter. It has been an age since I visited."

"Lucifer." Irrika held in a hiss and fractionally dipped

her head. "Welcome to my home. To what do we owe this honor?"

"Oh, you know," Lucifer said, slowly looking around her space, his eyes dipping to the body on the floor, although whatever his thoughts, his expression remained inscrutable. "Doing my fatherly duty and checking on my offspring."

THANK YOU & REVIEWS

Dear Reader, thank you so much for reading Keeper Of My Desire, the third story in The Immortal Keepers series.

As an Australian author I'm proud to bring you a story set in the stunning, unique landscape of our beautiful country.

And if you enjoyed Daniel and Amadis's story, I would be very grateful for a review on your favorite reading platform. As a new author, every review helps me pursue my dream of a career in writing.

ALSO BY HM HODGSON

The Immortal Keepers

Book 1 The Last Keeper

Book 2 Keeper Of My Heart

Relics and Legends

A Wreath Of Thorns

Anthologies

Mermaid Kisses

Guarded Hearts

FREE EBOOK GIVEAWAY

Can a cursed Merprince blackmail his way out of a fairytale nightmare?

Read now to enjoy this Beauty and the Beast retelling!

Get your free ebook now by joining my reader group.

ACKNOWLEDGMENTS

While I wrote this story, the book you've just read only came about because of the time, feedback and effort from a lot of other people.

My writing crew, the Romantics With Attitude: Jen, Jac and Mel. Once again, you've been with me through conflict and characters and plot holes. Frustrations and fatigue and excitement. Can't say thank you enough!

Next up is the Romance Writers of Australia aspiring authors eLoop, because over one flash fiction weekend, the scene I wrote from the prompts turned into one of my favorite scenes in the book.

To Sandra Greenhalgh, the best beta reader ever—thank you for your feedback and support.

To Brendan, thank you for your technical help with matters regarding the armed forces and returned veterans.

To cover artists Jacqueline Hayley and Marina Farcic, this cover rocks!

To copy editor Sarah Proulx Calfee, you are an editing genius and I love working with you. Somehow you take my mash up of ideas and see the story I'm trying to convey and help me pull it all together.

And to proofing editor Jo Speirs, your eye for detail, the extra care you take with my story and your support is magic.

And then to my family. Thank you for the countless

conversations and support while this story and these characters have evolved into what it & they are today.

And an extra special call out to the three most important people in my world—my children for understanding that my work starts early and spans weekends and holidays (and a giant hug to my eight-year-old son who wanted to show mummy's book to his teacher—not sure she was ready for my type of book!) and then to my husband, Henry. This book would not have happened without your support and love. And doing the house-stuff so I can write. Love you.

Last up, I have an important call out. This story touched on issues of mental health with Post Traumatic Stress Disorder. I would like to thank the amazing Davina Stone for her sensitivity read. This story takes place in a fantasy world, but it was important to me to represent the condition with respect.

ABOUT THE AUTHOR

HM HODGSON

Brisbane author, HM Hodgson, has always loved stories. Creating her own is the natural evolution of a passion for reading, a love for what makes people tick, and the fantastic places that can be imagined.

Today, she writes about romance (steamy scenes a must!) and magic. Magic that moves worlds and takes her to another place. When not writing or reading or reluctantly cleaning up after her children, she loves looking after her veggie patch and a little flock of chickens.

Keep in touch with HM Hodgson at: www.hmhodgson.com